STILL CHATTEL
AFTER ALL THESE YEARS

STILL CHATTEL
AFTER ALL THESE YEARS ©

VOLUME ONE:
STILL CHATTEL COLLECTION

written by

Angela Browne-Miller

afterword by

Dr. Angela Browne-Miller

Metaterra® Publications

metatерra®
publications

STILL CHATTEL AFTER ALL THESE YEARS
Volume One: Still Chattel Collection

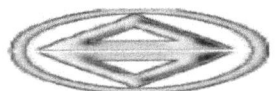

Published in the United States by Metaterra® Publications.
www.Metaterra.com
Library of Congress Cataloging-in-Publication Data.
Browne-Miller, Angela -- 1st Edition.
1. Fiction. 2. Women. 3. Drama. 4. Psychology.
5. Adventure. 5. Domestic Violence.
6. Violence and Abuse. 7. Browne-Miller, Angela.
Title:
STILL CHATTEL AFTER ALL THESE YEARS
Volume One: STILL CHATTEL COLLECTION
Library of Congress Control Number: (see website listed above)
ISBN 13: 978-1-937951-06-1 (Amazon Paperback)
ISBN 13: 978-1-937951-07-8 (Kindle eBook)
Published in the United States of America for US and worldwide distribution.
Metaterra® Publications, 1 Blackfield Dr 343, Tiburon, CA 94920, USA.

Ordering information and bulk ordering information available through: Amazon, Paperback and Amazon Kindle.
Also contact Info@Metaterra.com.

Dedicated
to
women who are liberated,
women who think they are liberated,
women who are not liberated,
women who know what liberation means,
and
women who do not know.

And the men and women
who love them.

publisher's note

This is a work of fiction. Names, characters, places, and incidents are either the product of the author's imagination or are used fictionally. Any resemblance to: actual persons living or dead, and actual locations, organizations, and events, is entirely unintentional.

•••••••

table of contents

Part One

In the Dead of Her Night

1.

HOTEL ROOM IN SAN FRANCISCO BAY AREA….

"Keep the damn press out of here whatever you do, jerks."

This potentially deadly sort of on-the-job learning had to stop. The morgue had wrongly been called in by an idiot. And then, the inept coroner-in-training, hungry for his first death, had readily misdiagnosed a body for a carcass. She was not dead, not yet. But now every minute wasted could kill her.

Quickly, the ambulance paramedics were rushed in to do their work. Stanger watched, frowning, disgusted as they uncovered the cold and clammy porcelain doll of a body left for dead and now put it on oxygen. Barely living. This was a big case, involving an influential family well known on two coasts of the US, one with difficult to prove but nevertheless real and serious underworld ties. Stanger looked around at the inept personnel the local authorities had sent. It was clear that he was going to have to handle this one himself.

Something under the bed caught his eye. Muttering profanities at a uniformed novice who tried to stop him, Stanger stubbornly pulled out his handkerchief, covered his fingers, knelt, and reached for it.

A photograph. Broken picture frame. Broken glass. Possibly dried blood on one corner. Eerily foreboding dream-like face of a pale, detached looking teenage girl who knew too many secrets and was not aware of an obvious anger brewing deep within her. She seemed to be gazing blankly at something off in the distance, something not quite yet in focus.

Stanger shook his head. This was not the near dead lady they were rushing to the hospital. So, who was this queer child? Why was her picture here?

The uniformed novice reached for the picture and Stanger pulled it away. "Hey, you, this is a crime scene, not a tea party, get busy and do something forensic, would you?"

The ambulance siren blared with accusation as it carried away the barely alive lady. Was it suicide or murder, detective Stanger asked himself. Yeah right, suicide. Not a beauty like that. Even on the verge of death, she could have any man, any thing, she wanted. It'll be attempted murder, if she lives. We'll get him this time.

Stanger marveled silently at his attraction to this near carcass, this rare and normally untouchable doll hovering on the edge of death, her porcelain skin calling hollowly, almost from the other side, for a touch.

2.

SECRET AIRPORT IN SOUTH AMERICAN JUNGLE….

The tall gangly young woman, her hair cropped short and slicked back under a beret, her military fatigues mud and blood stained, her pistols and knives barely visible and tucked away into her tattered boots, sat in the dingy little airport palapa in the desolate hidden Latin American mountain town, waiting.

Night had come again. Hours had gone by, almost twenty-four of them, since the time she should have been there. But, she had had to lose the cut throats who had followed her. Now tonight, this second night, the small plane had not yet re-appeared. Still, she knew it would come for her. It always did at the end of her missions.

Tired of waving off flies, and of seeing death, she dozed warily, in a seated fetal position. But what she had seen did not leave her. Visions of the bloody event she had witnessed a few nights prior high-jacked her mind: women, a long line of young women, their arms tied behind their backs, blind-folded, forced to walk along a high mountain ledge to the end of a narrow path. And then pushed one by one to their deaths, each one screaming at first then just falling, down down down the cliffs into the sullen coffee plantation waiting in its mists so silently below.

She had not been able to save them. In fact, she herself had barely gotten away alive, hidden and racing through the bush of the ancient land so riddled with sacrifice.

What a horror to lose those girls. What a horror to watch them murdered instead of freed because their sale had been blocked. Maybe in their next lives they would form an army, some sort of damaged but willfully avenging army – returning to kill their traders come killers.

The overly big blackish-red bird hanging, in a rusty cage, from the palapa ceiling squawked abruptly for no apparent reason. The guerilla bolted to her feet, studied the dead of night like a hawk, detected nothing. She sat back down, moaned, slumped over, and buried her face in her hands. Once in a while, but not very often, she wanted her mother. That poor broken woman. Lost in the shuffle of transition. She's just one generation older, or something like that, yet we're eons apart.

She doesn't see it, she thinks she's part of the "liberated generation" just because she's a woman who went to Harvard Law School in the early 1970s, a trail blazer. But she's so much a part of the old way, and I am so much a part of the new, even beyond the new. Worlds apart. How can we be so close and yet see the whole world and ourselves so very differently?

Her mind is so stuck in the old way, the old model of women, that she just cannot see how stuck she is. Some of the women who broke down those first barriers somehow forgot what women's liberation was really about. It's more than just gaining access to the man's world, the man's hierarchy, the man's values, the man's intellect. She misses seeing how very very profound the shifts in women's standing are, and yet how the job is in no way done. We've got a whole world full of women who need our help.

I'm the newest of the new, so new the world does not see me yet. Where is mom right now, I wonder? Mom, the thought of you eats at me. I'm so sorry I hurt you, so achingly sorry I left you, but I had to go. I was called to help bring on the new world order and the long awaited changing of the guard.

The sad guerilla gazed into the mist surrounding the walless palapa as the emotional monster lurking within her reared its nagging head, fleetingly stabbed at her heart and cut an opening in its wall, took a piece in its bloody jaws, then slipped away.

The gripping horror of the girls' mass murder returned. "Take another little piece of my heart," she whispered, thinking of their decomposing bodies among the coffee fields. Would their killers return, following back the trail of their blood, to cut out their hearts and offer these to the gods?

The big bird closed one eye.

3.

HOSPITAL ROOM IN SAN FRANCISCO BAY AREA….

So this is death. Ahh, like a sweet dream. Floating, swimming. Safe here. Nothing can touch me. No one can touch me. The raping of my soul is ended.

He can't touch me. There is no body for him to beat. No heart to break. Nothing to bruise. No pain. No more pain....

So glad. So glad to be away from that wicked dependence....

Sounds? Sounds! Sounds of people. Talking. People talking. But they can't touch me. They can't have me back. I'm gone now. Finally gone. Gone ... I found a way out ... I FOUND A WAY OUT!

A door is surely closing somewhere out there. Right here but so far away. I'm falling over the edge, falling away. ... yes....

Darkness. And more darkness, coming in waves. The welcome sea of darkness washing out that life. ... I have thirsted for this sweet darkness for years, years, years....

But what is this now? Pictures? Visions? A parade. Is this my death dream?

It looks like women. Long lines of women without arms, blind-folded, walking on tightropes that end in mid air. They form an army. Some sort of damaged, blinded, stranded, but willfully avenging army, their worn feet leaving a trail of blood in the black of their night.

And what woman is not in some way one of these? Or, is this still a question for the women of the future? Is their being held down, their so-called "subjugation," over now? Would they know the difference? Well, not me….

The women are whispering, what? What are they saying? Chanting: "Sister, what a bloody path we tread...."

Oh, I know who they are. .... Yes, the revenge of the Maxwell House wives. They no longer make coffee. They can't make coffee, because they have no arms. Broken dolls. They can't serve their masters now. They've been broken, and in their brokenness, their armless-mess, their complete inability to serve, to perform, their failure in their lives, their complete powerlessness, they've finally gained their power.

So they march into death like proud female soldiers -- soldiers who have won the ultimate battle -- escape from life failure -- escape from addiction to men -- escape from a contract with no other way out -- escape from the illusion of liberation into true liberation.

Oh but look, is that one me? Yes, wait, there I am! There I am! I am going away! Falling away. Away into the distant flame, the light. Away with them. Generations of women are gladly dead now. This is not surrender; this is the great escape! An exodus of will. A journey through all time, into the great time of the women's great return.

Into the time when the real woman will arise. Finally who women really are, and the power they really have, will come to us…. A most necessary step in evolution. Our survival depends upon this.

What in the hell am I talking about?

Oh wait, I am not talking. I am dead.

4.

MARKET DEEP IN SOUTH AMERICAN JUNGLE….

They searched the swarming sea of people for their tall gangly partner. Where had their soldier gone? Hadn't she made it to the market? They had been able to intercept the sale; had she then been able to free the human cargo? That particular delivery of those particular girls did not seem to be here, so maybe she had been successful. Or maybe not.

Finding one's way through this dense maze of desperate humanity was virtually impossible without a guide. There, at the core of the teeming jungle market, barely distinguishable amidst the array of color and blare of noise, was one of many small ramshackle stages cluttering the place. Here trades were conducted. Scrawny chickens, broken chairs, magic potions, old carcasses of all sorts of dead things passing for edible meats, and more, were bought and sold in an obscure bargaining process. A crowd was always gathered and scrambling, in multiple indigenous and modern dialects, for deals.

The cracking whip on human flesh and the girls' shrill screams coming from the compound behind the stage were barely audible over the cacophony. No one seemed to listen or care, except the two armed women who had somehow made their way in. But they were too late to stop the sale of three girls, now being hauled away in chains at gunpoint, and the murder of another one who had no intention of being sold. Her body had been left behind for someone else to clean up, or to salvage for organs or the skull, if anyone happened to want to.

Here, life, as strained as it had become, was but a commodity.

5.

SAME HOSPITAL ROOM….

"She's coming around. Yes, ... she is. It'll be a few hours before she's fully conscious, and even then she'll be in and out, woozy, for days, what with what she took and then what we had to give her, but we have her back."

Tears came to his eyes as he stared intensely at the beautiful creature: his doll, the Creation he called his wife. His. "Thank God. Thank you, doctor." He sounded humble. Sounded.

Falsely humble. Can't anyone see through his act? Those aren't real tears in his eyes! Such a slimy actor. He has none of these feelings for me. He's just embarrassed that something with his name on it is so broken. And that his public may find out about it.

He hates that he can't beat on my soul here. He's not grateful, doctor. Don't believe him.

A rush of birds' wings sounded in her ears.

Wait! What is this? I'm coming back? What? How can this be? I killed myself! No! No! They have no right to bring me back! I have a right to go! He even controls my time of death? My right to leave? He has no right to let them bring me back to life.

No! Don't leave the room! Can't you hear me? Am I not speaking? Wait! Take these cords and tubes and wires away! You have no right to bring me back. I want to leave, leave, leave with the avenging Maxwell House wives! Let us return when we are truly ready.

. . .

Now they're gone. Those bastards. How dare they? I'll show them. I'll go anyway, I'll die despite their tubes!!! Just watch me die in spite of you.

Wives turn away! Yet another generation of wives deceived by marital contract, by love, by false equality, fight by leaving ... it's the only way out. We will collect somewhere else, forge solidarity and return en masse, when the time is right.

Darkness. Ahhh, darkness comes in waves.

Time stops.

But time insistently resumes sometime -- minutes, hours or days -- later. Time stubbornly remolds itself into units out of the void. Some kind of fierce hand yanks her back into life.

Angrily, spitting fire, she opens her eyes into a room. The yellow fluorescent light is unwelcoming. A persistent nausea replaces the sweet darkness. Oxygen pours its forceful gases into her nostrils. Some kind of fluid drips into her veins. Some kind of intrusive electrode reads her body. Beeps and mechanical noises. Ugly. Such ugliness. She will simply detach herself from all this lifesaving crap with her own hands.

But what is this? She is strapped down? Tied down to her bed, chained to her sorry life, like a prisoner? A deep, cellular-level resentment, years of repressed anger, swept all through her as she came to.

6.

SAME SECRET AIRPORT….

Aided by the sallow light of the full moon, the small craft sputtered down the dirt runway and lifted off in the dark, flying without lights.

It was an empty win. Yes, the woman guerrilla had been retrieved, and her killer followers evaded, but clearly she was without the young women who were to have been rescued and released. A fly by the high mountain plantation revealed what appeared to be some of their bodies, transformed to broken porcelain dolls by the yellow moon, in ravines along the downward slopes of the cliffs that had received them. It also showed that there was more than one plant being cultivated there. Strip-shaped fields of coca wove their way through the night time canopy of blackish green, barely camouflaged.

Over half of their missions were failures. The good was that at least they were doing some good. She wondered if they were still waiting for her at the jungle market, or had moved on to rendezvous later. How many dead would they have to report this time? How many sold?

She was so deeply engrossed in thought, and the propeller of the small plane she rode so raucous, that she did not notice the other small aircraft that followed her through the night sky. Nor did her pilot.

Down below them, in a deep bed of freshly cut plants, a wounded and stunned young woman regained consciousness, sat up, and struggled blindly to loosen her hands still tied behind her back. One hand freed. She felt for her eyes. They were still blindfolded. As she struggled to remove the blindfold from her eyes, she remembered the ghastly sacrifice. She had blacked out during the fall from the cliffs above, blacked out and somehow survived. It had to be a miracle. Had to be. “Dios,” she whispered and crossed herself. “Dios mio. Solo de los manos de dios.” Only of the hands of God.

Her arms had been tied for days. She moved to stretch them and then froze when she hit the carcass of one of the other girls who had been pushed from above. She took an enormous breath, as if for both of them. To be sure the girl was not still alive, she shook her gently and whispered, “Hey.” Nothing. She put her hand over the mouth of the girl. No breath.

A delayed response, a core fear, welled up and whipped through her. She knew better then to cry out for help. She would become prisoner again. Prisoner and slave. And she knew better than to let herself die there and be salvaged for organs or eggs or maybe her skull. Or used in one of their macabre heart-tearing rituals. Not if she could help it. She would be no man's sacrificial fodder and no one's slave.

"Los muertes sabes...." she murmured as she pulled herself up onto her knees and surveyed the terrain. The dead know.

She gazed up toward the moonlit cliffs from which she had been pushed. Now she could feel her life force racing through her veins, as if she had never realized she was alive before this moment. She surveyed the plantation around her. She had to get out while it was still night. She crawled to firmer ground, stood, her legs weak beneath her, and realized she was covered in blood, glistening dark red in the moonlight. Was it her own? Was it the blood of this young woman, Revuelta, named for the great return?

She heard wings beating in the night air. A blackish-red bird flew by. Into the dark of the blood red night.

Freedom.

7.

SAME HOSPITAL ROOM….

She awoke from a strange dream about a large red bird. She was disoriented, mad, groggy, and already nagging herself as her logic and emotions blurred into one messy stream of thought.

Why hadn't it worked? She had planned it carefully. An overdose of sleeping pills, two kinds, two bottles full, plus a bottle of vodka, plus some poison in sweet fruit juice which she swallowed at the last minute as she was about to fall asleep. A rented motel room where no one knew her. The "do not disturb" sign on the door so the maids wouldn't come in.

How could this have failed? What kind of nasty twist of fate could have brought about her unwanted rescue? Who could have found her? How? Why?

It had been a gray day. A Tuesday morning. She had left a note, but it was a note in her safe deposit box. No note for her husband. Just a note for her daughter, Sheila, in case Sheila ever reappeared. Ever.

She had gone to John's office in town, on what was now the ground floor of his modified blue and brown Victorian house, unannounced. She had walked right in and made herself sit down facing him. "John, I need some help."

John had stopped working on his newest legal brief, put his pen down firmly, and leaned forward across his old mahogany desk. He looked at the ever beautiful Carla, her almond eyes, her ash blonde hair, her aristocratic bearing which the years had only served to refine. All her beauty was still there, but the glow was long gone. Carla seemed more and more like a talking mannequin, a lovely china doll, a robot wife unit, a mere copy of herself, as time went by.

"Sure Carla, whatever I can do." John studied her vacant face. Were there bruises under her make-up again? He couldn't bring himself to ask specifically about this. Instead he leaned further forward, touched her hand, and whispered, "You look troubled, really a mess, in fact. What is it?"

"It's really nothing, John. I just want someone outside the family to handle my things if, God forbid, anything should ever happen to me. I know that you do this for people, so I'm asking you to do it for me."

There was some activity in front of the mission across the street which could be seen from John's window, but John and Carla ignored it.

"Well, sure, I do, but it's usually for clients, not friends, Carla."

"Well, I'll pay then, John. Of course, I'll pay. No problem."

John reached for her hand again. "I'd never charge you, Carla. You know that."

"Either way, I want the security of knowing that certain things are in your hands. You're the only person I trust." Carla almost cried, but stopped herself just in time. She knew John would see her tears as an invitation to pry.

"Of course I'll do it, I'll do whatever you want. I'd do anything for you." He squeezed her hand. How could he reach this woman?

Carla pulled her hand away and tried to sound business-like. "John, what I need is --"

A sudden surge of clatter poured in through John's open window. They both looked up for a moment as two nuns and a teenage Latina girl rushed by, speaking a hurried Spanish and glancing in at them. John reached over and shut the window. The weird trio lingered a moment, staring in.

"God, what do they want?" Carla frowned.

"Probably lost, who knows?" John shrugged.

The trio turned and headed for the mission across the street.

Carla looked at John's kind face. John could have been just about any woman's Prince Charming, with his sweetness, and his quiet but rugged outdoorsman's good looks. Any woman's, but not hers, she insisted to herself, even though it was pretty clear he had years ago moved to Northern California, bought this house, fixed it up, one part as a home, one part as a law office, and spent his years there only because she had done so — nearby, but with Burt.

"Good, John. Thanks. You see, I want to be sure that certain things go to my daughter if something happens to me."

"Your daughter's gone, Carla." John tried to touch Carla's hand again but she pulled it further away.

Carla shook her head. "But she's not dead. I just don't think she's dead. I can feel that she's alive somewhere, John."

"Missing in action for years, though." John shook his head sadly. "Carla, stop putting yourself through so much pain."

"I should never have let her go to West Point."

"Carla, that was up to her, and quite an honor."

"That's what did it, that's what led to her disappearance, my not stopping her." Carla shuddered all over, feeling a guilty darkness washing through her sad heart.

"Oh, I don't know — and you don't really tell a young adult what to do. Once they are adults, no matter how young they seem to us, they are adults. Their life choices become theirs." John wondered why he even dared to give advice as he had had no children, and had never even married for that matter. Carla was the only woman he had ever wanted.

"Who ever heard of being taken out of West Point to work on a covert project while still enrolled there?"

John shrugged. Maybe she wasn't taken, maybe she had been offered an opportunity or had just volunteered for whatever it was. Maybe she was missing, or even dead. But she was gone.

Carla just would not get over the disappearance of Sheila. How could he help her? How could he sooth the terrible pain in her heart?

"Anyway...." Carla repressed her agony. She wanted to get back to her reason for the visit. "Please, John, just protect the little I have to leave her and the very personal things I've saved for her. Please, in case something should happen to me before she comes back."

"Sure, Carla, if you say so. But don't you want to ask Burt? After all, he is her father."

Carla was immensely irritated at the suggestion. "No. I don't want to ask Burt." She smothered her sarcasm and anguish as best she could.

A hearse pulled up across the street. And then three more. A woman in a dark red pant suit got out of the third hearse. She was greeted by a nun.

"How are things going with Burt, anyway?" John tried not to sound too concerned about this battered woman he was facing.

"Same," Carla said in a hollow voice. It was always the same. She had been stuck beyond all hope for well over a decade. Longer. And she had resigned herself to the fact that she and Burt were trapped in a never-ending, sad, and increasingly dangerous cycle. She wanted out but there was no exit (except death, she had decided). Burt, well Burt, he just wanted to do whatever he happened to do, whenever he chose to do it. And he had made it clear that her leaving would be a political embarrassment. He would do anything to stop her. "Don't you even think about it, because you will be more than sorry if you try. ... Anyway, you're mine for life and you know it," Burt had warned her many times. He would do anything to stop her except treat her well.

Plain wooden coffins were being unloaded from the hearses into the mission.

John always tried not to reveal his worries about Carla, as she resented these, but he was indeed concerned. He hated seeing the woman of his dreams end up like this. "Why don't you just leave him, Carla? Just pack up and move out. There's still a lot of life yet. You don't have to stay victim forever." Leave before he kills you, John wanted to say.

"We've been through this before, John. I've put years, everything I had, all he demanded, all of me, my adulthood, into the businesses he calls 'his' and I doubt I'll come away with any piece of any of it. I'd come away without any of what's mine if I left. And you know that's the least of it. He would come after me if I fought this. Or he'd have one of his 'guys' as he calls them do it. You know he has these guys."

The Latina teenager reappeared and passed by the now closed window, slowly, as if trying to hear the conversation inside. John looked over, caught her eye, and she bolted, her red scarf falling to the street as she did.

"First of all, Carla," John tried, as he had so many times before, to convince Carla otherwise, "the courts would see right through his arguments and games and doctored accountings. You'd more than likely come away with your half. And, second --"

Carla shook her head sadly. "Don't be so naïve. There's no guarantee, you know that, John. Come on, you know I know the law and the way things go in court, especially in these courts here in this county. Burt can get what he wants from a judge any day he wants to. He has the connections, and he has the information to hold over every one of their heads, and he is willing to blackmail and bribe who ever he has to. You know this. You've seen it happen in other divorces."

"But, Carla ---"

"And, John, you also know that Burt is not only the hottest attorney in the west, but that the public loves him as well. Really, he is highly skilled at deception. And, he's got the connections to get exactly what he wants, and he always does."

"Not everyone loves Burt, Carla. Believe me. Some of us see him for what he is." John's eyes were dark for a moment, and then he continued. "But anyway, you're right, there's no absolute guarantee. Still, this is a community property state. Even if you can't prove that you contributed equally to the businesses he calls his own, that you worked endlessly and selflessly, 24:7 -- you can prove you were his wife for many years. Definitely a long term marriage. And that's all that you need to prove — the number of years married."

"But I did contribute, John, endlessly."

"Carla, I know, but —"

"He demanded it. Year after year, I made endless cups of coffee, cleaned an infinite number of toilets at home and at the office, answered phone call after phone call, dressed him, wrote virtually all his legal briefs, came up with his most brilliant legal arguments, did all his research, wrote all his speeches, dealt with most of his clients on a regular basis, covered for him whenever he was out of the country (wherever he would go when he disappeared) -- you name it -- pumped my mental energy, my personality, my soul, and my brains into what he still insists upon calling *his* businesses and *his* career. I'm at least half responsible for making Burt into whatever degree of success he is known for today. At least. He couldn't have done it without me. And I'll never get credit for that. Never." Carla was certain about this.

"I know how much you've done for him. It's quite obvious to anyone really watching."

"It took the two of us to build the one of him, I guarantee you. And then there was nothing left for me. I'm all used up. And he wants me that way. Always did. I am just his captive resource, his 'brain trust' as he used to call me before he saw that with that label he was giving me the credit I was due. This is and has been my whole adult existence."

John cringed. He knew Carla was right about the making of Burt. Burt was a master at using people. In fact, he would be no one without this skill. And he sure picked the right woman to exploit, to consume, to use in every way, and to keep in the back seat for all these years. She didn't even see him coming, had no idea what she was in for way back when they were in law school.

"Well, Carla, I for one certainly know how true this is. But, even if no one else gets this, as I've said before, Carla, you will have a certain amount of protection under the law if you divorce. It's well worth the gamble. And, also, as I was trying to say a few moments ago, you'd come away with your self for your self. That's worth a great deal, worth it all. Right now you have very little of yourself for yourself, and that self is what's most valuable."

Carla was a little insulted by John's comment, but she knew he was right. "None. I have none of myself. I gave it all to him. OR he took it all. ... I feel so terribly ... disgustingly ... ripped off. Used up. The time of my life pilfered from me. He used my life force -- the essence of my soul, my libido, my intellectual, spiritual, creative, and sexual energy -- he used me 'til I was all gone, to build his kingdom, and now he says that none of it is mine."

"Well," John said softly, "whether or not he has really managed to steal absolutely all of you from you, this garbage with Burt's been going on for years. I want it to stop, but I can't help unless you let me. Let me know when you're really ready to deal with it, OK?"

"Sure." Carla waved his offer away. She'd be careful not to let John in, she told herself. She was so vulnerable right now. She had to keep everyone around her from seeing this. Had to. "But right now, I'm here on other business, John. I need to be certain that what I want to have go to Sheila will go to Sheila and not to anyone but Sheila, no matter how long it takes for her return."

"Sure, Carla, but is something wrong? Are you sick or something? You sound a bit as if your death is imminent."

Carla looked at John warily. Had she revealed too much? Could he tell what she was planning? Could he tell she was faking being OK? Could he see she was on the very edge, over the edge already? No. Good. "Why do you say that? You know you always advise people to plan for their children." She blinked back the hot tears that were threatening to surface. This whole thing was going to have to end, she told herself silently. The whole painful charade was too much to continue even one more day.

Carla felt as if she was about to cry blood rather than regular tears. But she stopped herself.

Red bird cry. Into the dark night of this woman's soul.

8.

SECRET LOCATION IN SOUTH AMERICAN JUNGLE….

A tattered nun peeked out from the thick of the tangled tropical forest. All clear. She raced across the overgrown dirt road to the entrance of a shed well hidden in the deceptive foliage. She was greeted by a female armed guard who, after pulling a gun and pointing it at her, recognized her.

"Jesus, Sister Seventy-Seven, it's you. I could've shot you. And, you're late. They've already started. But you're alive."

"Shit."

"And General Dame herself is here."

"Here? Now?" Seventy Seven whispered in amazement. "Why?"

"Things are getting real bad. Everywhere."

Hurriedly yanking her nun's frock from her lanky frame, stripping down to her bloody army fatigues, Sister Seventy Seven stumbled into the meeting. The bespectacled woman leading the meeting paused and looked out over her wire glasses. In the dim light it took her a moment to recognize her most reckless and most important underground agent. “Seventy-Seven.”

“General Dame.” Standing off to the side of the seated team, Seventy Seven came to sharp attention as she addressed with great respect Dr. Susan G. Dame, the Queen General of the secret International Underground Women’s Militia, the secret IUWM.

“Seventy-Seven, save for the fact that we are all most grateful that you are alive, we have no understanding regarding why you have had to disappear without any communication whatsoever for so long.”

“General Dame, I was followed and had to lose them before heading here.”

“That is a reasonable answer. At least in part. And so, tell us, where are the girls you were to take back after their sale was blocked?”

“General Dame....” Seventy-Seven suddenly wanted to disappear. She gulped back forbidden tears. There was no place for tears here among these militant women.

“Yes?”

“General Dame – I – they --”

A heavy silence saturated the hot room and held them all frozen still for a brief eternity.

“Yes, Seventy-Seven?”

The lanky young guerilla cleared her throat and prepared herself to announce her failure. She hated herself for trembling audibly as she responded, “Murdered, sacrificed, one by one, each pushed from a high cliff over a coffee and coca plantation.”

That silence again.

“You were spotted?”

“Yes.”

“Well, thank God you were able to get away. ... And we all appreciate your taking a detour to be certain you were not followed here. ... And, of course, we are deeply grateful for your survival.”

Seventy-Seven nodded.

“Be seated for now, and I want to meet with you myself, after this meeting for further debriefing.”

“Yes, General.”

“Be seated I said, and Seventy-Seven, remove that head dress, please.”

The lanky guerilla blushed as she discovered that the remnants of her disguise as a nun remained on her head. Off these went, replaced by the beret she carried in her rear pocket. She sat in the back and tried to disappear from the General’s view.

“Women of the 49th team, we are proud of your efforts here. Despite the recent casualties, we are saving more than we are losing, which is an improvement over the past three years of our efforts. And eighty percent of you are still alive and with us after three years since the inception of this unit. While we mourn our losses and miss the women who have been killed, we celebrate the survival rate we do have.”

The General paused and took the time to look each woman present in the eye. "I cherish each and every one of you. ... That includes you, Seventy-Seven."

Silence.

"Seventy-Seven?"

"Yes, General, thank you, General."

"We also have word that some of the women of this unit that we thought had been killed may have been captured."

Sighs of relief came from around the room.

"While we are grateful for this possibility, I have to be honest with you, ladies – capture over kill almost certainly means torture, rape, mental cruelty, and for those without full escape training, a future in forced slavery."

"For this reason, we are going to begin a campaign of intensified surveillance, with the mission of finding and liberating any of our members who may be captured. We are also going to begin an advanced on-the-job training program, better yet preparing each and every one of you to both evade capture as Seventy-Seven just had to do, and to survive imprisonment if captured, including torture if tortured.

"We will also prepare some of you to go undercover as girls, young women, who are to be bought and sold by the traders. We need more information on the routes and the transport systems, as well as the buyers. Those of you selected will have to learn methods of escape of course, especially if and when you find that your deaths or forced organ transplants or forced conceptions are immanent. Escape, and when needed, the rare suicide."

The women listening shifted in their seats as they looked around at each other wondering who might possibly be able to pass as a flesh trade girl.

"We have a brave new wave of also very dedicated and tough inductees which will allow us a broader group from which to select these candidates. Still, I think some of you will be more than adequate for this work."

Rifle shots were heard in the distance. The General abruptly stood and said quickly, "You are ordered to reassemble in the Mariana Assisi Mission headquarters in twelve days. We are expecting several other of your teams as well. Some are completing missions as we speak. Disperse in small groups and do not, absolutely DO NOT, be seen as you pass. You are dismissed."

As the women moved quickly to depart, the General added, "Seventy-Seven, you come with me. And don't leave that frock behind, it'll give us away."

"Yes, General."

9.

JOHN'S LAW OFFICE IN SAN FRANCISCO BAY AREA….

The painful meeting between Carla and John had stretched on too long.

John had belabored the sad point too much, he scolded himself. He had pressed her again and again, "Carla, what if Sheila never returns?"

"I told you that she will. And if I am not here for her, you will be."

Not quite seeing her logic, John shrugged a yes. He got up and moved around his desk to stand behind Carla. He started massaging her neck, her lovely neck. "OK, sure. As I said, whatever I can do for you. You know I've always been here for you. I just wish you'd feel safe enough to focus on yourself a bit."

Carla put her hands on his, not removing them from her neck, but stopping the massage. "John, no offense, but again and again you manage to make it sound like focusing on myself is basically giving my self to you."

"I'm not talking about you giving yourself away, just giving your self to love." John put his cheek next to hers and hugged her from behind. He still wanted her, still, after all these years. Why wouldn't she let him in?

Carla squirmed out of his hug and stood up. She faced him. "Stop, John, please stop. You know we'll always be good friends, the best, but we're like brother and sister. We go all the way back to high school."

"And college. And law school," he said wistfully.

"Don't remind me of my failures."

"Our failures, Carla. Or mine. ... But, if you'd been with me instead of with him, you wouldn't feel this way about your life now. I always wanted the best for you. I always believed in you and wanted you to shine. Without Burt sucking on you, you would have definitely passed the bar. You know you would. You were at the top of the class at the Harvard Law School 'til Burt. You were the best." John took her hands. "Look, I still love you. I can still help. I can still help you fix your life, whether you want me in it or not."

Carla took her hands out of his. "Enough John. I really do need your help, now. But not the kind you're offering. If you really love me, you'll do this for me. Let's deal with the subject at hand now."

"Sure," he consented reluctantly. "But only because I do love you. I've always loved you."

Carla again fought back tears. "OK. Fine, fine, you love me. I love you too, in some way. Whatever. We weren't on God's agenda, I guess. So let's stop all this. … Now, here's a letter addressed to my daughter." Carla handed John a large sealed envelope. "It's for no one else to see. It should be burned unopened if -- and only if -- she turns up dead."

"Uh, huh. Whatever you say, Carla."

Carla pulled a typed list out of her briefcase. "And here is a list of items which must go to her."

"Uh, huh."

Carla picked up an engraved silver box. "And here is a box of my mother's jewelry, which is to go to Sheila."

John put the envelope and the list down on his desk and took the box. He opened it and fingered the jewelry. "And to whom if she turns up dead?" he murmured.

"She's not dead!"

John put the box down and tried hard to stay detached. "OK. What else?"

"And here is the key to my safe deposit box, with the bank listed on the post-it on the envelope. Throw the post-it away or keep it somewhere else. Please sign this card so the bank knows that you can use the key." Carla picked up John's pen and handed it to him.

"Uh, huh." He signed the card.

"And here is power of attorney over any of my legal and or health questions. And here is a living will declaring that I want absolutely no life support or anything that would prolong my life artificially." She held the papers under John's nose.

"Uh, huh," he said, deciding that Carla's urgency was more than just evidence of her ongoing misery, it was some kind of anxiety attack. But he would humor her. "OK, got it, Carla. But what's the hurry? You're leaving town or something?"

"Nothing much, John. I just want to be very certain that you'll do this for me," Carla answered as nonchalantly as she could. "Then I can relax. Really get away."

"I said I would," he paused. "Now, Carla, I have an idea: will you go away with me for a weekend? Platonic only, don't worry. No love-making or anything. You just need a rest. And a friend and some tender loving care." John ran his hand along her high cheek bone. He loved the feel of her skin just as much today as he had so many years ago. He wanted to touch her all over and let her feel loved again. How could he make this come about? He'd waited so long for her forgiveness. They'd been so young and the abortion had seemed the only way to go. It had seemed as if it was a black and white choice for both of them – they either did law school or did baby.

Carla patted him as if he were a dog. "Thanks, John. I know you care. But not right now, please. I'm empty inside. I feel dead. No love. No sex left. And I've got to go."

John felt a hint of panic in his gut. What was this feeling he was getting? Being persistent but not too pushy, John tapped her hand very gently as she turned to leave. "Carla, wait. Please. What's going on with you? You worry me. Please sit and talk a while longer. Please. Nothing romantic on my part. Really, I won't pressure you anymore. I'll stop the love stuff. Just friendship, OK?"

Carla almost sat back down as a hint of deep longing surfaced in her heart. John and his family had been all she had left after her parents had died in that explosion. But his parents would never have wanted them to give up Harvard. Especially not John. Then she stopped herself. That was another life, a long time ago. She really didn't want to talk anymore. She couldn't risk having John talk her out of suicide: "No, I can't, John. Not now. Thanks for caring, really, thanks. It's just that I've something I have to do. An appointment. Right now. I'm late."

10.

JOHN'S LAW OFFICE….

John watched Carla leave, feeling carved out, hollow inside, and helpless. Why couldn't she see she still had other options in life? Why couldn't she see she had John? And this house, and this life to come to? Wasn't it obvious he had come out here to California and waited here for her all these years?

He tried to get back to his work, but couldn't concentrate. Heading outside for a short walk, this morning's unusual commotion across the street finally hit him. As many years as he had been there, he had never seen a series of hearses pull up to the mission and leave off a collection of coffins. In fact, he had never once seen a single coffin go into the place or a single hearse pull up.

But now all was quiet over there. Inquisitive, or maybe only trying to distract himself from the heartbreak of seeing Carla so distraught, he walked over and then into the mission church. There was no one there. Unaware that he was seeking solace, John took the liberty of exploring the place, telling himself he was in search of someone who could explain whether a group funeral was being planned, or what the event was that brought so much death in a box to this neighborhood this morning.

A few minutes search made it clear that everyone had departed. Contemplating a Mother Mary statue he had come upon, John sat down before her, quietly searching his soul for an explanation. He had just spent most of his adulthood waiting for a woman who not only did not want him, but who actually chose misery over him. If it weren't that she was so damaged from all those years of abuse, all those years of Burt beating on her, both mentally and physically, he would be profoundly insulted.

Burt. So many times over the years, John had found himself longing to kill Burt, to strangle him, to make him suffer, to beat him to death slowly, to shoot him in the leg and then the arm and then the groin, and make him beg for death. Or at least to confront him about beating Carla. Why hadn't he even done at least that? John chastised himself.

John's self-castigation was interrupted when a banging and a muffled yell sounded from across the mission courtyard. Startled, John looked away from Mother Mary in the direction of the sound. Again, banging. John looked around to see if anyone was there to respond to this obvious need for help. But no one appeared.

John headed across the courtyard toward the noise, feeling a fool for so doing. He opened a large old wooden door leading into a dank room. In the dim light, John saw coffins. He tensed a moment. Should he enter this room full of dead? He could make out a little design painted or maybe stenciled on the end of each box. A red bird. Some kind of phoenix maybe, he thought, maybe the coffin company's logo....

Again the banging.

It was not more than a few seconds before John realized that the sound was coming from inside one of the coffins. Revolted, he turned to leave and then caught himself.

Wait, someone needs help, he thought.

11.

GOODMAN RESIDENCE IN SAN FRANCISCO BAY AREA....

Right. An appointment.

An appointment with death. Her own. She felt piercingly rationale about it. First, a stop at the bank to put the letter and the jewelry box into her safe deposit box. Then the motel.

She could hear the pills and poisons jangling in her bag like good friends, loving hands caressing her into a soon-to-come permanent comfort. A great blanket of sweet nothingness to pull over her head.

She finished at the bank at 11 A.M. She checked in at the motel at noon. But then she remembered that she had left Sheila's photograph at home. Now she was desperate. She needed to say goodbye to her daughter's face. Had to. Had to. Had to. So, she went back to the house to get it. It would be an hour detour. Carla's date with death would have to wait just a while....

Carla rushed home and raced into her house. She berated herself for having forgotten to lock the front door, as if that mattered to her anymore. Not where she was going.

She tried not to look at the home she was leaving, not to see her paintings on the walls and the particularly artistic way she had arranged the furniture. She tried not to see her soul reaching out at her from every pretty space she had created. She tried not to see the love she had poured into this unloving home, into this bottomless pit, the hours and weeks and months and years that she had poured into building this life. This sick and empty farce of a life. Tears collected in her chest, in her heart. But she didn't cry. There should be no more tears.

Instead, she went straight into the bedroom, grabbed the picture of Sheila from the dresser, and headed out of that oh-so-empty room. Only, right then, Burt, who was never home at that time of day, walked into the bedroom, eating a sandwich, dropping his crumbs in a trail behind him, as if he wanted to be found or something. "Where are you going with that? That's mine," he said harshly, coldly reaching for the picture.

Carla held the picture against her chest. She was tense. "What are you doing here?" She cringed.

"Forgot some papers." Burt reached over and forcefully grabbed the photo away from her. "I said that's mine."

Carla grabbed it back. "Who says so?"

"Everything here is mine. I pay for all of it. It's all mine," Burt said as he grabbed the photo away again.

Insulted beyond words, Carla grabbed the photo back rather roughly. The corner of the frame scratched Burt's wrist. Burt, in an impulsive reflex, as if on automatic, slapped her face. Carla dropped the photo, her face stinging with darts of shame which instantly raced deep into her heart. She tried to slap Burt back to relieve herself of the insult.

Burt kicked her leg hard, knocking her to the ground. He mechanically dropped himself on top of her, as if he had this part memorized, and hit her a few more times, each hit, each time, much harder than the one preceding.

"How dare you strike at me, you hysterical bitch?" Burt growled in a monotone. Then he stood up, paused a moment, and began to kick Carla. She managed to roll over onto her chest to protect herself. He kicked the back of her body very hard several more times and then stomped out.

Carla lay there and cried for several minutes. She had been through this all many times before. The years of tears seemed to be squeezing out of her heart as if a fist was closing around it. But, this time, the excruciating pain turned quickly to detached numbness.

She abruptly stopped crying, struggled up, picked up the photo -- which Burt had forgotten or perhaps never wanted in the first place, and departed for the motel.

As she had already checked in, she went straight to her room. First, she put her daughter's photo, now under cracked glass, and the frame bent, by the bed. No one else's photo, just her daughter's.

Then a shower and clean clothes. Underwear too. Nothing sexy. Plain and simple. They would find her looking good. The exit mattered almost more than the rest of her life. Except the years she still had had her daughter around, her daughter who for some reason had left her. Carla thought about this and told herself: Of course, I have left myself, so why wouldn't she want to leave me. I was already gone maybe.

Carla was oblivious to the many bleeding cuts and massive bruises marring her flesh.

This would really make no difference. She would not miss her life. Carla had waited for her daughter long enough. If Sheila was still alive and was able to and wanted to see her mother, she would have done so. If Sheila was still alive and had not come home, she would forgive her mother for going. After all, her mother just could not take this life anymore. And after all, Sheila had left her parents years ago.

Carla had forgiven her daughter for her untimely exit. And if Sheila was alive but not coming back to see her mother because she did not want to see her mother, well, then, good-bye anyway. And if Sheila was dead, then Carla did not have any reason whatsoever for living anymore.

The impeccably closed logic of a suicidal woman is impervious to reason. People can't really know this about this kind of suicide. They can't know how much sense it seems to make unless they feel it for themselves.

Sheila was not dead. Carla just knew it. But Carla just could not wait any longer. Carla had to move on. She told herself that the will of a truly suicidal woman is as strong and unbendable as a tidal wave. People think that all suicide is a cry for help: well, they're wrong. A good amount of it is an intelligent decision to get out of a locked box, an exitless prison.

This suicide would not be difficult, because Carla was already dead. Life with Sheila's father had killed her. Killed her spirit. Killed her will. Killed her self-esteem. Had it killed Sheila too, or did Sheila get out in time? Can a girl manage to watch her mother live dead, live in the shade of perpetual disgrace, and feel any different from that mother?

Yes. Sheila was far stronger than Carla.

As for Carla however, a woman can be hit only so many times by the man she loves dearly before she thinks nothing of her self except that she is garbage, trash, junk to be kicked or hit or discarded. After a while, the tears hardly come. No feelings. What does it matter if the refuse she feels herself to be is hit? Kicked? Beaten? There isn't even any feeling sorry for herself. She just dies inside.

That's what Carla had done. Now, as of this moment, there would be absolutely no more tears. The dead do not cry. They just die.

It would probably surprise the world to know that such a bright, attractive, competent, socially respected, loving woman was regularly going into her beautiful upper class home and being beaten by her highly-regarded and very successful husband. And that he was telling her it was all her fault. And that she was believing him.

But she was. Or at least she had been. But no more.

That was all over now.

12.

CHURCH GROUNDS ACROSS FROM JOHN'S OFFICE….

There had been a young Latina woman in the box. John had pulled her out of the coffin, shaking so much he was not aware she was also trembling. She grabbed his hand as he helped her stand.

Now what? What should he do with this girl?

"Dios," she gasped.

"Habla Engles?" he hoped she spoke English, as his Spanish was deplorable, a lack of skill which was now embarrassing in California.

"Si, un poquito," she murmured. A little.

Once in the light of the courtyard, he saw that she was about sixteen, maybe seventeen. From what he could see through the film of filth coating her all over, she seemed to also be covered in cuts and bruises.

"Vamos a la policia," John said. We're going to the police.

The girl halted, refused to move, and looked horrified. "No. No. No." She struggled to impress upon him that this was in no way a good idea.

“Oh, OK.” Now what? “Let’s see .... Uh, uh, Donde vive?” Where do you live. It seemed like a good place to start.

“Soy soldada,” she answered with a brave tone.

Soldada. What was she saying? I am a — what? Soldada is — maybe soldier?

“Una soldada del los muertes.” A soldier from the dead....

13.

SAME HOSPITAL ROOM….

Suddenly, there was a rude intrusion into Carla's reverie of despair.

"Hello. I'm Dr. Achtentauf, the hospital psychologist."

Carla opened her eyes and found herself still in the visual disaster they called a hospital room. Don't people knock here, Carla said to herself. It's an intrusive and uncaring place, a lot like life. ... Oh, well, I'd better respond: "I'm Carla, but I suppose you know that. Failed suicide case number 388." Carla's voice was faint and her speech slurred. ".... I know why you're here. But I don't really need any help. Especially not therapy, thanks anyway."

"It's simply routine." Feeling challenged, the doctor pulled a chair close to the bed and sat down. This patient was exhibiting a rather common post-suicide attempt emotional state, Dr. Achtentauf mused inwardly. "We conduct psychological assessments of all attempted suicides."

Carla was irritated. First they force me to live, they then invade my space, then they label me. "So that's all I qualify for, the title of 'attempted suicide'? I even failed at that," she moaned.

Dr. Achtentauf raised her make-up enhanced eyebrows. "Failed?"

God, this shrink is a moron. Does she really think I fall for her trap? "Yes," Carla replied surprisingly matter-of-factly given her groggy fatigue. "Failed. I'm still here. I consider that a failure, just one in a series."

"Fortunately, Carla, you have a chance to get help now, time to reconsider your options."

Carla was angry, sleepy, and, at the same time, strangely amused. "Is that why you're here? To get me to reconsider my options?"

"Not entirely. My first purpose is to conduct an assessment of your psychological status."

"What for?" Carla asked.

"To recommend a treatment plan," the doctor answered patiently.

"Treatment plan? Doctor, I don't need treatment. I need death. Please just leave. Now," Carla demanded.

The doctor did not move. "I know you are still coming out of your drugged state. You drugged yourself as you know, and the physicians have sedated you on top of that. In fact, you will most likely be in and out of it for days. Still, I am required by law to determine whether or not you are a continued threat to yourself, and I have to start now."

Oops. Oh no, she's trying to decide if I'm going to try to kill myself again. If she thinks I am, she'll try to stop me. Carla softened her voice and tried to speak clearly. "I'm not. Really. I just get sarcastic when I'm embarrassed, and when I'm tired."

"Suicides attempts and suicides are often cries for help. Cries of the heart."

The doctor sounded so very insincere to Carla. "Oh," Carla responded callously. Don't you dare reach me and touch my feelings, doctor. Especially not falsely. Either way, go away. Let me sleep. Let me die.

But Doctor Achtentauf continued. "There are tens of thousands of officially registered suicide attempts each year in the US alone, but the real number is much, much higher."

So I'm not alone, Carla said to herself. But who are the winners? "How many actually succeed?" Carla wondered aloud.

"The data varies. Some say about one in every one hundred," the psychologist replied.

Good memory for facts. Was she showing off or what? "That's a high failure rate. ... So, doctor, this is your specialty?" Carla asked as she tried to sit up a little higher and look interested.

"No, not really. I'm not a suicidologist."

"Suicidologist?" Carla forced a faint chuckle. "You mean there are people who actually label themselves that way? How disgusting."

"So the thought of specializing in the study of suicide disgusts you?"

"No. It just seems to be frivolous, contrived work, like many so-called professional endeavors. Including yours, doctor, if you will forgive my saying so."

"What do you find more disgusting, the study of suicide or suicide itself?"

God, this shrink isn't even listening to me. Can't she go away?

"Neither."

She's not getting any more out of me in this direction. Carla studied the face of Dr. Achtentauf. It looked to Carla to be the face of a cold, confident, middle-aged woman, one who long ago surrendered to the lie of liberation.

The doctor made a note on her chart, as if retaliating for something. What did she have there, a check list? Carla fantasized that maybe they were fighting a war here: successful female doctors versus failed Maxwell House Wives. Round one.

"Look, Doctor Achten--, uh, do you have a first name?" Carla tried again to be kind. Carla was alert enough to realize that the doctor might be useful in some way.

"Phyllis."

Some name, Carla said to herself. It fits her perfectly. Carla shook her head as if to clear the fog out of it. "Look, Phyllis, I'm OK, I just need to get out of here. How long will it be?"

Dr. Achtentauf resumed control of the conversation, or at least she thought she did: “Well, first and foremost, we have to be certain your body has recovered and that you have sustained no neurological or other physical damage.”

“And then?” Carla tried to sound as if she was comfortable putting her fate in this woman’s hands.

“And second, although perhaps more important, still second, we have to determine your emotional state.” The doctor made another note.

But Carla was not comfortable. “Why can’t you just ask me about me? About my emotional state directly? I’ll save you a lot of time.”

“Because you may not know.” Now the doctor made yet another note.

Bullshit. “So someone else is better suited to tell me how I am doing than I am? Come on, give me a break, doctor, Phyllis.”

“You may be unprepared to diagnose yourself, Carla. Unprepared to assess the meaning, extent and consequences of your depression or whatever psychological state you are experiencing.”

Carla felt caged in. “Who says I’m depressed?” I am, Carla reminded herself: But who else’s business is this? My depression is so thick it’s like cement pouring over me. But I can’t let it show.

“Depression is one possibility. A significant number of suicide attempts act out of depression.”

"You mean people who attempt suicide?" Carla corrected, feeling stronger now that she was confronting the doctor.

"That's what I said."

"No you didn't, doctor. You called me an 'attempt'. You make it sound like I've been reduced to an act, an attempt, instead of a person. Try calling us 'people who attempt suicide'." Carla always had the sharp mind of a lawyer, even here and now, she told herself.

Dr. Achtentauf sighed, attempting to cover over her impatience. "A significant proportion of persons who attempt suicide suffer major depression by clinical standards. And another large proportion is addicted to alcohol or other drugs. Antisocial and borderline personalities comprise another group."

"So you are a suicidologist. A closet suicidologist."

"No, but I keep up on the data. In fact, I just returned from the International Conference on Suicide Behavior."

"You must be very proud of yourself." Carla could not say this without sarcasm.

"Look, Mrs., Mrs. --" The Doctor glanced down at her papers to get Carla's last name.

"Skip the Mrs., please. Carla is fine."

"Skip the Mrs.? Are there marital problems?" Looking a bit like a vulture descending in upon her now spotted prey, the doctor made another note, as if she had discovered something.

"Look, Dr. uh -- Phyllis, you are talking to me as if I'm either stupid or uneducated or both. You've got the wrong woman on both counts. Among other things, I'm a graduate of Harvard Law School. I can think. I see through your procedures. And your demeanor. Whose business is my marriage anyway? Just because I failed at suicide doesn't mean you have the right to invade my privacy."

Carla realized at that very moment that she had not talked to her husband, the "oh-so-good" man, Burt, yet. The great attorney-at-law, Mr. Goodman. Maybe Phyllis had noticed that Burt was not here by her bedside. Maybe it was obvious that there were marital problems. Still, it was none of Phyllis' business.

"I'm not here to offend you. I am here merely to determine your risk of further suicidality," the doctor made yet another note.

"Suicidality? Now there's a word for you. Makes you sound real learned, doctor. ... Well, there is no risk of this suicide or of this suicidality. Case closed. Now you can leave." Carla rolled her beautiful eyes sarcastically.

"Unfortunately, the very fact that brings us together, your suicide attempt, says there is a risk. A history of previous suicide attempts ranks as the number one predictor of suicide." Dr. Achtentauf sounded triumphant, as if she were playing chess and saying checkmate.

"I don't have a history. I have one attempt to my name -- first and last. That's all I have to tell you. You can go now. I really can't keep up conversation much longer. I keep starting to fade away again."

Phyllis stood up abruptly. Were her feelings hurt? Carla hoped so. Or was this just the lady doctor's poor bedside manner?

"Well, Carla, we have to end for now. I'll be back tomorrow about this time to see how you're doing. Hang in there. Your defiance is actually a good sign. You are turning your anger outward."

The doctor left. Disgusted, Carla shut her eyes and started to talk to her self under her breath: I'd better get a grip. Old Phyllis (well not so old -- about my age actually) will have me in a mental institution if I make her feel too badly. When she comes back, I'll let her feel like she's accomplishing something with me.

14.

DIRT TRACK IN JUNGLE LOCATION….

An obscure dirt track linked itself, almost invisibly, throughout Central and South America, like a chain, from road to train to port, and back to road upon road. Somewhere along its camouflaged roads, another set of female slaves – this time twenty-nine of them, ages nine through nineteen, were paraded at gunpoint into the hot and airless trailer of a large, old, dusty truck. These women themselves were linked together; they by rope from wrist to wrist, their fates and their market values intertwined.

Only one protested and struggled. She was most unceremoniously shot, cut from the rope chain, thrown into the bush, and left for dead nameless and faceless.

Straining for survival, the other girls and women repressed the wails their shared horror begged them to make. The trailer doors were slammed shut and locked. The silent slaves inside huddled in total darkness, just this side of death.

Quick as it all had happened, the truck sped away, leaving behind the discarded girl as dead, startled eyes frozen open.

The 38th team of female guerrillas arrived on the scene far too late. They too would have to report mission failure when they arrived at Mariana Assisi.

A big red bird flew by.

Mire, un pajaro rojo. Look, a red bird.

A red bird only the somewhat dead one saw.

15.

SAME HOSPITAL ROOM….

Time went by, yet Carla could not say how much. She was trapped, a prisoner of the hospital of all things. She waited for her release, trying to stay as calm and even as she could, to impress upon all watching that she was indeed calm and even.

And then there was a noise at the door of her hospital room. She hoped it would not be John. Seeing him would be too awkward. On the one hand she would be humiliated and on the other furious that he had not been there to keep her off all medical intervention and let her die.

Some guy in some kind of religious collar poked his shiny balding head into the room. He looked a bit like an owl. "Hello?" he said. "May I come in?"

At least he asked first. Strangely relieved, Carla pulled herself out of her half-sleep. "Sure, why not? At least you asked first," Carla whispered, using a kinder voice than she had used on the mind doctor. "Come in."

He did. “I’m Reverend Mastersen, the hospital chaplain. I hope you have enough energy for a brief conversation, Mrs. Goodman.”

“Well, that depends. First, you should call me Carla, please. And second, tell me, are you going to read me my rights?”

He laughed, surprised that this lady who had just tried to kill herself could be the least bit funny. “Your last rights? I hope not.”

“No, my Miranda rights.” Carla had to, just had to, smile wryly.

The Chaplain had to laugh. “Have you committed a crime?”

“I don’t know, have I?”

“I am in no position to judge.”

“But is God?”

“And I am in no position to speak for God. ... Anyway, I don’t even read last rights. I’m supposed to be in the business of saving lives.”

“You mean souls, don’t you, Reverend? Lives of souls?”

The Reverend smiled religiously. He emitted a strange, but not unappealing, kind of general, impersonal, lovingness. “That is the life to which I am referring -- the only true life.”

“Spare me,” Carla warned as sweetly as she could.

“I will.” He sounded a bit formal, but considerate.

“You can sit down,” Carla said. She felt like a queen granting an audience to a pawn. Queen for a day. “So I guess you visit all suicide victims.”

He sat down in the chair Dr. Achtentauf had left. “No. I don’t go to the morgue that often. I deal with the living.” The Reverend also had a sense of humor.

“Victims of failed suicide attempts,” Carla reworded her sentence.

“I visit all kinds of people who come through this hospital, including people who have attempted suicide.” The Reverend wondered whether Carla felt she was indeed a victim of her failure at suicide as her phrasing had just revealed.

“You get many? Am I one of hundreds here? People who’ve tried to kill themselves?”

The Reverend smiled and answered kindly, “You’d be surprised how many.”

“More than the morgue? I mean, more failed attempts than successful ones?”

“You could put it that way, although I prefer not to call suicide attempt survivors ‘failures’.”

“But we are,” Carla insisted. “Double failures, in fact. Failures at life and at death. Double whammy.” As tired as she was, Carla was resolute in her condemnation of herself and anyone who might be like herself. The Reverend noticed this.

“Well, if you turn ‘failure’ around, you get ‘eruliaf.’ ” The Reverend said it again slowly: “Er-yoo-lyaf.”

“That’s a meaningless word.” Why this empty, vapid, conversation? What was he getting at?

"Yep. You're right. But it helps get to the idea: 'err and you laugh.' You know, laugh at your mistakes."

"Do you laugh at yours, Reverend?"

"Not often enough. What about you?" he asked.

"No. I don't. What about God?" Carla tried not to sound too irreverent.

"Do you think God has a sense of humor?" he asked her.

"God better, because we humans are a real blight on Creation," Carla realized she was working to keep the conversation going despite her fatigue.

The Reverend grinned and was quiet for a while.

Finally, Carla spoke. "So why are you here? Have I sinned? I don't want to be forgiven for attempting suicide. I want to be forgiven for failing suicide."

"That's up to you, Carla."

"What is?"

"Forgiving yourself," he ever so slightly bowed his head at her. "That's the key to a shift in your world view."

"I suppose so. But I don't. I don't forgive myself for failing at suicide. I really wanted to be gone. Really."

He looked her right in the eye. She felt him come right into her with his heart. "It's been pretty rough, hasn't it?"

Carla stared at him, trying to wall out his empathy. "What?"

"Your life," he replied softly.

"Oh, just the last half," Carla pretended to laugh at her own joke under her breath.

"That's enough," the Reverend responded, "rough enough."

"You're right, Reverend. I've had enough of it, too."

"So you took action." He seemed to understand.

"Yeah. It's the first really strong thing I've ever done, and like everything else I've tried, I blew it."

He looked as if he knew exactly what she was talking about. "You weren't happy to wake up and find yourself alive, then."

"You can say that again."

"You weren't happy to wake up and find yourself alive, then." He said it again.

"Very funny, Reverend. No, I really wasn't. I was -- I am -- MAD! No one has the right to interfere with a person's decision to go, to die, especially when that person has taken care of all major responsibilities."

"You may be right. .... So, should I leave?" The Reverend stood up.

"....No. I'd like you to stay a moment and answer a question. Maybe you can explain what that obnoxious shrink was doing here, interrogating me, before you came in."

"Didn't she explain?" he wondered.

"Yes she did, a bit, but I had to pull the little I got out of her. And she's not an honest person. She had more up her sleeve than she was saying." Carla paused and then added, "Furthermore, I found her visit intrusive and offensive."

"I'm sorry about that, Carla. That's not my jurisdiction and I won't be able to save you from the assessment process."

"Can't you just slip me some cyanide? Or maybe slip her some?" The Reverend raised his eyebrows and so Carla added, "Just kidding."

He smiled and shook his head no. "All I can do is slip you some insight, Carla. Insight into another dimension of reality."

"Sounds profound. Maybe later. I'd like to go to sleep now." Suddenly she felt more tired than ever. And she had no sense that the Reverend or anyone else could change her reality, or any piece of it.

How tiring all this babble was. But would sleep offer any escape? No. Death is the ticket, she reminded herself. Absolute death.

"Sure. I'll check in later or tomorrow, depending on what your various doctors think about more visitors." The Reverend seemed to bow a little again.

"I have more than one doctor? But why ask them?"

"Just procedure. One of the hassles of life here on earth. More than most of us bargained for -- all this red tape."

"Bye." Carla closed her eyes and drifted into a floating sleep.

"Take care, Carla." He seemed to mean it. "And bless you."

16.

SAME CHURCH….

The mission priest was nowhere to be found. The shower in John's office was handy and John was able to lead this young soldada de los muertes, as she called herself, across the street to make use of it. After a long long time in the shower, the young soldada de los muertes emerged. She had finally decided she trusted John, at least somewhat. John was stunned to hear the story she told once he got his friend Enrico at the Sol Ray Café down the street to translate.

That many of the other girls had likely died on the way in was not surprising. Such a long trip in a coffin. This was days and days in a box.

They had wanted this! Yes, because for them the risk of death was preferable to life on the run. They had been helped to escape from the people who were buying and selling them, from that life of slavery and abuse they had been and or were being sold into. Were they caught again, they would surely be killed or spend their lives in chains until they were no longer strong, pretty, fertile, a source of healthy organs, or of other value, and then be killed.

People who did not live in their world could hardly imagine that this sort of thing was going on. Girls and young women, sometimes boys as well, being taken, their wills trashed, being denied ownership of their own bodies, of their own flesh -- their lives being bought and sold ... for work, for sex, for eggs, for anything — absolutely anything the buyers wanted.

This particular human trading company, *Cuerpas*, specialized in beautiful young women, White, Latina, and Indigenous American or Indio as they were called in many parts of Latin America. The girls were sometimes lured in, but most often they were "taken" — kidnapping was too simple a word for this "taking" process.

Every single aspect of a girl's existence was commanded, taken from that girl by whatever means possible. Certainly, threatening to take the lives of the girls' loved ones and entire families was often part of the process, a main key, as was threatening to take the girls' own lives. But the buyers had to be careful, because if the girls were sure they were already as good as dead, they would kill themselves and then be of no worth. Of course, in the view of their owners, there were times when the girls did have to be discarded.

Physical torture and abuse served as another one of the primary keys to having the girls acquiesce entirely, become entirely compliant and totally subservient. And then there was the psychological and spiritual abuse which, after all else was inflicted, proved to be the most powerful. Lock the girls up, feed them sparely on a rigid schedule, keep them always hungry, filthy and beaten. But allow them a shred of hope, a glimmer of possible relief, often enough that the girls would still want it, crave it, long for this relief.

At the same, time, offer continuous verbal degradation until it becomes almost a truth, then a kind word, then more abuse. A sort of step-by-step negative barrage with slivers of positive reinforcement for bowing ever more into subservience. First subservience for survival, then subservience for survival, then subservience because there is nothing else any more.

17.

SAME HOSPITAL ROOM….

"Knock-knock."

Carla was startled out of her sad daydream. She opened her eyes, rubbed them in order to focus, found herself still in the hospital, and moaned, "What now?"

Someone in an oversized trench coat and ugly hat came in. "Detective Stanger, City Police." He took off his terrible hat and, for a moment, looked as if he might salute. He wasn't really city police, but not good to explain this right now, he told himself.

"First I'm mentally ill, then I'm a sinner, now I'm a criminal," Carla told him groggily.

"I doubt any of those labels hold, ma'am," he said flatly.

Carla had no desire to talk to this stiff, Ken-doll sort of highway-patrol type, she told herself. "Why are you here? Do you really have to bother me?" she asked faintly.

"Just routine, ma'am."

"Cut the ma'am stuff, please." Carla tried to sound stern, but all she felt was eroded inside -- hollow and weak. Too many people, an unwanted parade. The wrong parade.

Carla could see that this Mr. Stanger was appreciating her looks. She hated it when men stared at her. "Stop staring. Please."

"Excuse me, ma'am, I'm just trying to get the picture."

"Sure you are. The name is Carla. And the picture is I made a mistake. And, given that, now I have to deal with people like you and that Phyllis --"

"Phyllis?" He obviously did not know her. Or was he pretending ignorance?

"Yes, the hospital shrink."

"Oh yes, Phyllis," he sounded as if a light bulb had gone off in his head.

"Look, I don't know what you want. But I'm not it." Carla sighed. She wished he would stop staring at her, undressing her with his eyes and trying not to look like he was doing so.

"I want to know if you're all right, ma'am."

"Ask the doctors," Carla answered. "They seem to think it's up to them, not me."

"And I want to know if you're going to be all right when you leave here." He was scanning her face for some kind of response. Was there any truth behind her beauty?

"Well, join the crowd. They seem to think I'm a potential future suicide." She was, of course, a potential future suicide -- actually, an actual one -- but she wouldn't tell him, or any of them.

"That is not what I mean." The detective sat in the same chair that the head doctor and then the Reverend had used. The detective would catch the doctor's idiocy, if it was contagious, Carla mused.

"Then get to the point, detective," she insisted politely.

Suddenly he was at a loss for words. "Uh --"

"I said please get to the point. I'm very very tired and I will definitely fall asleep soon, so you'd better say it quickly."

"OK, I'll drop all social niceties, Ma'am."

"Please do." Carla tried to laugh, but couldn't. Her chuckle came out like a sort of giggled snarl. "You're no good at them anyway," she suppressed her scoffing as much as she could.

The detective crossed his arms. "So, Mrs. Goodman --"

"Carla, just Carla, please." If she was called Mrs. Goodman one more time she would scream, she complained to herself.

The detective seemed to need to collect himself in order to get to the point. He sat up straighter, cleared his throat, eyed the cuts and bruises on this woman who had almost died just recently and asked, "Carla -- are you the victim of domestic violence?"

Carla's breath caught in her chest. What was this question coming at her? "What? Am I the what?"

"Are you a battered woman?"

"What?"

He knew that she knew what he was talking about, but he played along anyway. "I mean, has your husband hit you?"

Carla recoiled and tried to hide the fact that she was recoiling. Wilting a thousand wilts in but a second, she revived herself with anger. “What is this? This is such a rude intrusion. You have absolutely no business here. Get out. Get out!”

“I’m afraid I do have business here, Mrs. Goodman.”

“How so? I’ll call hospital security.” But Carla knew he wasn’t completely wrong.

The detective was uncomfortable having to upset this woman. “Over twenty severe bruises and contusions were found on your body when you were brought in here unconscious. It’s doubtful that you beat yourself. Most of the marks on your legs and torso were made from behind you. The force of most of the marks even on your sides and front had to come from someone other and stronger than yourself. There were several cuts of significance. Because of your life-threatening condition at the time of your admission, they did not receive as many stitches as they might normally have. Nevertheless, the combination of all your injuries, put together, looks like it could even be a felony-level battering, or even more than one of those over time, not some so-called forgettable misdemeanor. Either way, whoever beat you has committed a serious and punishable crime. Do you understand this?”

In her still somewhat anesthetized state, Carla had not realized that, in that last horrible interlude with Burt, she had sustained visible bruises and wounds, and had needed stitches.

Now she felt her heart sinking down into what seemed like a vacuum -- a black hole -- of misery. Now what?

“Do you understand this, ma’am?” The detective pressed for a response, “The ramifications of this, ma’am?”

Ramifications? Now what? Carla felt her stomach collapsing in on itself. She gulped. “I have absolutely no idea what you’re talking about,” she played dumb. She felt dumb.

The detective tried to speak calmly. “Do you mean to suggest that you were beaten while you were unconscious and have no memories of receiving any of these injuries? That can’t be. As I indicated a moment ago, some of the injuries are older than that. They happened some piece of time before the suicide attempt if — if — uh --”

Carla glowered at him from under her heavy eyelids. “What — if what?”

“If that is what this was.”

“What? I don’t understand you.” She did not. She could not get it.

“Ma’am, you have been severely beaten and more than once.”

“What are you talking about? What did you do, study my naked body while I was out of it?”

“No, not me,” he said, embarrassed by her reference to his looking at her beautiful body. Which he had indeed seen parts of while she was out, he admitted to himself silently.

"Well, the doctors must have mixed up my files with someone else's. You have the wrong person. I don't know what you're talking about."

The detective stared at her neck. She had not yet realized that hospital staff had washed off her make-up. There were the off-color remnants of hefty bruises there. In fact, there were even hints of something approaching strangling. "Ma'am, Carla, I'm just here to help you," he warned.

"Well, you're making me very sick. You're not helping. Please leave." She turned away and closed her eyes.

"Yes, I'll go soon. But first, tell me how you got those marks on your neck. It looks as if someone tried to strangle you. And where did that black eye come from? And why the stitches on your forehead?"

"What? On my forehead?" Carla touched her head and gasped. She told herself that the sedatives must have numbed her so much she couldn't feel the stitches. Carla thought about what the detective was saying. She had forgotten the most recent beating, the one that had happened when she had gone home for Sheila's picture, right before her suicide attempt. But Burt had grabbed her by the neck the beating before that, right before she had gone to John.

"Haven't you seen yourself? There are bruises and cuts all over your body as well as those on your forehead."

Carla realized that she hadn't seen herself. "I guess not," she said. She was going to have to play very very dumb very very convincingly. The bruises must have darkened the day after she was hit, after she took the pills and poison. They certainly hadn't shown when she had looked herself in the mirror to say good-bye to her sorry life. And the cuts, well the cuts, she hadn't realized these were so bad. Anyway, she had figured that someone would think she fell because she got dizzy on all those pills.

"Carla, I have to ask -- it's my job -- was someone in the room with you at that motel?"

"Was someone in the room...?" She repeated his strange question.

"Did someone come in and attack you?" He looked as if he believed this.

Carla acted befuddled. "Not that I remember."

"Carla, Mrs. Goodman, are you protecting someone?" Now the detective was starting to sound stern.

Yes, you fool, myself. Just leave well enough alone, Carla told him with her angry eyes and then she replied aloud, "No, I am not protecting anyone."

"Carla, who were the people you saw during the twenty four hours before you ingested the poison?"

"Um, uh ... I have to work hard to remember. It's all a blur. I'm groggy. But what are you getting at, and why are you bothering me about it?"

"Carla, let me get to the point," he said.

"Yes do," she responded impatiently.

"Were you forced to swallow all those pills and take the poison?"

Carla was silent. And she was startled. She knew enough to know that what he was saying sounded more like attempted homicide than attempted suicide. How could the detective think this? Finally she managed to whisper a shocked and indignant, "Absolutely not. Don't insult me with your inane questions. Now please just go. Get out."

"Mrs. Goodman, Carla. I wish I could just go and let you rest. But I have to be investigating any possible assaults and attempted homicides. Assault with the intent to kill is a serious crime. It's almost murder. Had you died, it would be murder."

Her porcelain skin turned red.

"Really, Mr. Strange or whatever your name is, I tried to kill myself. I have a sad life. I decided I wanted out. I made a mistake. I won't do it again. That's all. Now I'm falling asleep, really I am, so just leave."

He stood up. "All right. I'll be back. Think about it, though. Even if you weren't forced to take the pills and the poison, you were probably in a suicidal state of mind after sustaining such a severe beating. And the doctors tell me that there are old scars on your body, indicating that you have been hit and beaten a number of times over the years."

At this, Carla opened her eyes a little too wide and tried to act a little too tough. "What's the big deal?"

The detective cleared his throat. “Even though major efforts have been made to reduce domestic violence, and even to hold both perpetrators and victims (survivors) accountable for a larger share of it, and even though some of these efforts have had a positive effect in some ways, a man still beats a woman every ten or so seconds in the US. Worldwide, men batter many millions of women a year. All kinds of these women suffer permanent injuries including brain damage, speech loss, deafness, paralysis, sterility, miscarriage, damage to internal organs and, what would also be a pity, for any woman and certainly for a beautiful woman such as yourself, mutilation and permanent disfigurement. And, a shockingly significant percentage of women who are murdered are killed by their batterers. Sometimes the murder is an accident and sometimes it is not.”

“Detective, I haven’t been beaten a number of times over the years, and, I would have certainly called the police if my husband had beaten me even once. I didn’t. Ever. Check the records.” Carla hoped Stanger would not see she was lying, lying a lot.

But the detective wasn’t convinced. “Unfortunately, most women who are beaten by their boyfriends or husbands never call the police, ma’am. Even these days. They are afraid of retaliation, social stigma, and more.”

This sounded like something this man had learned in a seminar somewhere. Carla clenched her jaw. “Why are you telling me this?" Now what, she worried. This was a bizarre twist she had not foreseen.

"Because you may be one of those women." The detective stared into Carla's eyes, looking for the truth. "And, women in your social situation are quite ashamed when this sort of thing happens, and tend not to report it. Even these days."

"Good-bye detective." Carla closed her eyes and kept them closed, hiding her panic. Get out now. Oh God, go away.

The detective looked at the battered woman a moment longer and then shook his head and left the room. He was determined to get to the bottom of this, even if it pointed to the well known Burt Goodman himself. Which it had to, the detective thought again.

18.

ALONG SAME DIRT TRACK IN THE JUNGLE….

Several hundred miles of rugged terrain lay between the cadre of rescued girls escorted by the back-up group, the 23rd team of female soldiers, and the safe haven where the other teams would be waiting. Going was slow, and food and beverage was limited to what one of the soldiers, disguised as a Catholic nun, could bargain for in small marketplaces they found in villages along the way.

Stopping for anything was always a project, as the two jeeps and the stolen truck and girls had to be hidden and guarded each time. The soldiers knew their cargo was precious, more precious now that they had "stolen" it. This cargo would be desired by many a bandit, including the human trade and organ smuggling operation they had rescued the twenty-nine girls from, *Cuerpas*. Well, actually, twenty-eight girls plus one they had found passed out on the road covered in blood. Apparently she had been killed unsuccessfully, and then thought to be and left for dead.

Now, the soldiers were on alert. Anyone who found out that there were that many “captive” girls in the cargo compartment of the truck would want to take a piece of the hefty sum they would bring on the black market, especially as a package deal. And by now, word that this slave cargo had been “stolen” from its “owners” had to be out. Of course, travel was more perilous than stopping. The threat of detection and ambush while in motion was constant.

The back end of the truck had been tied loosely closed, with the doors banging open a few inches at each bump, so that the wounded and still bleeding girls could breathe and see. They huddled inside like wounded bloody red birds in a cage, wings clipped, blinking with each jolt.

19.

SAME HOSPITAL ROOM….

Carla forced herself to block out the shock and confusion caused her by the prying questions Mr. Stanger had asked her. She had to. She had to un-hear what she had just heard. She had to not-know what she now knew. She had to run away, deep into her mind. She desperately raced back into melancholy reminiscences of times long gone.

After her parents had been killed, Carla had grown quite numb. She had kept on with her work, her studies, her various jobs to help pay her way through college, and her senior year applications to law schools. But she had switched to running on automatic. Running on empty. A troubling hollowness had started to invade her but she was able to hold it at bay by being busy.

Carla had no living biological relatives. Her parents had left her a letter which stated that, in event of their untimely deaths, John's parents had agreed (years prior) that they would help Carla handle the affairs related to their deaths. Carla was told that her parents left enough money to pay all her tuition through graduate school should she choose to go, and to hire a trustee, one which they had already named. Most of the business was handled by a trustee, but John's parents helped a lot. Carla made a very private decision to work her way through graduate school in order to stretch the money, the only contact she still had with her parents, on as many years as she could.

Daily life had then grown more and more demanding, until it finally took her on a long long journey away from herself. And, in a way, Carla wanted this, because she felt so alone here in this life, so very stranded without her parents who had understood how different she was because they had been that different themselves. Carla wondered if she'd ever find any other members of her tribe.

Life went on. Not long after her parents' deaths, Carla realized that she was pregnant with John's child. She then told John right away.

"Sorry," she had apologized, as if it was her fault. "Sorry John."

John, although stunned, was a gentleman. "You don't have to apologize. I'm as responsible for this as you are. I'll do whatever you want. Just tell me. You know I love you, Carla," he pledged.

But his heart wasn't in it. Carla could tell. John looked scared.

To make matters worse, although under other circumstances the pregnancy could have been cause for celebration, both Carla and John had just been accepted to Harvard Law School. Carla had watched John's parents' faces when they were told John was accepted. They were ecstatic. They had worked their entire lives to see such an opportunity unfold for one of their children. And John was their brightest. And their only son.

Carla had watched the family congratulating John and decided that she would not impose. She would not interfere. She would not want to see the shock and horror on John's mother's face when she told them that she was pregnant with their first grandchild.

Carla had an abortion. She had told John that she probably would and John had not tried to stop her, not at all. So one day she went and did it. Later, John whispered, "thank you" in her ear. Hearing these words, Carla was deeply hurt. She felt rejected. She felt alone. She felt that the one source of unconditional love and connection to her tribe she could have found now that her parents were gone was the love she had just murdered -- her baby.

After that, Carla and John remained friends, but they grew apart. It was sad to see. They both went to Harvard but saw each other only sometimes. John seemed to never quite understand why it was that Carla had pulled away. But he never actively tried to win her back. He felt horribly guilty about the abortion but he never told Carla. He didn't think he deserved her anymore.

Time went by. Harvard was challenging and the challenge distracted Carla from her pain and loneliness. Carla was at the top of her class in all her classes even though she was working two part time jobs.

She had one rival. He was six or seven years older than most of the students in his year -- and thus almost ten years older than Carla who was several years younger than the average age there. This rival had earned an MBA at the Harvard School of Business first, right after graduating from college, and then had traveled around the world, then had started his own business, which was running successfully when he finally began law school. His name was Burt. Burt Goodman.

Burt noticed Carla immediately. Who didn't? She was bright, beautiful, articulate, competitive but kind, and she was number one. And she had a tremendous amount of energy.

Burt had sidled up to Carla one day in the hall. "If you can't beat 'em, join 'em."

Carla had forced a smile. "You talking to me?"

"Yep. As I see it, you're the only real competition I face here. The rest are pushovers. So what about dinner?"

Carla looked at him. He was olive-skinned and blue eyed -- and stunningly handsome, a stud. Not at all her type. She forced a testy grin. "I plan on graduating at the top of our class. Can you handle that? Most guys can't."

Not to be one-upped, even in flirtation, Burt replied, "So do I. Can you handle that?"

Carla just laughed.

Burt and Carla had started out neck in neck. He was older and more worldly, but no brighter. He came from a relatively wealthy family and had also already made a significant amount of money on his own. He drove an expensive car. He had all of what he wanted materially. Except for Carla; Carla was left on his wish list.

So he got Carla.

It was that simple.

20.

JOHN'S OFFICE….

John was extremely troubled by the coming into his life of this soldada situation, let alone having this go on while he was agonizing over what had happened with Carla. Extremely troubled.

John forced himself to determine the appropriate and most responsible way of dealing with this young soldada. He was allowing her to stay in his home until he could find the priest who he supposed had been expecting those coffins. However, no one knew where this priest had gone, no one had seen him in weeks. And, this priest had left no instructions regarding coffins or anything else for that matter.

John worried that other girls could still be alive in those coffins, and went to the FBI. He chose the FBI instead of the local police because of the international aspect to all this, these coffins seeming to have come in from outside the country. He thought later it should have been the CIA. The FBI took the young soldada del los muertes into custody while John, at a loss for what to do here, began proceedings to adopt her, as she had expressed to him that should she be sent home, she would be killed.

And then there was Carla, who had actually attempted suicide. How could he have missed the signs, how stupid could he be? John wrenched with disgust, he hated himself. This was the woman he loved, the only woman he had ever loved, and she was trying to kill herself over a man who did not love her, and who would beat her until he killed her or drove her to suicide. Well, we were there now. Suicide. Almost.

John had to do something, take some kind of action.

But what? Would he be so brave as to ask Carla to marry him? Finally, after all these years?

21.

SAME HOSPITAL ROOM….

Again, someone broke into her troubled journey into her troubled past.

"Carla? Hi."

Carla's close friend, Deanne, came in and sat on the bed. Deanne's wild red hair was a mess, as usual, her wire rimmed glasses crooked, as usual, and she was out of breath, as if the wind had just blown her in from somewhere, as usual. She tried to no avail to make her hair neat and then said, "I've been trying to figure out if you would want to see me or not. So I finally decided to come down and ask. Do you want to see me? Or not? I can go if not."

Carla sighed, "Of course, Deanne, you -- always."

Deanne gulped. "Always wouldn't have been so easy if you'd managed to kill yourself," Deanne scolded as she pushed her glasses back up her nose.

"Well, we would have eventually met again, next life," Carla said dismissively.

Deanne was nervous. “Sure, next life. ... You know, Carla, you’re always talking like that, this next life stuff, but what good does it really do you? Anyway, next time, say good-bye first. If there is a next time. I mean, I hope there isn’t. I mean, oh ... you know what I mean.”

“Deanne, sometimes things are just too extreme to deal with anymore.”

“Carla, did he beat you up again?”

“That’s not it. It’s bigger than that.” Carla looked at Deanne blankly.

“Carla, let me help. Come and stay at my house when you get out of here. Don’t go back to him. Make a clean break. Do it now. This is the time to do it.”

Carla looked at Deanne as defiantly as she could manage to. “Deanne, the only clean break I can make from the pain that man has caused is death. He’s worn the very negative belief he has about me into my nervous system. And, I’ve let him do this. Now it’s my own belief about me: I’m worthless. My life is a total failure. I’m no one. He’s made this clear. He’s taken me down. He’s broken me. I just can’t come back from it anymore. I can’t.” Carla had tears in her eyes.

“Carla --” Deanne was crying.

“Deanne, please stop that. You know I love you, you’re my good friend, but don’t -- I’m too tired for emotion right now. Please. Maybe you can read me the cards on the new flowers. The new ones are sitting on the floor. We ran out of room there're been so many."

Deanne got up, wiping her eyes with her hands, wiping her hands on her plaid skirt, and read every card aloud. "Oh, here's one from John. I meant to tell you he's been here three times, and each time you've been asleep. He's beside himself, really upset, Carla, and he blames himself, which makes no sense. But I guess we all blame ourselves, in some way. Anyway, he's a wreck for sure."

"Why? That's ridiculous, this is no one else's thing. Why?"

"Carla, come on...."

Carla stared at Deanne.

"You know what I mean. Anyway, John is hurting, he cares about you, he really needs to see you."

Carla was hugely upset with John, for allowing her to be kept alive, especially after she had given him strict instructions otherwise. But, maybe she had gone ahead and done it too soon for John to even put the papers into effect, or maybe he was not around, or maybe no one notified him. Wait, how would someone know to notify John? He wasn't anyone the hospital would know to look for, not a husband, not a family member. A wave of forgiveness washed through Carla. Of course she had forgotten to have her in-case-of-emergency notify note in her wallet, and had she, it would have said notify John.

Deanne was now going through the cards on all the older flowers. Deanne tried to make a point by asking, "None from Burt?"

"Does that surprise you, Deanne?"

"No. Well, yes, actually it does. He's so glib. So slick, so concerned with his image, you'd think he'd realize how bad it looks for the husband not to bring his own wife flowers, especially a husband of his social standing."

"He hasn't been in to see me, Deanne. Not since I came to."

"God, he's disgusting." Deanne sat back down on the bed. "Why do you protect him? Why do you let him go on treating you like this?"

"Deanne, you're the only one who really knows even a bit of what he's done, and even you wouldn't believe it if I told you the rest."

"I would. Really. Try it. Tell me."

"No, I can't," Carla looked frightened and exhausted.

"But why?" Deanne asked.

"For one thing, it's private and you should never tell anyone about any of it. For another, I don't know how to describe the cruelty. Its so complex, so Machiavellian, so hidden --"

"Try. Try, Carla. Come on, you're a good writer. You have a way with words. You can do it. You need to tell someone. You really need to. And you know you can trust me to keep it confidential," Deanne pleaded.

"I can trust you never to tell anyone -- absolutely no one -- about Burt's violence?"

"Of course."

"For sure?"

"Yes, for sure. You already know that, Carla," Deanne winced.

"But even so, the situation is so complex, I don't know how to talk to you about it."

"Try. Just try." Please, please Carla, Deanne begged silently.

"But, I don't know how to explain the complicated way he treats me. I just don't, Deanne. There really aren't words to describe it. I mean sometimes I even think he *is* trying to be good to me and just doesn't know how to, you know. Sometimes I am sure he doesn't want me anymore and then at the same time, he tells me that if I ever try to leave him he will never let me get out. He beats me almost senseless, yet tells me I am the love of his life. It's confusing and heart breaking. But it's far more than this. It's sick. He's sick."

"Carla, stop protecting him. Stop or he'll kill you. Or, you'll kill you for him."

Carla heard Deanne's words echo in her head: you'll kill you for him. There was a preciously astute bit of truth here, but Carla could not admit this to Deanne – or to herself. Carla closed her eyes and pretended she was dozing off.

Deanne thought Carla had fallen asleep. She stood, went to Carla and hugged her, while sobbing openly. How could she save her friend? How could she stop the process of Carla's complete undoing? Her murder? One way or another, Carla was being destroyed.

Carla could not find a way to talk about the hidden abuse. Not just the bruises and the cuts. Those were hard enough to talk about, humiliating. But the inner bruises, the wounds to her heart and soul which were bleeding endlessly like an infinite stream of pain -- there were no words which could describe such emotional devastation. She was trapped in a system designed to destroy her and she could find no way out, no way to kill the miserable pattern, except death, Death.

Red darkness, blackish red death ….

22.

ALONG SAME DIRT TRACK IN THE JUNGLE….

It was along that same dirt track, in the same place the twenty-nine rescued women had been loaded into that truck, minus the girl that had been removed, that a rusty jeep sputtered and braked abruptly. Three lean silhouettes leapt from the jeep, anxiously pulling their pistols out and prying the dark with their flashlights. It seemed to them, there in the dark, that they were surrounded by some sort of cultivation, perhaps a coffee plantation. Or maybe it was coca, or both.

"Here! Quick!" one whispered. The other two ran to help load the found bleeding girl into the back of the jeep.

"Any more?" another asked.

"No, they took them all."

They sped away down the illicit trail through the troubled and bloody Latin American underground.

Sisters, what bloody paths we tread….

23.

CARLA'S MIND….

Burt. The great Burt Goodman, Esquire. For a few moments, Carla let herself remember Burt as he was in law school. He was indeed brilliant. And stunningly handsome. And an athlete as well. Carla remembered how every woman at Harvard Law School wanted Burt. And, back then, they all definitely had their pick of men, as there was something like seven male students to every female student. Every woman wanted Burt.

But Burt wanted Carla. She would be his trophy.

And he got her. He got every last bit of her. At first they dated casually. Then they found themselves joining the same study groups. Burt's handwriting was virtually illegible. But Carla could read it. Burt's typing was lousy. So Carla typed his notes for him and also for the study group, once in a while at first and then quite regularly.

Burt paid Carla for her typing in the beginning. However, once their relationship became more steady and they moved in together, Burt stopped paying Carla for her typing. He just expected it.

It made sense to Carla. She always tried to be fair. When they decided to live together, they went out to look for housing. It soon became clear that Burt wanted a more upscale place than did Carla.

Actually, she just couldn't afford her share of the rent in the neighborhood Burt picked. Not unless she spent all that little nest egg she had, the money her parents had left her. "Burt, it's lovely, but I just can't pay my half of our rent here. Let's take that place I showed you this morning. It's a nice place. We can give it personality."

"Carla, darling, I can't live like that. Maybe you can, but I can't. Let's not make a big thing out of it. You just pay the rent you'd be paying if we'd taken the cheaper place and I'll make up the difference."

"But Burt --"

"That's it. Say no more. It's all decided. I already signed the rental agreement."

Carla didn't really want to live in the house Burt liked. She actually thought it rather pristine -- antiseptic – and also a little pretentious. It lacked soul, but she told herself that relationships were made up of compromises. And anyway, she also told herself, look at how Burt just assumed more of the rent without blinking an eye. Quite a guy.

They moved in together. Something unspoken happened. Carla, pretty much unbeknownst to herself, felt beholden to Burt. And there it was: The first glitch in a seemingly perfect system. But, the glitch was overlooked. After all, the Carla-Burt team was brilliant, was bound to do great things, was gorgeous, was highly visible, was the ideal pairing of the ideal male and female of our times. Or so it seemed.

Perhaps, Carla thought to herself as she looked back on the evolution of her life disaster, many women have let this happen, even the ones who think they don't let this happen. Who knows? Back then, all the law students and professors knew that Carla was an exceptional young woman. She was by far and away number one in her class. And this was a class made up of the nation's cream of the crop. But no one saw that Carla took the second seat at home. She typed, she picked up, she cleaned, she cooked, she shopped, all in the name of paying her way while Burt paid more rent.

Carla was proud of herself for this, for a while -- until the next set of grades came in. Carla's had dropped a little. Now Burt's grade point average was higher than hers. Burt said nothing, but Carla sensed that he was pleased. Maybe it was just her imagination. She kept telling herself it was all in her mind and she also told herself that people with Carla's high level of intelligence should make room for others. Burt was not exactly others, but his mental ability was slightly more commonplace than Carla's. At least slightly. So she would have to be gentle with him. Noblesse oblige, her parents had taught her. The obligation of those naturally as brilliant as Carla was to – to – not just be humble – but to let life dumb her down. Or at least to appear to do this.

Still, Carla found herself studying harder. Despite the fact that she was holding down two jobs, and was also virtually Burt's personal assistant and maid, she managed to catch up with Burt the next semester. In fact, she pulled her grade average ahead of his again. This took beating Burt's semester grades by the same degree that he had beat her the last semester, and then some.

Burt was quite displeased. Or was it just her imagination? Little things revealed that something had changed. Was Burt a bit threatened by Carla? She sure didn't want to lose him. Carla actually felt a little guilty about beating Burt's grades. She would make him better dinners. Spend more time on her looks. Be better in bed. Whatever it took, maybe even let the grades drop a bit from time to time. Yes, willingly dumb down ever so little.

Burt and Carla remained neck-and-neck in the race to graduate number one until their last year of law school. Then things changed. Early in the semester, as that academic year started, Carla got pregnant. She had been using birth control religiously, but, there she was: About to enter her third year at Harvard Law School, up for top honors though she was by far the youngest in her class, and pregnant.

She decided she would not tell Burt until she was sure. It wasn't really confirmed until well into the semester. And, by then, there were all kinds of things going on. The academic pressure was intense. And, for the first time since he had started law school, Burt's business needed serious attention. New people had to be hired. Letters and other materials had to be written. Details, large and small, had been neglected too long. Of course Carla was helping Burt with all these things.

There was one aspect of the business that Burt didn't want Carla's help with. He kept everything about it in a locked file cabinet, and told her -- warned her -- that it was strictly hands off. Stay out. Carla thought this was odd, because it was the business Burt seemed most worried about. It had something to do with the shipment of something, but Burt told Carla never never to ask. Carla wondered briefly what was so very hush-hush about this hidden activity of Burt's, whether it might even be somewhat shady in some vague way, and then she got busy with life and lost interest in her question.

Time just raced by. Carla managed to ignore her own morning sickness. As Carla approached the three month limit on any relatively legal abortion, she found herself clearer than she had ever been on one thing: She would not give up this baby. She would not lose the only blood relative she had in this world. Not this time. This baby was her tribe.

Suddenly it was time for the holidays. As in the past, Burt took Carla up to spend the weekend with his very large family. When they sat down to eat, Burt's mother said, "Carla, you look absolutely wonderful. Glowing."

Burt put his arm around her, "Yeah, she's gorgeous isn't she, mother?"

"Oh Burton, she's always gorgeous, but something's different. .... Are you two keeping a secret from us?"

Carla winced. His mother was asking the question of the hour. How could this be happening? Why now?

Burt looked perplexed. All the other noise at the table stopped. Everyone stared at Carla. So did Burt. "I don't see anything different about her. It must be her hair. She's wearing it up today. Right, babe?"

Carla laughed stiffly. She thought she would sink right through the chair, down through the floor, deep into the earth. Oh, God, don't make me tell him this way.

But her future mother-in-law would not stop. "Carla, tell me now, are you expecting?"

Burt wasn't getting it. "Expecting WHAT, mother?"

"Excuse me, Burt, I was asking Carla."

Here goes, Carla said to herself. She looked into her plate feeling like the mashed potatoes. Here goes, she said to herself: "Yes," she muttered, "I just found out and haven't had a chance to tell Burt."

Burt dropped his fork. (Or did he slam it down?) Everyone else clapped.

The family pestered Burt and Carla about wedding plans the rest of the weekend. Burt spoke to Carla when the family was watching them, but he said not a word to her when they were alone.

In fact, Burt hardly spoke to Carla for almost eight weeks after that. It was impossible to plan a wedding, or even to set a date. Carla finally told Burt's mother, who kept calling about the wedding, that they would get a marriage license soon, and have the big wedding right after she had the baby and right after graduation, late June or July.

Carla prayed that she could take her last exams before the baby was born. She hoped and prayed.

Eventually, Burt started speaking to her again. He felt that she'd deceived him, that she hadn't given him a choice as to whether to have a child or not. Pushed to the limits of her heart, she offered Burt an option: "You don't have to have a child. I can go and have it on my own. I've been on my own for years. I'll be fine."

"I thought you always argued against children being born out of wedlock, that parents couldn't predict the morals of the future enough to know if the stigma of being an illegitimate child would hurt that child years later," Burt said mockingly, sounding mechanical and heartless.

"I have, Burt. And, if I'm really still worried, I can find someone to marry to prevent that problem. You don't have to be involved. Not at all."

"Ah, come on, Carla, who would marry you like that? Who else but me would even consider taking that body to his bed?" He grimaced at her swelling belly, the belly that was now in the way of their sex life, the belly that turned his gorgeous doll into what he described as a cow. "And what would my mother say?"

Now, as Carla looked back on that interlude, she realized that all the degradation she had experienced in all her years with Burt could have been predicted right then and there. Why hadn't she seen Burt for the man he was in that moment?

They'd been sitting in their pristine living room. She looked down at the floor, feeling shame about her fat belly. "I'm sure one of my friends would, Burt."

"Would what? Marry you? Yeah? Who? Who on earth could be so stupid? You're wrong, Carla! There's no one who would! Don't jerk me around. And don't you dare threaten me."

Carla stood up. She was near tears. "I'm sorry if you feel threatened, Burt. I'm not threatening you -- I love you, but -- it's up to me what I --"

Burt jumped up and yelled extremely loudly into her face. "Shut up, Carla. If I don't want to marry you pregnant, then you can be sure no one else will. It's up to me whether that baby will be illegitimate or not! Me alone!"

Carla shouted back at him, "I don't need you! You're wrong! I know there'll be someone who'll help me with this." Carla hoped she was right about this someone.

Burt came closer. He was furious. He pushed his face in closer to hers. Carla tripped backwards and dropped down into the chair behind her. He loomed over her and scowled at her big belly. "Like who?"

For the first time, Carla was wary of Burt. What was this she was seeing? A volatile man, maybe even a monster, behind his perfect face? No? Yes? No. Of course not, he is just nervous, Carla told herself.

"Who, I said!" he demanded.

Carla did not answer.

"WHO?"

Carla was silent.

Burt grabbed her by the shoulders and began to shake her. "WHO?"

Carla still did not answer.

Burt started to stomp around the room shouting, "WHO? WHO? WHO?"

Carla finally stood up and shouted back. "John of course!"

Burt leapt at her and shoved her so roughly that she almost fell. "John! That wimp? Maybe he's the father? Maybe this is all a set-up."

Carla caught her balance and sat down. She was shaking. She answered in a pleading voice. "No. No, it's you, Burt. I swear on my parents' graves. It's your child."

Burt turned and marched out the door. He knew she was telling the truth. It was his. But he would let her think that he was afraid it was John's.

Carla curled up in bed, hugged the infant coiled in her belly, and sobbed until all the tears stopped. By then, she was asleep.

24.

SAME MARKET IN JUNGLE….

Number 77 had let her hair grow about an inch to soften her look a bit. Her youthful face, so young for her age, was so innocent for what she had seen of life so far. And, her boyish twiggy-like figure rendered her pretty and to the feminine side of unisex. Would she truly be of interest to the flesh trade merchants? She was not so sure. Still, her newly acquired revealing clothes actually created the look of a sort of would-be fashion model in late adolescence. So today all of Sheila's twenty plus a couple of years of life condensed back down to maybe nineteen. Or seventeen….

That she had been ordered to roam the more hidden sections of the sprawling jungle market in Belem, Northern Peru, appearing to be soliciting men who wanted sex, made her feel quite uneasy. She found herself musing that she could conduct raids, rescue women and girls, fight hard, shoot a weapon very effectively, but was having a difficult time dealing with this prostitute role.

Heat-drawn perspiration, dank jungle dust, and something very strange in the air there, mixed to cover her skin with a thin layer of almost living filth. Swimming in this sea of people, she was perhaps too invisible to make the correct connection. She made her way deeper into the heart of this particularly unusual jungle market, selling particularly unusual things, this cross roads of humanity and inhumanity. Time went on, hours, and no sign of the human traders that she was positioning herself to be discovered by. On and on, until ... she thought she heard screams of women somewhere nearby. Where?

Follow the sound, she told herself.

25.

SAME HOSPITAL ROOM….

Carla tumbled back into the now. She opened her eyes from a nap, startled to see Burt, of all people, Burt, the part-time monster, sitting next to her hospital bed, holding her hand, with his head on her wrist. She jerked abruptly.

He whispered, "Carla, it's me, Burt. Are you awake now? I've been waiting half an hour." He sat up and let go of her hand.

Even now he was complaining at her.

"Sorry to keep you waiting," she whispered, mildly apologizing to Burt out of habit. This time there was a slight tone of facetiousness in her voice.

"No, I don't mean that you shouldn't be resting. I just mean that -- that --" Burt's face was expressionless. Either he had no feelings or he was hiding his feelings. Or maybe he didn't know what to feel.

Carla tried to sound flat. Why care how he feels anymore? "You don't like to be kept waiting. Even by someone who has almost died," she murmured.

"No. Forget it. I've been talking to the doctors, trying to find out when you can come home, Carla."

"Get real, Burt. I don't want to go home. Why would I try to kill myself if I wanted to go home?"

"Carla, please, I love you. You are the love of my life." Burt took her hand again. "We have such a tough time with each other, but you know I do … love you. We're both in pain, you know. My heart is aching, Carla."

What bullshit, Carla said to herself. She took her hand back. "No, you don't love me. You love to control me, Burt. Everything is all about you and what you need and how you look. And look how you even make my suicide attempt all about you, your pain."

He took her hand again, this time less gently. "Stop it, Carla, not here."

Carla shuddered inwardly. "Here is as safe as I'll ever be when I'm telling you what I think. You can't hit me here. You can't beat me here, at least not literally."

A hint of hateful anger swept through Burt's eyes, then he caught himself. "Carla, please, not now. Not here." Burt sounded as if he was practically begging. "Don't get silly on me here, not here."

Carla sat up, somewhat dizzy. She had things to say. "Silly? Burt, they've seen the bruises. And there are cuts with stitches too."

Burt blinked hard but looked otherwise unfettered by this news. “What do they think?” he asked far too calmly, far too cooly.

“Probably they think domestic violence. I’m domestic and you’re violence,” Carla replied.

“Carla, stop. You know there is no domestic violence. Stop.”

Carla responded in a quietly serious yet clearly tired voice. “What? Stop? Why? Why Burt? Am I supposed to continue to lie for you, to go on helping you hide your sick and cruel, abusive and violent, side? Even now? You can’t be serious. You’re the secret poster boy for the perpetration of secret domestic violence. Abusers everywhere could learn from you.”

“Carla, and you, you are the ultimate victim. Poor you. … Come on, let’s stop this, please.”

“No. Do you think I care any more? I’m tired of protecting your reputation. My whole adulthood has been about you. Now my whole death, or miserably botched attempt at death, is also going to be about you.”

“Whatever you say, Carla. But for the record, I never hit you.”

“You know that is absolutely untrue. You didn’t just hit me, you beat me, and you beat me for years.”

Burt gritted his teeth and whispered sternly, “Carla, not here.”

“You just don’t care, do you? All I am to you is the thing you need to control to feel like a man. Really, what do you care,

Burt? Honestly, what do you care? Remember how you threatened me with taking Sheila away when she was little, taking her away so that I'd never be able to find her, stealing her, if I ever tried to divorce you? Remember how you blackmailed me with my motherhood, blackmailed me into fear and then confiscated my life?"

Carla took a deep breath. This encounter with Burt was depleting her far far more than all the others – more than the ridiculous visits from the Reverend, Deanne, the shrink, and the detective.

Now Burt stared at her so coldly it scared her. And it scared her that this did scare her. What was this new piercing intensity Burt could barely restrain? He always played at being threatening when he wanted his way, but this was something else. Something else was going on with him right now. Why? Why now? Why here? And why this new fear she was feeling?

Then, the next moment, Burt's face changed and, for the first time ever, Carla thought he looked almost honestly, sincerely, sad. He shrugged. "I just came by to say I love you," he said quietly, sounding terribly hurt.

But Carla didn't trust his words. Burt's radical personality shifts and mood swings were always unnerving, but now they were quite scary. "How kind. How appropriate. ... How Hallmark card of you," was all she said in response to Burt's sudden profession of love.

They were quiet for a while and then Carla asked, "So, did you bring flowers?"

He looked at the mass of flowers on the dresser. "Uh uh," he fumbled, "Let's see…."

"Don't try to fool me, Burt," Carla warned, "You didn't. Deanne read me all the cards. Yours wasn't one of them."

"God, that Deanne, she's so nosey. Tell her to get a life and to --"

"Burt --"

"Oh God, Carla, I'm sorry. I forgot. I was so overwhelmed by this whole thing, I forgot. I'll get some right away." The angry tango, the orchestration of love and hate conducted by Burt and Carla, was camouflaged with another blast of Burt's insincerity. "Dear, I love you so much, I do."

"Sure, yea, right. Don't bother trying to convince me of your lies anymore. I've had enough of the hearts and flowers act from you. It grew old and meaningless long ago. Flowers don't really matter. The thought does. And don't apologize to me. At this point, I really couldn't care less, and couldn't believe you less. Love is not lies. Love is not abuse."

Irritated that Carla was not falling for his play at caring, or for his attempt to convince himself he was sincere, Burt looked around the room. "Who sent you all these flowers?"

"None of your business." Carla demanded.

But Burt went over and began reading the cards.

"I said stay out of my flowers, Burt," Carla demanded again. But Burt did not respect her wishes.

Carla pushed the call button. A nurse came rushing in. "Yes, Mrs. Goodman?"

"Please, I feel real sick, like I'm going to vomit. Right now! Can you help? Can you do something?"

The nurse turned to Burt and spoke hurriedly. "Mr. Goodman, I'm sorry, I have to ask you to leave. Try back tomorrow."

Burt almost objected, then shrugged, looked at Carla with an immense amount of feigned hurt in his eyes, and left. The nurse began taking Carla's pulse.

Carla pushed the nurse off gently. "It's OK, I'm OK, I just needed to be alone, to have him leave. And I do really need some Seven-Up for my stomach."

"I understand, Mrs. Goodman. You just can't be around your husband right now. It's alright. Call me anytime. I've been in your shoes. All kinds of women have. Most of us, I bet." The nurse looked at Carla so knowingly.

The nurse left to get the Seven-Up.

Carla wondered to herself: My shoes? Who could ever have been in my shoes? Who can know the convoluted messed-up misery I've been in for so long?

Carla wallowed there, in her own pain. She was separating herself from her own role in her pain, from her failure to ever leave Burt, from her failure to be a modern woman who would stand up to abuse. She was also separating herself from the anguish of so many women around the world, women who were also still feeling trapped and hopeless, still on some level or on many levels slaves to an old model of reality which was killing them, still slaves to their forced or institutionalized -- or even unwitting -- dependencies on old definitions of power and control, old values.

Slaves to their definitions of themselves. Slaves to society's definitions of them. So this is the women's liberation we all have been living, Carla wondered.

Or did I just get it very wrong? Am I the only one who does not get it? How can I have been set for liberation and ended up so trapped? Me?

Slaves, the modern way? Or just me, she wondered.

26.

SAME JUNGLE MARKET….

Out of this morass of humanity, deep in this remote jungle marketplace, a strong hand grabbed Number 77, Sheila.

Next she knew, she was gone.

27.

SAME HOSPITAL ROOM….

Carla went back to daydreaming of her past.

Burt had been such a large part of her life for so long that Carla had a hard time separating "her" past from "his." Back when he was eighteen, which was some years before he met Carla, Burt had, via a one night stand (or maybe a one hour or fifteen minute or thirty second stand), impregnated his mother's young Hispanic housekeeper.

Burt's parents had offered to pay -- actually had insisted upon paying -- for her abortion, but the young woman had tearfully declined; for religious reasons. So, nine months later, there was a baby. But, long before the due date, the young woman had been whisked away, set up in an apartment in another town, and guaranteed a monthly stipend for a certain vague number of years in order to take care of the child. Marriage was never discussed, presumably for Burt's parents' class and racial reasons. Burt occasionally sent the child a present. At the insistence of his parents, he visited once a year to deliver a birthday gift. He was not particularly interested in the child.

In fact, when that child disappeared a few years after Burt and Carla were married, Burt seemed amazingly unfazed. He told Carla that it was because he had never wanted the child. He had never married or even lived with the child's mother and thus never formed a bond with "that kid." Burt told Carla that he would have never married someone of the "likes of the child's mother." Burt said that the mother had not been "wife material" and that the child had not been "offspring material" either.

At first, Carla had been deeply shocked at Burt's comments. But then she had thought that he was just being dramatic, as was his tendency, and that he did not mean any of this. Still, on some level, Carla suspected there was more to the story. How could a girl in the early years of adolescence simply disappear? That girl had been too young to move away from her mother. And how could the father of the child, Burt, honestly be so very unconcerned? Was he just hiding his pain? Denying his great loss? Carla had wondered this back then. She had, but she had not voiced her wonders, as she had not wanted to see Burt's reactions. He just didn't want Carla prying in his business.

The girl's mother disappeared shortly after the girl did. When Carla tried to help Burt by offering to find a good detective to investigate the disappearance, Burt came unglued. He stomped his feet, yelled and threw things. Something about the look in Burt's eye said stay out of this or else. Carla had no intention of finding out what "else" might be. Carla dropped the subject and never mentioned it again. But, again and again, deep in the back of her mind, she always at least faintly suspected that Burt had something to do with the disappearances of that mother and daughter.

Whatever it was that happened to that child and her mother, Carla was a different story. So was her daughter, Sheila. Carla was considered appropriate wife material, at least by Burt's parents. Carla had the looks, the manners, the intelligence, the education, the style. They would overlook the fact that she was an orphan. This sad fact was actually in her favor in an indirect way, as Burt's parents would never have approved of the politics of Carla's parents.

Carla thought back to her own pregnancy, and the wedding. Being appropriate wife material, being pregnant with their son's child, and about to be a Harvard Law School graduate, Carla had been ushered into the role of daughter-in-law with aplomb. Everyone had been overjoyed except Burt. "But he'll come around, don't worry, Carla," Burt's mother had told Carla when she observed Burt's lack of interest in the forthcoming baby and in Carla.

Burt had not come around. But he had agreed to the marriage -- agreed by default. He had never said no. No one, not even Burt, wanted two of Burt's children floating around out there, illegitimate. That would be political suicide for a future politician, which he surely was. So finally, when Carla was most definitely showing her pregnancy, they got themselves a marriage license. That was it. Or about it. Suddenly, one Friday night, when some people were over and Burt realized that one of the men was an ordained minister, Burt suggested an impromptu ceremony. Carla was touched, at least at first.

But then she realized that she would not even have time to invite any of her own friends. Burt said, "It'll be OK. We'll save the big one for your friends and my parents and everyone who should be there. Let's just do something now so we'll feel like we're really married." He actually put his arm around Carla and kissed her on the cheek. His guests saw this and they all clapped. Burt smiled at them and bowed a bit. Great show.

So Carla agreed to the ceremony and it ended up being rather charming. One of the guests played the piano, singing sixties folk songs. An all night bakery delivered pies. Burt was kind to Carla and fed her bites of pie off his fork.

After that, Burt was somewhat warmer. "Well then, we're husband and wife now," he said the next morning. "Guess that means this is for real."

"Well, I should hope so," Carla said with a joking lilt in her voice, hoping she was covering up the sadness she felt at the thought that Burt had perhaps been contemplating getting out of the whole thing. Of course, she had been prepared for such a decision on Burt's part. She had even offered him the option.

But that was all in the past now.

Life went on. The last semester of law school was well underway. Carla was tired a lot and could not keep up with the typing she had been doing for Burt. She could barely contribute her own notes to the study group she belonged to, as now, for the first time ever, she was falling asleep during lectures. Being bright, Carla was able to appear to keep up, but now she was always a bit behind. She dropped out of the study group because she felt she could not contribute her share of the work. What this meant was that she had to make certain she studied all the right stuff on her own, while everyone else had a team to work with. And Burt wasn't much help.

Once she asked Burt to stay home from his study group and study with her. He turned his back to her. On his way out the door he said, "Carla, I'm willing to marry you. I'm willing to be a father to this baby, but I'm not willing to blow law school because of all this. You're smarter than I am. You just remember the stuff without having to force it into your brain. Your natural smarts are going to get you through, but me, I am smart, but not enough to slack off. And skipping study groups is slacking off. Don't ask again. Nether of us can afford to have me blow it this semester. You yes. Me no."

Carla stood up and made her way, with the slight waddle of her pregnancy, across the room to Burt. "But Burt, I really need the help and the companionship. Please. Just this once. I hardly ever ask anything of you."

"Hah," he stood in the doorway and snorted.

"What does that mean: hah?" Carla asked.

"Who do you think has been paying your rent all this time? How do you think you got to live like this while going through law school? And how do you think you got to marry into a family such as mine, one you'd never have qualified for if you hadn't gone and gotten pregnant?" He narrowed his eyes and stared at her. "Don't say you never asked anything of me."

Stunned, Carla reached out and grabbed Burt's hand. "Burt! You don't really mean that. You're not really this kind of man. This isn't you talking. Please take it back. Take it back now. I don't want to see you this way."

"Let go of my hand, Carla." Burt started to turn to leave.

Carla let go of Burt's hand but then she held onto his arm with her other hand. "No. Wait, before you go, just say you didn't mean it."

"I meant it all right. Now let go of me." Burt was angry.

"No, Burt. Don't leave after talking to me like that. Please. I can't take it."

"Carla, let go, I'M LATE. YOU'RE STOPPING ME FROM STUDYING!!! YOU HAVE NO RIGHT."

Shocked and humiliated by his treatment of her, Carla did not let go. So, Burt hit her on the side of the head, quite hard. She fell to the floor. Then he said, "Don't blame me, you asked for that." He turned and walked out.

Burt had never really hit her before. She found a bruise on her neck by her ear. She covered up the bruise with makeup. When he came home, Burt didn't ask her if she was all right. But Burt never asked Carla if she was all right. And he never said he was sorry. It was always as if he had not hit her, he had not done anything in any way out of line.

Carla never asked Burt to stay home again. Ever.

In the remaining months of law school, Burt and Carla separated their studies from their marriage, almost as if they weren't in the same classes and weren't both heading for the same major set of final exams before the same graduation date.

Carla was tired a lot. She continued getting sick long after the morning sickness should have worn off. Suddenly, all kinds of foods nauseated her. The increase in crackers and reduction in other foods seemed to affect her brain a bit. Or maybe it was hormones. She was not thinking as quickly and clearly as usual.

Carla went to her doctor. "I feel like I'm suddenly retarded or something. Is it the pregnancy? Is it sapping my intelligence?"

The doctor told her that some women do feel this sort of thing is happening to them while pregnant. It was nothing serious and certainly nothing permanent.

The doctor suggested that Carla drop out and do her last semester of law school the next year. Carla said she could not because her husband already had an offer at a prestigious law firm in California. They were going to move there and take the bar exam there.

So that was it. Carla decided to do her best, to finish the semester, to graduate and forego any thought of the number one slot. At least she would graduate; there was no question about that.

Carla graduated twentieth in her class. But Burt graduated number one. His family was very proud. Carla went into labor during the big party the family threw for them, a party which was basically celebrating Burt's "number one" title. Burt was not very happy about Carla's timing.

Carla whispered to him: "I'm in labor, Burt. It's starting."

"Not now, Carla," he said,

"Burt!!!" She clenched his arm. He threw her hand off of him so roughly that Carla lost her balance and fell against the wall. Burt checked around to see if anyone had noticed. No one had. The room was far too crowded. Carla felt the impact of her banging against the wall in every bone in her body, in her uterus, in her baby, in her heart. She tried to ignore the depth of her pain. Burt walked away.

Shaken, Carla slipped out of the room, found one of her girlfriends, and begged that friend to drive her to the hospital. "We'll call Burt when it's closer to the time," she promised her friend, revealing nothing of the recent scene with Burt.

Her friend agreed reluctantly. Problem was, Carla had an extremely short labor. The baby was born before Burt got there. When Burt and his family arrived, Burt whispered to her only one thing: "I wish it could have been a boy."

"I'm sorry you're not happy, Burt," she whispered back. "I am."

She was in love with her daughter, Sheila, from the moment she laid eyes on her. In that instant, all past loss, all sense of being family-less, all sense of meaninglessness and hurt was gone. The baby answered all the questions. So this was what life was about!!! This was family. Tribe.

Burt forever denied that he had told her that he wished the baby had been a boy. But Carla never forgot. She came to know that Burt was willing to lie -- lie to her and to himself.

She was not surprised that when she later mentioned that he had hit her while she was pregnant, and that she had been relieved to see that the baby was all right anyway, he had denied hitting her. "Oh come on, Carla. You know I didn't hit you," he had said. "It's just like you to over-dramatize things. You need a shrink."

It was just like Burt to rewrite history. He seemed to block out any memories of his own dark side, and to exaggerate all of his memories of hers. In Burt's eyes, he was a great and kind man. A gift to humanity. Virtually a saint.

28.

SECRET FLESH TRADE HOLDING CENTER….

Number 77 had been taken by exactly who she was sent to be taken by. From one moment to the next, she went from being women's freedom and liberation fighter of the IUWM to being the very sort of captive she sought to set free. The shock of the transition was more than she had expected. Of course, being a captive would be unpleasant, of course the fear would run high, of course protest could mean death. She had expected all this. She had even expected to feel this wooziness as she came to after being tranquilized by her captors.

What had come as a surprise was the captivity itself. One minute free, the next crunched up in a crate, its air holes giving it a cage-like ambience. An animal in a trap.

Hours went by, no food no water. But they have to feed me, don't they? Don't they? They have to keep me alive and healthy to sell me. Don't they?

The waiting for she did not know what gave her extended time to think. The airless heat as well as the residues of the tranquilizer made her light-headed, and the thinking poured through her in rocky waves.

Suspended there, trapped, a what-have-I-done feeling came over her first. Fearing that she would slip into life-endangering panic, she felt herself hear the voice of her captivity trainer: DETACH DETACH DETACH. She was able to keep the fear and panic at bay by silently repeating to herself DETACH DETACH DETACH until she could focus on something not there in this crate. Focus, focus, focus on – on – on --

What? What? Oh, wait, here's something. Anger, focus on anger. Anger, anger, anger. Anger will do. Anger and then....

She angrily remembered the letter she had sent her mother shortly before her disappearance. How cruel of her to do this to her mother. How could she have done this, she asked herself. Now she grabbed onto this anger at herself as if it were a life raft, as a way of staying sane in this cage. Her disappearance had been carefully staged, so that her enlisting into this underground militia would remain a secret. Regret, a sharp pang of regret, seared through her. These were tough words she had written to her poor mother, who by now most likely thought she was dead. Tough words for a poor woman caught in a mess she could not escape. Trapped. Her mother just did not get it, she did not and could not get it, Sheila told herself. But was this a reason to hurt her?

So did she read it all alone, let alone by now? Now? Now?

Mama! I want my mother! Sheila held her anguish silent. She forced herself to be very still and stay quite. Her life was at stake.

A new surge of panic threatened to engulf her, and she wanted to scream. But she had to let them think she was still out, drugged, so that she could buy time to prepare for what might be next. Panic. Panic. Shiver. Stop. Stop! Do not let go. Detach. Detach, Detach.

Number 77, number 77, 77 of the IUWM.

Finally this chant bored her, and she slept, all crumpled up, dreaming about this puzzling and life-threatening directive from General Dame, accompanied by her orders to " ...escape and, when needed, the rare suicide."

29.

SAME HOSPITAL ROOM….

"I'm back, Mrs. --, no, Carla."

"I am no longer available to speak with you, detective."

"I'm afraid you have no choice." He sat down in Carla's hospital room, rather unsteadily, knowing how unwelcome he was.

"How can you say that, detective?"

"Easy. I just did," he answered.

"Get out of here. Just leave." Carla turned away.

The detective stood up and started to pace. "I can't. Look, the fact of the matter is that the medical reports, and thus the police department, claim there is reason to believe that you were violently beaten not long before you ingested the sleeping pills and poison. And the view is that the beating is linked to what is either your own attempt at suicide, or someone else's attempt at murder, a murder designed to look like your suicide."

Carla was still facing away. But she was frozen with an irrational fear. She did not know exactly why.

He went on pacing. “You can either help with the investigation of this crime or you can make things difficult. Just keep in mind, your life is still in danger. And, in a strange way, you may be an accomplice to your own murder. Well no, not really, but you are still in danger.”

Carla made herself turn to the detective and mutter defiantly, “Thank goodness.”

Taken aback by her comment, the detective sat down and massaged his brow. “Mrs. Goodman, Carla, it’s pretty obvious that you’re protecting someone, most likely your husband.”

“Him? Why would I want to,” Carla caught herself, “-- I mean, need to -- protect *him*?”

“Because, Mrs. Goodman, your husband is being investigated for attempted homicide.”

“WHAT?” Now Carla felt as if she was the subject of a bizarre practical joke.

“I said your husband is being investigated for attempted homicide.”

“Oh, this is madness. Just get out of here. Just give me a break! This is beyond belief! Can’t a woman just commit a simple suicide and be left alone?!!!”

The detective stared at Carla. What sort of bizarre denial was this woman in?

“Leave or I’ll have you thrown out,” she said.

The detective didn’t move. Carla began to buzz for the nurse.

"OK, OK lady. I'm leaving the room." He stood up and shoved the chair back. "But you can count on one thing. I'm not going to drop this case. So many women who die violent deaths come out of domestic violence situations. And, we always start the investigation with the husband, ma'am."

He tried to slam the door as he walked out. But it swung, most belligerently, back and forth on its slam-proof hinges.

30.

SAME HOSPITAL ROOM….

The chubby nurse answered Carla's anxious buzz. "Yes, Mrs. Goodman?"

"Please, no more visitors. They're all upsetting me -- not exactly upsetting me, but tiring me. I just can't find the energy to deal with so much so fast. Especially that detective. He's horrible. Disgusting. Rude."

The nurse rearranged Carla's sheets and shrugged her shoulders apologetically. "Oh, well, you know, we can't really interfere with a police investigation."

"Well, I know it's not up to you, but you could maybe call my doctor and ask if they can tell the police to wait until I get out of here or something." Carla stopped the nurse's work on the bed by putting her hand on the nurse's arm. "Please. Please. Please."

"I'll try, Mrs. Goodman. I'll do my best."

The nurse left.

Detective Stanger was dangerous. He was on to something, and he knew it. But he was wrong. No one, not even Burt, had tried to kill her. Why would Burt bother when he had killed her so thoroughly so long ago? She was already living dead. Why would Burt risk being put on death row when he'd already succeeded in getting away with the secret and prolonged psychological murder of his wife? No way.

Carla paused in her thinking a moment.

But Burt! *Burt had been trying to kill her*! Of course he didn't brutally coerce her to take an overdose of sleeping pills and rat poison. He didn't need to. He would get her to do that to herself. She would indeed be accomplice to her own murder.

Burt was indeed a murderer. Burt was indeed a wife killer, just an invisible one – invisible to the outside world.

And, he would have her stay dead one way or another. All he had to do was continue with the intricate cruelty that he was so very capable of exacting at home while looking so wonderful to the outside world.

Burt was as cold, calculating, and vicious a murderer as they come, only he was far more subtle and sophisticated. He would never be punished for his crimes. And not even in his own heart would he ever feel remorse. Remorse was not in his emotional repertoire. Not honest remorse, only pretended, acted, remorse when it suited his self-image purposes.

Carla was shocked. Why hadn't she consciously seen Burt as a killer before? How could she bring justice to this situation? How could she restore her dignity? Her honor?

Carla dozed off and began to dream about her long missing daughter. She awoke with a start. Of course! Of course!!! She knew what to do!

Detective Stanger has called it! He is completely wrong about it, but it doesn't matter! He thinks that Burt forced me to take the pills and the poison. He wants to arrest Burt for attempted murder!!! What an irony! But what a justice!

Had her suicide been successful, Burt might have been charged with murder! So that's it. The only way to catch a murderer who doesn't kill with his own hands but who nevertheless kills ruthlessly is to let them FRAME HIM! Carla was exhilarated with her realization. Burt would be punished for the slow killing of his wife, the long drawn out and hidden wife-killing, which was normally totally legal. If Burt would be framed for the final step, the last murder, a murder which makes real, which actualizes, which culminates, years of his ongoing assault and abuse, then Burt would meet justice his way. It would be out of Carla's hands, and up to fate.

In that moment, Carla determined she would surely commit suicide again, this time dying. Burt would face whatever the consequences were. Carla would not be here to cover for him anymore. The Maxwell House wives would have their revenge after all. What a righteous way to go.

Part Two

These Broken Wings

31.

SAME FLESH TRADE HOLDING CENTER….

She was out. They pulled her out, almost dead. She was virtually a throw away, and vaguely conscious. They realized this. In fact, through the fog of her dulled mind, she could hear them haranguing each other, in Spanish, about their horribly poor care of her. There would be trouble, the jefe, the boss, would be very angry, they were telling each other.

This talk went on for a while, as they stripped her, probably naked, she did not know, and laid her out on a tabletop, perhaps a surgical table, she did not know. Her numb stupor was interrupted by a blast of cold water shooting at her as they hosed her off, turned her over, and hosed her off again.

Almost awake, she recalled enough of her captivity training to keep her eyes closed. She knew to pose sleep, or semi- or even un-consciousness, until she could brace herself, and even do some contingency planning. Out of the din, there then came a stronger, louder, still male voice, but this one in English.

"Get rid of that one, over there. And this one – wait. Not yet. She's beautiful. Maybe we can still sell her whole."

32.

SAME GOODMAN RESIDENCE….

Carla was home from the hospital. Deanne knocked at her front door several times, but there was no answer. Strange, Deanne said to herself, strange because Carla was expecting her. Deanne sat on the porch and waited five minutes and then began knocking again. She was uncomfortable. What if Carla had --

Deanne refused to let herself finish the thought. She stopped knocking and tried to open the door. It was unlocked. Deanne went in, softly calling Carla's name. Deanne rounded the corner into the living room and saw Carla on the couch under several blankets, with her eyes shut. Deanne immediately went over to check to see if her dearest friend was still breathing. And fortunately, Carla was still breathing. However, it seemed that the breaths were few and far between.

"Carla, Carla. ... are you asleep?" Deanne shook her friend, "Are you asleep?"

"No, I'm dead," Carla opened her eyes and looked exasperated.

Deanne gasped.

"What are you doing, Deanne?"

"I, um, I, well, we planned that I would come by and take you out to lunch, remember? And when you didn't answer the door and it was unlocked, I came in. And then I saw you like this and I thought, I thought --"

Deanne had tears in her eyes.

Carla looked at Deanne as if she were crazy. "Yeah right, Deanne. I would decide to kill myself, to do it here, to leave the door unlocked, and to have it all coincide with our lunch date! Very smart of me." Carla knew that her feigned sarcasm would distract Deanne from legitimate concerns about Carla's still wanting to commit suicide.

"Sorry, Carla."

"It's all right," Carla laughed just a little and then took the blame. "I forgot what time it was, and I was tired so I took a nap."

Deanne helped Carla stand up. "But why are you so wobbly?" Deanne asked her friend suspiciously.

"It's nothing Deanne. … Well it is something, but it's nothing I've taken to kill myself, I mean. They have this nurse type coming over three times a day to tranquilize me. They won't let me do it myself. They don't trust me with the pills," Carla laughed, "of all things."

Deanne laughed as well, although she did not exactly see the humor. But what are friends for? Deanne sometimes wondered.

33.

REMOTE JUNGLE MISSION IN SOUTH AMERICA….

Dr. Dame, dressed as a nun, made her way through the people sitting on the steps, watching faces carefully for anyone who might look in any way suspect. So far, for several years now, the protection this Mission Assisi offered was complete, and Dr. Dame wanted it to stay that way. There was a sign on the door of the church which read, "serrada, ahora no entrada," closed, no entrance right now, yet she entered anyway, which was not at all suspect given her nun-like appearance.

A few people still lingered in the dim light, having not cleared out after the morning prayer session. The head priest, Father Coro, saw her and waved her over. He patted the pew next to him and said, "Please, sit a moment, Sister."

Sister General Dr. Dame sat, glad for the brief rest.

"Look at them, Sister," Father Coro whispered, slightly emphasizing the "sister." "They just do not want to leave the house of God, do they?"

Dr. Dame chuckled. She studied the women cleaning the feet of Jesus, at one end of the cathedral.

Father Coro saw her seeing this. “Such a myth, isn’t it?”

“Not sure what you mean, Father,” Dr. Dame whispered.

“Well, Sister, you do know that they are not cleaning the feet of Jesus per se, so much as washing the tears away.”

“Tears of sadness over that changing of the guard you mean?”

“You could say that. The coming of the male-dominated religions, taking the place of the female goddess worship that had guided so many for so long.”

“We should all be wiping our tears away now.”

“Oh?”

“Next changing of the guard is coming, has to. Or Mother earth will die, Father.”

Father Coro took Dr. Dame’s hand. “Yes, I think I hear the stampede.”

“Funny.”

“Thing is, the true meaning, the time into the future meaning, of ‘set the captives free’ has yet to be understood by the great religions of today’s world,” Father Coro mused.

“Yet to be, but will. … Hard to get it across to people that we are captives too, prisoners of a gross distortion, a wrong path in history,” Dr. Dame answered.

“Those of us who know are very quiet.”

"In your line of work, I understand. But for other reasons, as you know, my team must be quiet to be safe while setting the captives free. ALL the captives, whether or not they know they are captives."

"Amen."

"I have to go, have the meeting. Is the coast clear?"

"Yes, all safe and set. Go the back way, and then through the seventh underground tunnel, yes?"

"Yes, and always thank you, thank you, for hosting us."

"The honor is mine."

"Kudos in heaven."

"Yep."

"Set the captives free." General Dame left the church through the back, dipped into a small hidden doorway, traveled down a hall in the dark a while, and then headed into a tunnel lit by hanging lanterns. Minutes later, she emerged into a large underground room full of women and girls.

An armed female guerilla, standing at guard at the entrance, greeted her. "General, hello."

"20, how are you?" General Dame replied as she moved some of the guerilla's hair out of her eyes and straightened her beret. Other uniformed women who happened to notice this exchange immediately checked to see whether their own berets were sitting on their heads at the proper angle, and whether their collars and weapons were being worn correctly.

"Alright, General."

"Any word from or about 77?"

"None."

"Did you ask around?"

"Yes."

"She must have made it in."

"Hope so."

"We hope and pray for her in her work."

"Yes."

"Time to call everyone together. Let's start the meeting."

"Yes, General."

The women and girls formed an unusual crowd, a mix of uniformed military women and then young women, mostly girls, in what appeared to be Catholic schoolgirl dresses. Somehow, the sense of community overrode the disparate images they all together presented. The girls were living there, having been brought in after their rescues of various sorts all over the Americas and other continents. Many were still in shock after great maltreatment of various forms. Some had moved past the shock and wanted to join the militia, the women that saved them, the IUWM. Few wanted to be helped to go home, as they were all afraid of being caught again, captured and sold or killed. And many had no homes to go to, having come, nameless and faceless, living dead, throw aways, from the streets.

Some, many, of these girls would indeed be trained to serve in the IUWM. And some would even be smuggled into the US to help crack open the American-based seat of the international human trading business, and the secret but powerful American center of *Cuerpas*. The secret trip into the US would be dangerous and frightening, but nothing close to the risk they faced being returned to the streets as freed flesh trade captives. They would arrive in the US anonymously, nameless and dead, soldiers of the dead, in coffins.

34.

CARLA'S MIND….

For their daughter, Sheila, going away to West Point was more than getting an education, it was getting away from home. Sheila never told her parents about the cold hell of the beginning weeks at West Point, about the bizarre form of harassment coming from the upper classmen, the tests and frivolous drills, the trivia forced down the throats and into the minds of the new cadets, the "plebes." Sheila never complained or even reported to "mom and dad" about the sweating, the isolation, the stress, the absolute nastiness of the tyranny. But why would she tell home? She had chosen to leave them, to go her own way. And with good reason.

The facelessness of a military education was a relief from the naked inescapable identity of being the only child, the ever present, very exposed offspring, of overly invincible Burt Goodman and his overly vincible wife, Carla. For their daughter, Sheila, as much of an honor as her admission was, West Point was a retreat of bleak emotions, an orphanage of the heart, a kind of safe haven from pain. So, duty, honor and country, and a formalized form of machismo, no matter how difficult the initiation into it, was a relief.

And furthermore, Sheila hated her father. She hated the way he treated women, like things to be bought and sold. She hated the way he acted when Sheila needed money, as if she should beg for it, bargain for it, or do something degrading, she could never figure out exactly what, for it.

And she hated seeing what her mother had allowed herself to become -- or not to become. A girl cannot stand to watch her mother fail at life. This has probably always been so, but now, after all that the women's movement and feminism had brought women of Sheila's mother's generation, the failure was obvious. Sheila's mother had had all she needed to be a great success, all the brains and looks, and education. Still, she had nevertheless failed at life. Sheila couldn't stand it.

So Sheila left home. Of course, going away to college was typical among her high school classmates. But going away to West Point was, back then, very rare for anyone let alone a female, and was nothing encouraged by Sheila's parents. In fact, they had been against it. Her father said that it was no place for a young woman. Her mother said she had no desire to see her daughter in a military uniform.

"Why Mom?" The tall slim Sheila, who had beautiful eyes like her mother's, had asked Carla before she sent her acceptance form in to West Point. "Just give me a good reason and I'll decline them." Sheila would never forget her mother's response. Carla had picked up a feather duster and started dusting the living room.

"Answer me, please, Mom. Stop all that silly dusting and sit down and talk to me, please."

But Carla just dusted more feverishly. Sheila started walking around the room behind her mother, saying, "Mom, you already dusted that -- and that -- AND THAT!" Finally Sheila had grabbed the dust mop. When Carla reached out to take it back, Sheila whirled around and started dusting even more feverishly than her mother had been.

"Sheila, I already dusted that -- and that -- AND that -- and THAT -- AND THAT!!! Oh, all right, Sheila. You win. Sit down and I'll answer you."

Sheila sat down and laughed. "OK, shoot."

"Women don't shoot," Carla announced.

"Women have as much right to shoot as men do, Mom," Sheila felt so much wiser than her mother, her old fashioned, out of place in these modern times, mother.

"This isn't about who has what right, it's about not losing what womanhood is about," Carla tried to explain.

"Mom, what do you think womanhood is about? Dusting? Making coffee? Failing the bar forever so you won't have to do battle? Don't tell me not to shoot. One of us has to."

And Sheila went to West Point.

One of them had to.

35.

GOODMAN RESIDENCE….

Someone tapped on the beautiful hand-carved front door of Carla's very fine house, a fine but crumbling fortress. A voice said, "Mrs. Goodman?"

Carla had been going through one of several boxes of keepsakes, newspaper articles, letters, and old photos. She did not want to see anyone. "Who is it?" she called out reluctantly from the living room couch.

"Mrs. Goodman, it's Dan Stanger, City Police. You remember me."

Carla stared at the door with resentment. She should not have asked who it was or responded to the knock in any way. But now he knew she was home. Carla got up and went to the door, but did not open it. "I'm busy right now. I'm not receiving visitors." Carla was indeed busy, shutting the world out.

"It'll be short, Mrs. Goodman."

Carla went back to her boxes and hurriedly stuffed away the keepsakes she had been examining, her past collapsing to almost nothing as she did. One photo slipped out and blew under the couch. As it did so, Carla saw that it was a photo of herself at some sort of Burt Goodman event: she was serving coffee, as usual. A message from the army of Maxwell house wives, or a jab from them as they watch me, still here, Carla told herself.

"Mrs. Goodman, please," Detective Stanger called.

Carla went back to the door but still did not open it. "I have nothing more to tell you."

"Look, Mrs. Goodman, I can always have you subpoenaed," he threatened gently, feeling ridiculous talking to a door. "Just open the door."

"No, you can't have me subpoenaed, detective."

"Well, I can certainly try," he retorted, "or do something to that effect."

Carla sighed, pulled her bathrobe closed, opened the door, and frowned at the detective. She spoke to him slowly now, emphasizing each word as if he were foreign to the English language, which she knew was not the case. "Why do you bother me? You know I have been through a major trauma and can hardly handle anything let alone the likes of you."

The detective pushed his way in. He looked around. "Nice house."

"Who asked you?" Carla was ready to call the police, but then she reminded herself that he was the police.

"Mrs. Goodman," he said, sitting down uninvited and making himself comfortable on Carla's spot on the couch, "I am not here to be a nuisance. I am here to continue an investigation which could save your life."

"First of all," Carla said as she sank down into a nearby lounge chair, "there is *no one* threatening my life except for *me*. And secondly, given that I just tried to commit suicide, I am hardly likely to care if my life is threatened. In fact, I might be happy about it."

His eyebrows went up. She realized that she must have indicated something which, in the mind of this strange man, implied that someone was indeed trying to do her in. How could she get him out of her living room?

Carla had to get this detective out of the way if she wanted to plan a successful suicide, and, yes, maybe, if she cared to, plan to frame Burt. The detective, as wrong as he was about Burt, could end up interfering in exactly that which would prove him right. "Really," she repeated herself to emphasize her message, "there isn't anything or anyone threatening my life except for me. And, I don't think you can possibly have a case without me knowing that you do. I'm the supposed victim, remember?" Carla paused as he eyed her. "So you can leave now," she commanded.

"Mrs. Goodman, or Carla, as I have said before, the wounds found on your body were inflicted upon you by someone other than yourself. We have reason to believe that this someone is your husband. There are various persons who claim that he has been violent with you many times before. Moreover, we have reason to believe that you were *forced* to take the sleeping pills and the poison."

"So what else is new? You have some silly reason to believe this nonsense. You did tell me all of this before." Carla tried to laugh at his suspicions. She tried, but it was difficult.

"Without your cooperation, we can do very little. Even if we can prove that you were beaten shortly before you ingested the poison and pills, we cannot prove that you were forced to take them unless you are willing to testify as such."

Carla smiled innocently. "Now, why would I do that?"

"Because you are an honest person."

"For God sakes, detective, of course I *am* an honest person. My husband did *not* force me to try to kill myself. Why would he want me dead?"

"Does anyone else want you dead?" he asked. The detective's eyes were boring through Carla's eyes, right into her mind.

"Yes … *me*," she said honestly, "I want me dead."

"I find it highly unlikely that a beautiful, educated woman such as yourself really wants herself dead. I very much believe that you are protecting your husband."

What an irony, Carla thought to herself. I am in no way protecting him. I want to get out of a life with him. Why would anyone really think that I would want to protect a man who has been beating me? And, the detective actually seems to think -- *to know* -- that Burt *has been* very violent with me for years.

Then a new thought crossed Carla's mind. Maybe there was more to the story than the detective was letting on here. "Detective," she said, "you were using the word 'we'. 'We cannot prove,' you said. Are there people working on this case with you?"

"There are a few doing some research for me," he replied and shrugged. "Why?"

"Is there someone who wants you to build this case -- someone ordering you or pressuring you to get some sort of evidence against my husband?"

A hint of surprise flitted through the detective's face. He thought he had camouflaged it, but Carla caught it.

"I wouldn't put it that way, Mrs. Goodman," Stanger said.

"I would, Mr. Stanger. Someone in the department or connected with the department is out to get Burt for some reason. Is it that he has successfully defended one too many a criminal? Has he shot one too many of your district attorney's supposed air tight cases to bits?"

They were always out to get Burt on some level. He was a threat to every one of their egos. But why drag Burt's wife into their conflict? Why make her the centerpiece of their campaign to debunk and probably even disbar Burt? Carla couldn't help but wonder.

"Well, Detective, should you ever force me to make a statement, an official statement, I will say precisely what I am saying here and now, and it will be the absolute truth: Burt did not force me to take the pills or the poison. He wasn't even in the motel room with me."

"But did he inflict those wounds found on your body?"

"I stand on the fifth," Carla answered as she crossed her arms.

"You see, you *are* protecting him. And I don't think the fifth would apply here, but what do I know?"

"There are several legal concepts that would apply here." Carla tried to appear confident, leaning back and crossing her legs. "Detective, you may not realize that you are talking to a Harvard Law School graduate. There is nothing you can slip by me, no trap you can lure me into."

"Have it your way, Mrs. Goodman. Have it your way. But you'd better believe that I intend to build a case against your husband. I *know* he has brutally beaten you and I *know* that you are protecting him. I can just *feel* it. You are protecting him for some reason. But it's not uncommon. I probably already told you that many women whose husbands beat them refuse to report even the worst of the beatings. If and when they manage to call the police, they change their minds about reporting their husbands before the police arrive. When confronted with the facts, these women even deny them. They deny and deny and deny, until one day they – or at least some of them anyway -- are found dead."

"What good wives," Carla said facetiously. Such good Maxwell House wives. She could hear the coffee percolating obediently in homes all over America, an homage to days gone by, days when women were truly the second sex, and quite proud of being that. Now, they were playing at being equal to men, but what did that really mean? Carla laughed at what she viewed as the myth of gender equality. All these modern women buying into men's value systems, hah, Carla mused.

"What are you mumbling to yourself, Mrs. Goodman?"

Carla had not realized that she was mumbling. "Just a private joke between me and myself."

"I will leave you now, Mrs. Goodman." The detective stood up.

She looked up at him blankly. "Carla. The name is Carla."

"I will leave, but --"

"Good, please do," Carla stood up and headed toward the front door.

The detective followed her to the door. "But the case is not closed. I'll do everything I can to collect the evidence required to bring your husband in."

"You're making a mistake, detective," Carla said as she opened the door, "a major career error which could ruin you."

"No, Carla, you are." The detective stopped very close to her as he headed out. "A woman like you deserves better, much better." For a moment, he looked at her slightly sympathetically. And then, without thinking, he slipped, loosing just a little control of his taut demeanor, and sent Carla a fleeting, a mini-microsecond-long, a barely legible flirtatious glance. Right away, he caught himself, snapped to and was certain that Carla had not registered it directly.

But she had. She grinned sarcastically and shook her head. "You're really all the same, aren't you? You're criticizing Burt, but look at you. You're making a little play for another man's wife, for a woman who has just tried to kill herself, for someone you think is in danger of being murdered. What on earth do you think you're doing, detective?"

The detective's face had already reassumed its professional facade. "You must be reading me wrong, Mrs. Goodman. Perhaps your doctor is sedating you with the wrong drug. You should get that checked. I'll be leaving now."

He left, silently berating himself. How could he have let his guard down and looked at her that way?

Carla watched him leave. She felt numb, and, at the same time, for just a moment, a little lonely. She almost found an excuse to call the detective back when she caught herself, and shook her head no, as if she were a mother scolding a child. She silently berated herself. She made sure the front door was locked, and headed for the couch to retrieve the photo of herself serving coffee.

There it was: Carla, the Maxwell house prototype herself. Carla ripped the photo to shreds and determined to get every photo of herself serving coffee out of all her boxes of keepsakes and burn them.

On a fervent mission now, she went back to the box she had been digging through when the detective so rudely touched her reverie. Yet, trolling through the memories for other signs of her failed coffee-making-and-serving persona, she found instead the last letter she received from her daughter, received just before Sheila disappeared. It was so confused and angry. What had her child been trying to tell her? What kind of rhetoric was this? Had her daughter joined a cult? Was she still alive but a prisoner of some form of brainwashing?

Maybe this time, this reading, Carla could finally make sense of Sheila's intense message -- her last message to her mother before disappearing without a trace. Taking a deep breath, Carla dared to read this shocking letter again one more time.

What on earth had her daughter been thinking? What on earth was all this crazy talk….

36.

OLD LETTER FROM SHEILA….

[Mother, only read when you have lots of time to think about what I am saying here.]

To my flesh and blood,
Mother dear,

You should have known all this for me. Instead, you failed me in the stupor of your denial, feeding me fresh baked cookies in place of hard won truth. But now I am your teacher, your avenger, your armed daughter, your woman warrior. And I will set the world straight for us, my dear. I am the women's militia, arising from the heart of a territory not yet on the map. Come into my world, Mother, the one you should have given me.

You must wake up, Mother. Time for a changing of the guard, Mother.

Disgusting things like a husband beating his wife and then setting her on fire do not happen as often as they used to. But they still happen, in many other forms, forms much more hidden now. Even to women like you. For a moment though, take the case of Amalini Avalatra, who was married in a small village in India at the age of fifteen and who died the same year after being beaten and set on fire by her husband. Her husband claimed that she had not brought enough money -- a large enough dowry

-- into the marriage. This sort of "dowry death" and similarly motivated wife killings have been traditionally overlooked by authorities in several cultures. Of course, Amalini's death was one of so many literal and figurative dowry deaths in her country, and in other countries in other forms, that year. And still every year. Now dowry death is frequently much more implicit but happening everywhere in subtle forms.

We can be glad that such crimes against women are becoming increasingly unpopular. At least the more explicit ones are. Yes, people say the stubborn grip of patriarchal history and its mind sets have finally given way. In but a brief time span, women have made tremendous gains socially, politically, and economically, in almost every part of the world. A new woman is emerging. Her daughters face freedoms virtually unheard of but a few centuries ago. We must rejoice, Mommy. Or must we? Dare we?

We must be very careful not to overlook what is even now locking women into an ever more invisible but ever more extensive kind of second class citizenship. There is a hidden war against women's gains secretly whipping its way through every culture in the world, in courts, in think tanks, in homes, etc. Yes, a hidden backlash. Now there is a new kind of wife killing. The crime has taken new, more invisible forms. Right, Mommy? And women are helping the new murder of themselves by doing nothing to truly change the still deeper-running river of their oppression, the invisible but deep river racing far beneath the skin of history like a hidden vein. Even the most successful women of our times are missing the point. This river runs right through their minds, right through their genes.

So dear, dear woman who gave birth to me by the bloody labors of her own flesh, carefully examine the changes we call "progress," even in what we think of as the most "advanced" societies. Of course, in many parts of the world, more and more women can vote and attain educations and pursue real careers. Of course most women are no longer men's property, not explicitly. (But their minds may still be. They may still use their minds to support and perpetuate an economic, political, structural, mindset that is not women's.) Of course fathers no longer sell their daughters into "suitable" marriages. Of course the virginity of daughters is no longer a selling point to be ensured and marketed by fathers. Of course women can no longer be legally beaten, raped and murdered by their husbands, Mother. Of course women cannot be sold into prostitution against their wills. At least not in our country, not in the U.S. of A., we say. Not against a woman's will, Mom.

The question is: what is her will? How close to the past is she? How much freedom is a woman prepared to take for herself at this moment in history which finally offers so much opportunity? Can a woman actually take what is rightfully hers? How deep is her commitment to take changing herself and the world all the way? Can she take leadership in establishing her freedom in the face of lingering and ever more hidden, implicit, but deep opposition to it? Does she know how to? Does she have the will to? Or do all the centuries of domination linger on, enslaving her even though she has, at least on paper, been declared free? Even though she believes she is free, is she?

Mom, don't tell me that the balance of power has shifted far enough. Look at your own life. How can you say this? What is the puppet, the broken doll, I see hiding behind your wrinkling eyes? Who are you now? What haven't you become? And why?

And what does this make me: Who are we women who have you puppets, you only half way liberated women, for our mothers?

Can't you see the truth? You are virtually no freer than a flesh trade slave. Think about your connection to these "less fortunate" women. We are all connected. If one of us is not free, then none of us are. Don't think you know freedom, full freedom, because the chains upon your mind are still there. And don't think one woman is free when another is not.

Even now, Mother dear, every year, around the globe, there are massive numbers of women and girls being enticed, tricked, forced, and sold into slavery and prostitution against their true wills. The flesh trade industry -- in the East and in the West -- is considered an excellent opportunity for business investment. Although boys and men are also bought and sold, girls and women are the big commodity. Much of this huge business is secret, hidden. But we know it's there. How can we look the other way? Do not ask me to put down my arms, Mother. I will kill to finally right these wrongs, to set the captives of inherited naiveté, of trained powerlessness, of institutionalized blindness to truth about power, and of truly ongoing injustice, free.

Do not think Western nations are uninvolved. They just cover up their participation more efficiently. Millions of dollars, slave trade profits, are pouring into Western businesses and bank accounts, usually labeled as other earnings. Millions of women and girls, often imported from other parts of the world, are trapped into flesh slavery in big cities, including Western cities such as Berlin and Amsterdam, and in other major cities in Europe, North America, Africa, Central America, South America. This is also going on all over Asia.

Does anyone think about what this really means? Does the ongoing buying and selling of human lives say anything about human beings? Does anyone care that, once flesh trade, slave trade, girls are sold, many are beaten, abused, mutilated, even hung for killing their masters after or while they are being raped and beaten by these masters? Yes, this is happening right now, Mother. Wake up. This is still going on, explicitly as well as implicitly.

Buyers, recruiters, employers, kidnappers, and professional "child catchers," the footmen of the slave trade, are sweeping the planet, collecting, ensnaring, extorting, women and girls, as well as boys, to sell. The continuing of this forced flesh trade is a horrible reminder of the past. And, it is, if we look closely, a horrible reminder of the present.

If we are honest, the modern flesh trading of females in particular is a reminder that women everywhere, even in the most modernized parts of the world, even you, Mommy, are, in so many ways, trading their lives, their flesh, their feminine spirit, their will, their power away. Many of them are selling themselves into an invisible bondage to an old and dangerous model of reality, and an old and limited way of thinking, without realizing what they are doing! Have they become willing parties to their own enslavements, to their own deaths -- to their own wife killings?

Wake up, Mommy. What have you sold yourself into? Where is your power? If you really believe you have some power, prove it. Stop trading yourself away. Hear this. The trading will end. We women are today still chattel even where the currency exchanged, the trade being made, has become invisible. Where are we free, our minds, our thought structures, truly free. We women today have accepted the illusion of liberation as a substitute for true liberation!

Today's women should no longer stand by and not see. And they should no longer pose as liberated when their spirits – their means of seeing reality -- are still so captive. It is their daughters who shall finally seek and inherit the earth, take back the throne for Gaia, the planet spirit so long dominated. And I will see to this.

It is time for women, and the men who know them, to look very closely at their relationships, to look for the remaining forms of behavior most modern people think they have left far behind, to examine the often invisible but frequently profound power trades that they are making. Power trades in terms of whose model dominates, for example.

The unspoken agreements, the contracts that we women make with our partners in life, are always, at least as long as we live in these bodies, flesh trades. Were it only physical flesh being traded, perhaps we could turn the other cheek for a few more millennia. But it is the greater and even more precious flesh of our souls, and the collective feminine spirit, the very Gaia of Mother Earth, which we have, for so long, allowed to live in actual and conceptual, visible and hidden, chains.

The time has come to set the captives of an old power structure and on old mind set free.

That means you.

Love,

Your daughter.

37.

SAME FLESH TRADE HOLDING CENTER….

Number 77 was awake. Her eyes were open. After such maltreatment and deprivation, the fresh bathrobe, the clean drinking water, and the soothing chicken soup they were indulging her with made her feel for a while like a queen.

That important man who spoke American English came in, waved the others out of the room, and sat down facing her. "Tell me who you are and where you come from," he commanded in an almost welcoming tone. Threatening but welcoming. Some kind of unspoken deal was being offered, something like: cooperate and things will go better for you. Fail to, and you will be back in that box, or dead.

But he was speaking to her in English, what might this mean? He probably wanted to see if she could understand English, perhaps for marketing reasons. Sheila knew better than to trust this human trading company higher-up. Questions raced through her mind: Was he the owner? Would he be out in the field like this?

Could this company be *Cuerpas*? And where was she anyway? What country? Where had they brought her while she was boxed up and drugged?

Sheila was thinking quickly. She had most likely indicated in some subtle way that she understood this English, so hiding this now would be more of a red flag. She would have to speak a broken English in the accent she had been trained to apply to her near perfect Spanish.

She swallowed. In all her training and planning, she had never expected to be asked this in this setting by an American, let alone an American in this business. She could not pretend to be someone she was not, or could she? Her Spanish was excellent, as was the accent she used when she spoke it, as was the accent she used when she spoke English from within that language. She sounded quite credible she had been told. But credible in what context?

"Lisa Moreno," Sheila lied in her perfected special Spanish accent English.

She saw the man startle ever so slightly, and realized in that very moment she had inadvertently used a name which was well known in this business, Moreno. (Moreno was, in fact, a partner in *Cuerpas*.) She hoped the man would decide that this was just a name so common that it was coincidence.

"And Lisa, where do you come from?"

Where was she from? For a moment, she could not remember what she had planned to say when asked.

"I said, Lisa, where do you come from?"

Sheila's training and memory of it kicked in. "I ran away from an orphanage in Baja California when I was thirteen."

"So you are a Mexican then?"

Silence.

"So?"

"I think my father might be American, that is what someone at the orphanage said, but I do not have his name or an American Visa or passport. They gave me the last name Moreno so I would have a last name. My mother is dead. I do not know where she was from. I do not know her last name. They never married. I have no identification papers. Maybe this makes me a Mexican?"

"This will not matter. Your lighter skin will make you easy to sell."

Sheila pretended to be surprised. She absolutely had to. She could show no sign of being aware of this business and its ramifications. "Sell?" She made herself sound not only surprised but scared. She was in fact quite scared. No amount of training could totally prepare someone for this experience.

"Yes, you must have realized this by now."

Silence. Sheila was quiet, appearing scared, and in actuality, both scared and highly but secretly alert. Was this the time to begin to look for a way out? Had she collected any useful information yet? No. Did it matter? Escape or suicide were her only options, Dr. Dame had said, with escape being preferable of course.

Sheila gulped, visibly both for show and for real. She could see no way out at this time, and were she to attempt, she would be killed on the spot. She knew this.

"Do not worry. If you cooperate, this will be a better life for you than in the orphanage or on the streets."

Sheila knew to very play dumb here. She looked at this man even more fearfully.

"Seriously, if you are good, you can be sent to one of the hidden cities."

Sheila put fear on her face again. She had to think about this, without being caught thinking. *Hidden cities*. Sheila had not heard of these. No one she worked with knew about them, so far as she knew. General Dame had never mentioned them. Was this a new aspect of this slave trade? Or something even more secret than the business itself?

"Fine new locations off the grids, places where new social orders are being created, enforced and protected with state of the art military technology. One day, eventually, the new world order. But then, this is all too sophisticated for you. Just know you will be there, if you are lucky, if you do what you are told."

Sheila completed this man's description in her mind --- yeah right, be there with no escape, as a forgotten nameless slave to men who want women back under their control, back as property, chattel. Now this new world order this man was describing was indeed big information. It was the opposite of the new world order the IUWM planned to eventually bring about.

Except that the IUWM did not want to enslave men, only to free women and return their full power to them. In this moment, quick flashes, images, of future war between the two new world orders popped into Sheila's mind. A huge realization whipped through her: so this is what it is all about!

She stiffened her body and made her face look fearful again. She could not afford to look at all surprised or eager to know more. "I do not understand." Sheila coughed to clear her throat. "Is this a place you want me to go? I would rather go home."

Now the man looked a bit surprised, and a little irritated at her insolence. "Home? You have no home. You have nothing to go home for. You are not a person, you have no name, you are invisible. At least in a hidden city you can be given a citizenship."

"Citizenship?"

"In small nations of men where women serve."

"Serve?"

"As many wives for one."

Sheila tried to look confused. And she was confused.

"Hidden cities being set up by men who are designing the new way. Each man can have one hundred wives there."

"I have never heard of one hundred wives, not in modern times," Sheila said, acting naïve, although she knew of many modern instances of this.

"This is a much improved model of an age old and most effective institution. Anyway, enough of all this. You just behave, be quiet, be good, and you can be one, you can go there, you can live in a new place with a new name, and a new life, and all you will ever need."

"No one has heard of these lands with one hundred wives. Where are these?" Sheila had to be careful not to be too curious. She had to come across being afraid and wanting to know what was going to happen to her.

For some reason, this man felt comfortable talking to her, now his captive for life, a bit more, most likely because he wanted her to be afraid but cooperative, as it made her easier to sell. "Far away, young lady, far away. It will not matter to you where you are when you are sold, sold for resale to the men there, as you will never go anywhere else again. … You know, the great Virracocha had one hundred wives or more. You know who he was?"

"No." Sheila knew, but said no.

"The ruler of the ancient Incan empire, his kingdom being centered in Macchu Picchu, now in Peru. There are still the cells where his wives were kept. One hundred eighty, actually."

"Sir, I do not know what we are talking about." The "sir" was a good touch, as Sheila had to appear non-threatening, even subservient, here.

"A great leader who, like many other great leaders of past times, and a few of our times, had many wives, and many children by these wives."

Sheila tried not to look too hard at this man, not to appear at all impudent. In the slip of a second, with only the bat of an eye the wrong way, the turn of her mouth one ioata hinting that she was not a girl from the streets who knew nothing and presented no threat, she could be dead meat. Being cooperative, even kissing ass, she told herself, was the only way to go here.

"Sir, do you mean I could have a good life there, in the hidden city?"

"Maybe, if they think you are worth the bucks. You are definitely pretty enough. This helps."

"What?" Why was he talking to her about all this? Was this his usual approach?

"Oh." Sheila pulled her knees to her chest and rocked a bit in fetal position, a sure sign of insecurity. "What if they say no?"

"We will see. Now we must get you some food, a little meat on your pretty bones." He stood, walked to the door, and shouted orders in Spanish. Food, decent food on a plate, came almost immediately. With it came an armed guard. He was given orders, again in Spanish, to watch her every second, to let her eat, to take the plate and utensils when she was finished eating, to leave and lock the door when she was done, and not to touch her, not to touch her or he would die. She was clearly a valuable item. The American man, the boss, this man who was a woman dealer, left without another word to her.

However, Sheila heard him in the hallway ordering someone else, perhaps a medic, to place a temporary contraception patch beneath her skin….

38.

ANDREA'S APARTMENT IN SAN FRANCISCO BAY AREA….

Andrea Villayorona was thirty-seven and on her way up. She had graduated from Boalt Law School at the University of California at Berkeley years after Burt and Carla had graduated from Harvard Law School. She had passed the California Bar Exam immediately. She had managed to develop a neat little reputation for defending women of color who had been brought up on criminal charges. As a female Latina attorney, Andrea was quite unusual and quite visible.

It was her specialty that first interested Burt. Andrea represented competition in that she *could* specialize in such an area. Although everyone knew that Burt was one of the best criminal attorneys in the country, Burt could never be a female, especially not a Hispanic female attorney specializing in criminal law for women. It would be best for Burt if someone like Andrea was not only an ally, but on the same team. Andrea ended up agreeing to join Burt's law firm. It was as simple as that.

Almost.

Andrea was difficult to be around. She was show-stoppingly beautiful, with gleaming dark eyes, glowing dark skin, and shining black hair. Burt could not avoid staring at her. That they would become lovers was inevitable. He just had to convince Andrea of this.

She was, at first, quite difficult to convince. She brought with her a strong moral structure, perhaps because of her many childhood years in Catholic schools, perhaps because of her visibility as a relatively young woman of color in a highly competitive, dog-eat-dog area of the legal profession.

Burt found that the way to get closest to Andrea was to work with her. So he managed to bring her in on some of his very important and time-consuming cases. The opportunities to do so just seemed to appear. One case involved big time drug smuggling. Another involved a multinational hierarchy of several illicit flesh trade businesses. Another related case involved an international kidnapping ring leader and his very young girlfriend. Bringing Andrea in was a natural response to the challenge of defending the women in the lives of these men. All three cases involved underworld type figures of various nationalities, many American. Many had in some way involved their girlfriends in their criminal activities.

Burt and Andrea's long hours of working together went unquestioned by all involved. The cases were visible, complicated, and intense. No one wondered why Burt was working at Andrea's apartment many evenings a week. Not even Andrea.

One night, Burt arrived and found that Andrea had made a lovely dinner. “What’s this?” he asked, hoping it meant she was interested in him.

“I thought it was about time I thanked you for the opportunity to work with you on such important cases. I know what this is doing for my career, and I know how brilliant you are. There isn’t much time to thank you, so let me say thank you this way, since we have to eat anyway. Gracias.” Andrea stood by her chair and beckoned Burt to come to her table.

Burt obliged her. He stood next to a chair but did not sit down, and lifted the lid on the largest pot. “It smells delicious, Andrea. What is it?”

“A special kind of chicken molé I invented, you know chicken with chocolate sauce, only I add some Thai flavoring and other things such as artichokes to the mix. And, on the side, Spanish rice, but it’s really Mexican rice. I hope you like spicy food. It’s muy picanté.”

While standing, Andrea served Burt and watched him taste the food. He was still standing as well. She looked at him, awaiting his approval. “I also hope this isn’t inappropriate. I mean, we both know that this isn’t a date or anything. We’re here working together, as usual. We usually order pizza or Chinese. But, I just, I just want --”

“Want to say thank you, I know,” Burt concluded her sentence.

"Si. Yes, to say that. And, to say that I know what else is going on between us. And I know I've been putting your subtle advances off. And, under other circumstances, I would not be. There is no way that I would be rejecting you if you were not married and were not the most senior partner in the firm where I work, your firm, actually. I admire you more than anyone, but I can't get closer than this."

They realized that they both were still standing near the table. Andrea sat down and beckoned Burt to do the same. He did.

Burt tasted the food again. "Mmmm. You would definitely make someone a fine wife."

"Oh, thanks a lot," Andrea laughed. "But I don't do coffee."

(Somewhere in space, the Maxwell House wives shuddered.)

Burt eyed her as if she were part of the meal. "You'd also make someone a fine lover, I'm certain."

"Burt--" Andrea promised herself to make her boundaries even more clear to Burt.

"Never mind," he said. "Let's enjoy this lovely dinner."

They ate and talked and laughed. It was a relief for both of them, as they had been working hard and feeling a great deal of pressure. Dinner finished.

"Desert is simple." Andrea stood up and went into the kitchen. "I'll be right back."

But Burt followed. "It's working," he whispered.

"What's working?" Andrea looked puzzled.

Burt leaned against the kitchen counter near Andrea. "Don't you think I know that hot food and artichokes and chocolate are aphrodisiacs?"

Andrea stepped away. "They are? Not where I come from. They're just common fare."

Burt stepped in closer to her this time. "Well, maybe nobody acknowledges it, but everyone feels it." Burt grabbed Andrea's arm. "I want you."

Andrea froze. Her hot eyes were gazing at Burt, burning into him.

Burt did not let go of her. "Tell me you want me too, Andrea, just say the word."

"The word?"

"Just once, Andrea, just once. Just make love with me once. And then we can work together without all this tension. Just once."

Andrea looked dangerously fierce as she gazed at him through her dark eyes. She pulled away from him. "I would hate myself, Burt."

"No, you would love yourself, Andrea. You would be ecstatic."

She shook her head. "How can you know?"

Burt grabbed both her hands. "I can just tell. You can too. You can feel the chemistry. I know it. I can tell."

Andrea pulled her hands out of Burt's grasp. Burt took her hands back. He leaned toward her, put his face in close to hers, his lips about two inches away from hers. He poured himself into her eyes. “I know you want me. Tell me that you don’t. Tell me that you haven’t thought about me after I leave here, that you haven’t undressed and crawled into your bed and touched yourself, wishing it was me.”

Andrea grimaced then grinned just a little and shook her head no. She looked wistful. “I have never ever wanted another woman’s husband. Never.”

“Until now.” Burt held her with his eyes. “Admit it. Until now.”

“Until now,” she admitted, looking ashamed. And then she pulled away again. “Let me put this whipped cream on the berries. Desert would be a good idea right now.” Andrea pushed the bowl of cream between them, to create some distance.

Unfortunately, Burt’s hand landed in it. He laughed and began to lick his fingers. But then he changed his mind. He moved around the counter to Andrea and roughly pushed a finger full of whipped cream into her mouth. “You should have to taste this first. It’s your concoction.”

That was it. The discussion ended. They were kissing and undressing in the kitchen. They barely made it to the couch before Burt was on top of Andrea. They made wild love and then fell asleep.

When Andrea opened her eyes, she knew that she was in love with this man. She had tried so hard not to be, but she was. It was a done deal. And she had been so very alone until this moment in her life.

Burt was right. It was easier to work together after this. They could smile and laugh and, when no one was looking, flirt, without attempting to suppress it. They had much more energy for their work.

And for their sex.

39.

GOODMAN RESIDENCE….

In tears, Carla put Sheila's last letter back in the box and put the box away. "Sheila, Sheila, Sheila, what happened to you, to your mind, to you?" Carla sobbed as she wandered around her house aimlessly, in a slow kind of hurry, waiting for the coming relief of her death. But not yet. It was not set for today.

Things looked so messy. Carla could see that the house was relatively neat and clean, but for some unexplainable reason, everything looked out of place and dirty. She kept walking around and putting things away, opening drawers and refolding things, dusting and redusting, straightening pillows and rugs. First the floor was dirty. She mopped it. Then the sink was stained. She scoured it. And then the windows looked filthy. She washed them all. Twice.

Why all this? She had a regular and very efficient maid service. Why did the world look so unkempt to her? Was it because death, or as close as she had so far come to it, looked, by comparison, so intensely clean?

But no amount of straightening up made her house look cleaner, neater, more organized, nicer. Finally, Carla turned on the radio and laid down on the couch in exhaustion. She closed her eyes and realized that she was listening to a very melancholy symphony, a symphony which had somehow turned all the forms of sadness and pain in the world into music. How could it all be captured in this one place? Who wrote this? She couldn't remember.

The music grew louder. The air around her seemed to be crying notes, each one a heavier tear that the one before. Now the tears were in her eyes. Now the tears were in her body.

Her heart was crying. She could feel the wrap of deep deep sadness like a hand around her heart. Oh, how to escape these feelings? How? How? How?

She cried oceans of grief and pain.

Obviously she was not dead yet.

The dead shed no tears.

40.

SAME FLESH TRADE HOLDING CENTER….

A man in a white lab coat came in, followed by another man in uniform, carrying a gun.

"Stand up," the man in the lab coat ordered in English.

Sheila stood up.

"Turn around, your back to me."

Sheila hesitated.

"Turn around, I said."

The man with the gun moved closer to Sheila, visibly placing his hand on his gun.

Sheila obeyed the order and turned around.

The medic lifted her shirt to look at her back. He then touched various places on her skin, pressing on spots, and saying to himself "yes" and "no" as he did so, seeming to be searching for places where the skin was not too thin.

Finally finding a place in the small of her back, he said, "Oh, here, good." He placed something very cold over the area, likely alcohol to disinfect it, Sheila hoped, and then something even colder which numbed the location.

"Hold very still. Very," he ordered sternly.

Sheila thought about trying to stop this process, but saw no way out and no way to mount a successful attack against both these men in the same instant. And grabbing the gun of the armed man would likely result in her being shot. So the choice for her, in this instant, was to succumb to the procedure conducted by the man in the lab coat, or to fight and risk death right now.

In that moment, the man in the lab coat injected her with something. She could hardly feel this, as the area was so cold and numb. Then it felt as if there was a small slice being cut into her skin, she could not know for sure what this was. She guessed that the process was a sub-dermal installation of the birth control patch she had thought they were talking about in the hallway.

She felt herself being bandaged there, where he had done this. Then the man in the lab coat took something else from the metal plate he had carried in, a syringe.

"Hold still, we must draw some blood, test your blood." The needle went in, the blood was drawn, the needle was removed, and a cotton ball was placed over the spot where the needle had entered her skin. "Hold this here for a while," she was ordered.

The men left the room with the medical tools, locking the door as they did.

Sheila pulled her shirt back down. What did this mean? Was she, from this moment on, available for "safe" rape? Safe rape, she warned herself, probably wasn't totally safe. It most likely meant safe from an impregnation as this would lower her market value a great deal, but not safe from HIV and other infections. Or were they going to protect her from these? Doubtful, she told herself. But how could this be, Sheila tried to understand the situation. Being HIV positive would mark her for death, make her virtually impossible to sell to anyone testing, and render her a throw away having no sale value. So maybe this would not be an issue, Sheila wondered. Or maybe they wanted no HIV in their hidden cities.

Maybe there was another explanation. … She could be sold as not pregnant and clean for sure, with the buyer having the option of removing the contraceptive now or later or never. And she would likely be very protected up until the point of sale to be certain that she had no diseases and that she was not pregnant. This was good, she was safe from rape for a while, maybe. What a relief?

And then she was anything but relieved: wait a minute, being sold and shipped to what the boss had called a "hidden city" from which there could be no escape and the existence and location of which no one would ever know!!! Life there until she was of no use. Then no life.

But then, Sheila reminded herself, she had been trained to deal with such things, even to escape once she had the critical information she had been assigned to get.

41.

JOHN'S HOME…..

After massive mounts of paperwork, there came a moment when the feds knew they had nowhere to send this nameless faceless girl, who simply did not exist. Surprisingly, an official order, allowing John temporary foster parent status while they decided what next, came about suddenly. Even the officials seemed surprised by it, and hinted that the orders had not only come in from high above, but from outside the FBI, and instead, from the CIA. Someone, somewhere, was overriding immigrations, etc.

The entire process was confusing and rather troubling. Still, from one moment to the next, John had a daughter, a temporary daughter.

She seemed quite pleased.

John immediately took her to Enrico, to have an easy conversation with her. Enrico immediately told John that this young soldada wanted to know what John had had to pay the officials to free her. When John said nothing was paid, the girl was quite surprised.

But John was not. He knew there was a deal being made here. He just needed to understand what all this was really about. And he didn't. Was he being pulled into something beyond his ability to handle it?

42.

ANDREA'S APARTMENT….

"Andrea! You have to know she's making it all up! I did *not* try to kill her. She's a madwoman! Look at me! Do I look like that kind of person?"

Andrea looked at him and answered quickly, "Of course not, Burt. But why, why would she make up such a hideous story?"

Burt was stomping around Andrea's apartment. "She's sick, Andrea. Obviously she's sick. Don't you get it? She's suicidal. She's depressed. She wants to blame me for her failed life. So she does this. She's gotta' be sick, absolutely delusional."

Andrea leaned against a wall, watching Burt stomp. What if there was another explanation for all this? "Burt, maybe she didn't make it up. Maybe someone else did, Burt. … Burt, are you listening?"

Burt stopped moving. He narrowed his eyes in thought. "Someone else?"

"Yes. The police or someone else involved with her case … or with some other case … such as one of our cases?" Andrea tipped her head a little to one side. She was thinking.

Burt sat down on the floor and put his head in his hands. "But how on earth could anybody imagine -- or expect anyone else to believe -- that I, Burt Goodman, well-known criminal lawyer, future political candidate, with everything to lose and nothing to gain, would risk losing everything I've worked so hard to build this way?"

Andrea shrugged, "Don't know."

Burt looked up at her, as if expecting the answer. "How could anyone think I could be so incredibly stupid?"

"They would have to think that you are quite sick, criminally insane, some kind of socio-psychopath maybe, that the criminal minds you've been working with so long have finally rubbed off on you," Andrea mused sullenly.

"Can you even imagine such a thing?" Burt moaned.

Andrea eyed him for a moment. Could she even imagine such a thing?

"What are you doing?" Burt asked.

"Trying to imagine such a thing," Andrea responded. "It's difficult, hard to imagine, but a tabloid-trained mind could, Burt."

Burt put himself back on his feet. "Well somebody's going to be brought to court over this one -- brought in for defamation of my character." He started marching around the room again, but this time more slowly.

Andrea moved in front of him and stopped his marching. "Burt, I really must talk to you about something else...."

"Something else?" He looked at Andrea as if she had insulted him. "How can there be something else when my career, my reputation, my life, is on the line? Tell me, HOW?"

Andrea was surprised that he had raised his voice at her. He saw that she was startled and reached out to soothe her. At first she pulled away, distressed, and then she forgave him.

"Sorry --"

"Sorry --"

They both spoke at the same moment, but she managed to begin the rest of her sentence before Burt went on.

"I -- I just, I just wanted to tell you --" Andrea struggled to pull the words out of herself.

"Tell me what, sweetheart?" he said hugging her. He must never show this woman his abusive side, he ordered himself, because, on some level, he did know he could be quite abusive.

For some reason, she felt, for the first time, that he might be upset to hear that she was pregnant. "I mean -- I just -- wanted to -- ask you if you would like to eat here, or to go out for dinner?"

"Here, please, Andrea, if you have anything here. I just can't face anyone tonight. Thanks for being so concerned. I know how much you care. Finally a woman who cares about me."

They should eat in. She agreed. Her other news would just have to wait.

43.

SAME FLESH TRADE HOLDING CENTER….

They left Sheila alone for a long time. The only way out, the door, was locked. She had checked it several times. There were no windows. The absence of sound outside the door caused Sheila to wonder whether she had been left there entirely alone, but under lock and key.

After scanning the corners, walls and ceiling for any possible escape routes, Sheila finally allowed herself to feel as demoralized and exhausted as she truly was. She tried to keep fear at bay, as fear could render her blinder to the dangers that awaited.

No way out. No way out? No way out! Was this the most stupid thing she had ever done? She chastised herself. No, it was not. The most stupid thing was the way she had said goodbye, or not said goodbye, to her poor mother. How could she have done this to her mother? After all, now she was under orders. Back then, she was just rude. No wait. She had already been under orders back then. But still, how cruel not to let her mother know. Instead, she had just left her mother that strange letter.

Now Sheila cried. She actually cried, something rare for her.

"Mommy," she whispered several times very quietly as she huddled in fetal position on the floor in a corner: "Mommy."

Finally, she slept, for at least several hours if not longer.

When the sound of helicopters awoke her, she was not sure what she was hearing. Helicopters and gun shots, then silence. Then shots. Then nothing. Later, doors slamming. Then shots. Gun shots. The slamming doors getting closer. Closer. Then banging on this one.

Wait, this one, this door, her door. Here! Now what? Who were they?

Sheila did not reply. Who could be out there -- could be anyone ranging from flesh trade thieves, to murderers, to casual rapists, to drug dealers, to soldiers who could be any of the above, to police who could be the same.

"Stand back," someone, a female, shouted in American English. English? Female? Sheila cowered in the corner.

There were gun shots. The door sprung open.

"CIA," said a woman in a man's suit as she pointed a gun at Sheila.

"CIA?" Sheila whispered, doubting this.

"Name?"

Silence.

A badge came out. CIA. Was this CIA or someone wanting to appear American CIA?

"Name?"

Silence.

"Su llama?" The agent tried Spanish.

Silence.

The CIA agent pulled a weapon and ordered one of the men with her to frisk Sheila, to search for weapons and ID.

Nothing.

"Come then," Sheila was ordered at gun point.

Sheila could not tell this woman that she was with the IUAM, even if she believed this was CIA, as the IUWM was an *underground*, secret army, which the CIA should not know of. Sheila could say nothing about herself, Sheila told herself. No name, no identification, nothing.

She was led to the helicopter containing two more Americans.

Once in and taking off, Sheila spoke to the woman who had found her. "How did you know I was there?"

"CIA knows." The woman looked Sheila in the eye.

"About what?" Shelia looked back as blankly as she could while still holding the woman's gaze.

The woman who had found her spoke into Sheila's ear, under the noise, so that no others could here. "Escape or the rare suicide."

Sheila's eyes widened involuntarily. "What did you say?"

"Nothing has been said," the CIA woman said into Sheila's ear.

The pilot turned around and shouted, "Where can the US Government take you?"

Home was Sheila's first response. But she could not tell them this, could she? What would General Dame say? Did she have permission to talk to these people? Sheila was not sure, but remembered General Dame had once told her that the American CIA was no friend of the IUWM.

"Your General will OK this," the woman from the CIA spoke again under the din, again into Sheila's ear.

Sheila's eyes widened yet again. Could it be that this woman was IUWM or IUWM-friendly and had somehow hidden this fact from the CIA? Had the IUWM infiltrated the CIA?

"Just one thing," the woman again spoke under the din into Sheila's ear. "We're going to have to transport you home in a coffin, to smuggle you back into the US."

44.

GOODMAN RESIDENCE….

A woman can point to all kinds of reasons for mid-life depression. And most of these are valid. But ferreting out its origins does not necessarily eliminate this depression. This may just give the depression more of an excuse, more of a justification.

Dr. Achtentauf had the gall to visit Carla at home....

“But, Carla,” the doctor insisted, “mid-life does not have to be a guaranteed crisis. It is after all, for a woman, a second coming of age. It’s the stage of life when, no matter what has come before, there is something new on the horizon.”

“I haven’t seen anything new on my horizon, Phyllis,” Carla tried to get through to this woman without being direct about it. Carla was done with her life. That was that. And this should be fine with everyone.

“It all depends on that which you choose to see, to focus on, Carla.”

Carla laughed. "My dear Dr. Achtentauf. You can tell me this. I can hear this. But none of it makes me feel any better. I still feel like killing myself from time to time, but don't worry, I won't." Carla felt she had succeeded in disguising her intentions here.

The doctor was undaunted. "Well, it is a bit like dying, this coming of age. Certain things, certain parts of your life, certain pieces of you, are gone, Carla. Nothing will bring them back."

"The hard truth," Carla's sarcasm was unsuppressed.

"Yes, Carla. The hard but true truth."

Carla tried to be patient with this Phyllis woman, but she was tired of it all. "This is supposed to cure me? I'm supposed to feel better now? ... I'm an intelligent woman. Don't try to feed me trivia – or crap." Carla was immediately a bit sorry for her outburst, but just a bit. She sensed that, somehow, Phyllis identified with Carla's state of mind. Too bad, Phyllis, go commit your own suicide. Leave mine alone. Get a death, your own death. Mine's taken.

Carla fell asleep while the doctor was talking. When she opened her eyes, Phyllis was gone. Oh, if I could only get rid of my life so easily, Carla wished.

For some reason, on the cusp of that wish, a sad but powerful memory, a memory of another way Carla had tried to change her life, snapped into Carla's mind. There was one time, one, when she successfully stood up to Burt and he knew it. This act had almost made Carla feel strong. The memory came back to her from many years in the past, from a time when her daughter was about eight years old. Why would Carla suddenly think of this?

Little Sheila had been arguing with her father about why she should have to rinse the breakfast cereal out of her bowl (before it dried and became difficult to wash off) when her father did not. She had made a good point, but back-talking to her father so insolently was wrong. Carla saw and heard the entire discussion from the next room, but, as Burt had insisted of her so many times before that day, Carla did not interfere in his disciplining of Sheila.

So Carla never interfered. Until this time -- until she saw Burt grab little Sheila, throw her down onto the floor and stand over her, shouting, “Don’t you dare ever argue with me again young lady!”

Carla was on the scene in half a second. “Go to your room, Sheila, now.” Sheila obeyed immediately. Carla followed Burt, who was already stomping off. “Burt,” she whispered, “I may let you get away with batting me around, but if I EVER see you lay an angry hand on Sheila again, no matter how difficult she is being, I will have the police here. I don’t care what it will do to us, or to your career, or to your license to practice law or anything, but you will never be violent in any way with Sheila and get away with it.”

Burt had heard her, she knew it. It was the kind of certainty you feel deep in your bones. Solid certainty. He might abuse his wife but never his daughter, plain and simple.

Burt took this strange arrangement for granted. Of course, neither he nor Carla ever tried to understand why it was alright for Burt to beat Carla. This beating of Carla was just an unspoken given. Or was it Carla's way of keeping Burt's volatility and abuse aimed at her rather than at the child?

45.

GOODMAN RESIDENCE….

It couldn't have been much different from any other time it had happened. It, the violence, just emerged, just came into the room as an uninvited guest who felt somehow welcome.

Violence always waited in the wings, waited for a justification for its appearance on stage. In this way, violence had been the silent partner in their marriage from day one.

But this was not day one. It was more like day 8,031 or later of their marriage or day 8,761 or later of their relationship. Something like that, but definitely not day one. It was early evening well over two decades into their sometimes at least superficially sweet, often strained, and mostly turbulent roller-coaster ride relationship.

So it was that Burt came home earlier than usual, unannounced but expecting dinner although he had not eaten at home the past four nights. As usual, Carla found it highly unreasonable of Burt to assume that Carla would have dinner waiting any evening he happened to show up and wish to eat it. Carla was more disturbed by the fact that this was so *illogical* of Burt than that this was so *abusive*. If Carla made him dinner every night and he happened to show up and want to eat it two out of seven days at most, what would Carla do with all the wasted meals?

Furthermore, why should Carla waste her time and energy preparing dinners that would go uneaten? Carla's time and energy, the time of her life -- had gone into serving Burt. And what did she have to show for it? Not even a thank you from him. Basically, the time of Carla's life was worth less than the time of Burt's. If even that.

She used to ask Burt why he could not just call a few hours in advance and let her know, one way or the other, whether he was eating at home that night. Burt had always found this request an insult. "Carla, my work is so unpredictable and so demanding, I often don't know when and where I'll next get to urinate let alone when and where and even whether I'll have dinner," he would explain in a falsely hurt voice.

"But why make me suffer for this, Burt?" Carla would inquire righteously. She could see through his feigned pain.

"Suffer?" Burt would say. Then he would wave his arm pointing around at the view from and the furniture in their very upscale home. "You call this suffering?" he would shout. "You live so well because I work so hard," Burt would shout at Carla.

"I would gladly live in a smaller place with fewer things and a smaller overhead. I would trade all this away for happiness, Burt," Carla would tell him sadly but calmly.

"Happy?" Burt would shout and stomp. "This *is* happy. Are you so sick, such an ingrate, that your don't acknowledge this?" Burt would continue to stomp and pace. He would yell, "Are you so out of touch with things that you think we're not happy?"

At that point, Carla would try to hold his hand, in hopes of getting through to him, of talking to his heart. "Burt! Burt! No, this is *not* happy. Please, Burt, please," she would beg, "we have to sit down and try to communicate. We have to *try* to connect somehow," Carla would shout to be heard over Burt's yelling: "It's my life too, you know, Burt! It's the time of my life too!"

Burt would push her away and say, "Who cares, Carla? Who cares whether you missed a hair dresser's appointment or you didn't get your little article into the paper on time? Who cares if you lost a little writing job that might have made you a few thousand puny little dollars? For Godsakes Carla, what do you contribute here? What makes *your* needs, *your* schedule, *your* dinner menu more important than *my* work? Where do you get off making demands on *me*?"

Carla would always feel deeply degraded by such comments from Burt. It was as if he could, in one fell swoop, erase all of her contributions to his career, to their family life, to their household, to their social standing in the community where she had been at Burt's side all the way as the wife, half of the public face of the great attorney and future candidate for Senate -- the public face of Burt Goodman completed so beautifully by her presence.

"Burt, I'm part of all this. I've worked very hard too. Hard every day of this marriage. And I've had to give up my career for yours. You know this."

"You've given up what? What career? And you've worked hard on what?"

"On everything I've contributed to our family enterprise and to the Burt Goodman show. And any career I would have wanted was back seat to what you wanted – which was me, all of me, all of my energy."

At this point, Burt would usually sputter and sometimes sound as if he were suppressing an urge to vomit.

About now, Carla would feel the insult rushing through her nervous system like hot acid. "You are a pig, Burt! How dare you invalidate my contributions like that? Really? I have written two-thirds of all your legal briefs."

Burt would come and stand over her and yell down into her face, his saliva flying at her as he yelled: "Because you are a nothing, a no one, a little meaningless housewife and you have no right to tell me when to come and go or report in. Having dinner ready in case I want it is the least you can do. You owe me at least that much!"

"Owe you?" she would shout up into his face, "Owe you? I owe you nothing!" And then she would shove him away as he started to yell into her face. But he would yell into her face anyway, and in so doing, spray his saliva into her face again and again.

Once he had provoked Carla, once he was shoved away, he would somehow manage to feel that he had his license to kill -- or to just about kill -- to hit, to beat, to throw Carla, to grab her by the throat and press in on her airways, which he often did at that point. Then he would walk out. On his way out, he would shout at her that it was all her fault, “If you had the brains to stop yourself from pushing me, you wouldn’t be on the floor now.”

Carla would try not to cry.

“And don’t bleed on the rug you bitch.” The door would slam.

He would never check to see if he had hurt her or tell her he was sorry. Not even hours, days, or weeks later.

Tonight wasn’t much different, although both of them threw in a few new lines.

46.

GOODMAN RESIDENCE….

There he was, staring in at Carla through the kitchen window. Now what?

"Mrs. Goodman, let me in or I'll come back with a search warrant."

A vicious chill raced through her. She made sure her robe was closed, and she pulled the collar of the robe high around her neck to cover the bruises. She motioned him to come in through the kitchen door.

"Sit down," she pointed at the kitchen table and proceeded to pour two cups of coffee. Somewhere in the recesses of her mind, she could see an army of mindless, bubble-headed Maxwell House wives shipping off to war, fiercely angry at their own stupidity. What on earth could they know of military strategy? They had never been trained to fight. Why should they even bother to try now?

Carla gazed into her coffee, transfixed by the relentless procession of housewives marching through her mind. She peered into her imagination more closely and saw that each woman was wearing a price tag.

After a while, she heard the detective talking to her. Had she been talking to him while she was daydreaming? Could she have told him anything she did not intend to tell him? She was still being administered mild sedatives by the doctor.

"Mrs. Goodman, are you all right? Mrs. Goodman? Mrs. Goodman?"

"OK. OK. That's enough, detective. I hear you. I've been tired lately, which is probably quite typical of people who come back from the dead."

"Especially when they're being tranquilized," he noted. "So let's go on," he added.

"Oh, let's do," Carla mocked the detective.

And he proceeded to continue to ask her the same question over and over, worded differently each time. And Carla proceeded to continue denying Burt's involvement in her attempted suicide. With each new question, Carla looked more irritated. Finally, the detective stopped asking questions.

Carla glowered at the detective a while longer. She was triumphant when she realized that he had finally run out of prying questions. But now he just sat there and stared back at her.

She could not know, he told himself, the real reason for his being there, the real motive behind his desire to frame her husband. But she was protecting her husband anyway.

Ironically enough, the detective had actually convinced himself that Carla's life was threatened by her husband, Attorney Goodman. And, ironically enough, he was starting to care about her far too much. The detective insisted to himself that Carla could not know what her husband, Burt, was actually involved in. She could not possibly know that Burt was not only a flesh trade attorney but that Burt was also an international flesh trade mogul. This was very big business.

The detective was certain that Carla had no idea of what was going on around the world: women and girls being bought, sold and shipped across international borders; flesh traffickers, networked around the world, tied to a growing and pervasive but underground flesh trade Mafia; women ending up being marketed objects of this flesh trade -- falling into the clutches of this Mafia sometimes when they are kidnapped or captured, and other times when they apply for other kinds of jobs and are trapped before they realize what they have gotten themselves into. The detective was certain that Carla could not know that, if these female slaves balk, when they rebel in any way, they are cruelly beaten and tortured and threatened with unspeakable abuse, and or killed. She could not know that some of the girls and women are actually sold into the flesh trade by their husbands and their fathers! And mothers! Carla could not know that no matter how they find their way into the flesh markets, even if they arrive voluntarily, and some do (or at least think they do), they almost always end up as bonded labor with no hope of breaking free; that if by some slim chance they get free, they often find themselves in foreign countries, illegally, with that illegal alien status being punishable by law; while many of their own countries and even their own families do not want them back.

And some of these women are forever lost, hidden away in places no one could ever find, radar-reflecting colonies living entirely off the grid – in a growing number of places around the globe where women and girls are only property, chattel. Places ever more armed with high tech weapons being bought on the black market. And why should Carla know anything about any of this, let alone the plights, the sufferings, of these women? Carla was very different from them; she knew nothing of their worlds or of her husband's work.

Of course, Stanger told himself, he himself was not supposed to know so much about all this, especially about the highly secret hidden cities project. He would be killed by any number of factions if anyone knew he knew.

The greater irony here was that Stanger had learned about this during his spying on Carla's husband, Burt, as Burt was defending and saving Moreno from prosecution.

And then there was Carla, herself, the unexpected piece of this project. Stanger cringed. Relax, he told himself. She could not possibly know what he was seeing in her. She could not possibly know that he was taking it all in, the particular way her neck merged into her collar bone, the timeless grace built into her hands with their long graceful fingers, the intriguing message wailing out from behind the forced glaze of her sullen eyes, the way her voice revealed so much more about the kind of woman she was than did her words. Maybe those eyes revealed more about Carla than she knew about herself. Maybe those bruises he chose not to mention he could see did too.

Detective Stanger allowed himself such a close, almost intimate look at this woman because he had actually come to believe his frame-up -- that this woman's husband was indeed trying to kill her and that she was actually letting him.

Now, why would a man want to kill such a woman? Wouldn't he rather have her to talk to, to touch, to lay with naked night after night? Why? Wouldn't her husband be more likely to want to charm her, to have her all to himself for all his life?

But would something about this Carla always remain just a bit out of reach, a bit unattainable for a husband, or for any man?

Carla fractured his reverie. "What are you staring at? What are you thinking about? You are a rude and intrusive man, Mr. Stanger." She tightened the collar of her robe around her neck again.

The detective shook himself out of his thoughts. Maybe a woman like Carla was forever unattainable for a guy like him -- maybe that's what he was really thinking about. No, he was trying to understand the mind of Carla's husband.

He still wanted an answer to his question: “Why would your husband want to kill you?” he asked.

But now Carla had her own line of questioning to pursue. “Why are you looking at me like that, detective? Don’t you think I feel you looking at me? Do you think this overly personal style of yours is professional behavior? I can report you for this.”

“I don’t know what you are talking about, Mrs. Goodman,” he said.

“Yes, you do, detective,” she replied.

“I was merely wondering why your husband would want to do you in, Mrs. Goodman, why a man would want to get rid of such a spectacular woman as you are.”

“You forget -- the name’s Carla, not Mrs. Goodman.”

“Carla,” he said apologetically.

“I am not here to explain, to accuse, or to excuse my husband,” Carla admonished him. “That’s not my reason for being. So there is no discussion so far as I am concerned.”

“It’s just that you’re a very attractive woman. Not the image of a throw away wife, Carla.” He liked calling her Carla. Did she like it when he did?

“Throw away? Are some wives disposable, then?”

“No. I don’t mean that. I mean that some men are that terrible to think that way,” Stanger answered, more friendly now. “But some do seem to take on that view, maybe because they have come to feel that way about themselves.”

"And me?" Carla wanted to know, "Your assessment of me?"

"You are definitely no throw away from my perspective," he said, almost gaping at her beauty as he acknowledged it to himself. "So, the motives for your murder or suicide must be more complex. No easy obvious here."

"What if I said that I wanted to be a throw away?" Carla posed a strange question to him.

The detective laughed awkwardly and looked at his shoe. He reached down to retie his laces. As he did, he looked at Carla and said, "Well, I guess I'd say that if *you* really didn't want *you* and *you* were throwing you away any way, that uh, that --"

"That what?" Carla interrupted abruptly. "That what?"

"That, maybe then *I* could have you." Now the detective had embarrassed himself. He felt hot under the collar and went on with what he hoped was an adequate cover-up, "Metaphorically speaking, that is."

When he realized that Carla was blushing, he felt relieved. "You're blushing," he said quietly.

"So what?"

The detective eyed her sympathetically. "It would be such a waste to lose you. ... I mean, for you to lose yourself."

For an instant, Carla's face revealed her deep pain. "I already have lost myself. I am already gone."

"I don't like your finality. It worries me. Couldn't something or someone find you again?" The detective tried not to sound as if he were suggesting himself to her.

"I don't think so. I really feel too far gone at this point."

"What about love?" the detective asked, trying again not to reveal his personal interest.

"Love is an idea that sells romance novels and greeting cards. And wishing for it ruins lives." Carla closed her eyes.

"Well, Mrs. Goodman, should you ever need a friend, I am available."

"I think you mean a date, don't you?" she replied.

The detective laughed again, "Well, that too."

"Dating your suspects now?"

"You're not a suspect, Carla."

"And I am not a date, detective."

"OK, I stand corrected." Feeling like an absolute idiot, the detective stood up. "Please excuse me if I've overstepped my bounds. I don't exactly know what it is about you that I find so attractive, but you are very special." He tried to put his coat on, but dropped it. Bending over to pick up the coat, he could hide his red face. "I'll leave now, before I humiliate myself any further."

"Good-bye. Your compliments were sweet and I forgive you for overstepping your bounds. You are, I am sure, overworked, drained, not thinking clearly, and simply trying to raise my morale by complimenting me. But you can't fix my life so please don't try."

Carla closed her eyes and pretended that she was falling asleep, which had become her favorite way of dismissing people since her time in the hospital.

The detective gazed at her a moment more and then left the room, shaking his head and reprimanding himself under his breath for his unusually forward behavior. But why do the bad men get the good women? He silently defended himself against his reprimand. Why don't guys like me ever get a chance?

After all, this woman's husband was no good. He had been bought by his biggest client. In fact, he had owned a good-sized piece of the international flesh-trade industry for years. He had to be involved in the invisible hidden cities project, the one he, Stanger, had discovered by mistake and told no one about. This Burt was involved in the entirely underground, multinational buying, selling and shipping of hundreds of thousands, even millions, of women and girls. He may have even sold his first daughter to them, and the girl's mother. Did Carla know? Did she even suspect? Detective Stanger was certain she did not. But, was this man, Goodman, going to kill Carla anyway? Detective Stanger was certain that he was.

Could he, merely Detective Stanger, save her, he asked himself.

47.

JOHN'S HOME….

John said that daughter soldada needed a name. Enrico promised to help get this accomplished: Revuelta, Return. It was the name she wanted, and John could find no logic for protest. So it was.

Miss Revuelta sat and stared at the television for a couple of days, clearly in shock even though Enrico had explained the circumstances and even though John was quickly mastering basic Spanish.

"You'll be safe here for as long as you want to stay," John told her, believing he was right.

Now, a few days later, Revuelta dropped the remote control and sprang to the window, watching additional coffins being unloaded into the mission across the street. Was any one coming in alive?

48.

ANDREA'S APARTMENT….

The scratching of pen on paper and the turning of page after page was about all that could be heard while Andrea and Burt worked on the Moreno-Milmar case. Fifteen minutes, half an hour, almost an hour, passed before either of them spoke.

And then it was Andrea. "It doesn't look good, Burt."

Burt pulled his reading glasses off of his eyes, in order to see her better. He yawned. He was tired. "What doesn't look good, sweetheart?"

"The evidence," Andrea groaned. "It looks like we're defending people who are very much guilty."

Burt put on his fatherly voice. "Either guilty or not. That's the way I see it. It's a little like being pregnant, you can't really be a little or a lot, much or very much, you just are."

Andrea winced, because she hadn't yet told Burt that she was pregnant. "They're big time criminals, international crime syndicate types, with a corporate cover. We can't know how many dirty deals they're involved in."

"No different from so many others." Burt went back to his work as if he cared not a bit about this conversation.

Andrea tapped the table with her fingers, each one hitting a little harder than the one preceding it. "No, Burt, these people are different. They sell women and girls, Burt. That's different. They kidnap them and ship them away from the country where they found them and then sell them. It's even happening here, in the US. That's what this whole kidnapping case we're on is about. Think of all the women and children that disappear every year, even in the US. Moreno's guys buy many of them. And then they market them elsewhere."

"You can't be sure they do. You sound like the prosecution not the defense." Burt looked at her quizzically. "Are you nervous about defending them?"

"No, not nervous," Andrea answered hesitantly.

"Then what?"

"Repulsed. Disgusted. They do sell women and girls. We can be sure that they do. They told us, remember? They're making hundreds of millions of dollars, more like billions, in the global organ, baby, slave, and sex industries -- they steal, buy, sell, blackmail, bribe – even cut open for organs, or rape for sex, or force conception: even force the "chosen ones" of them to have baby after baby which they sell – they do all these things to women just like me."

"Now Andrea, don't get over emotional. The women they sell are not women like you."

"Oh no? Although the largest market is for Asian women, others, Black, White, and Hispanic like me are used too. The market for Hispanic and related mixed-race females is growing. I know about the flesh trade business, Burt. All kinds of girls disappear for good out of the towns in Mexico where my cousins live. Everyone there knows what happens to them and who takes them away. And everyone is afraid to try to stop the process."

To Burt's amazement, Andrea launched into a pretty good assessment of the business: "Burt, you don't think I know about woman trafficking, do you? Well, you're wrong. I know a lot. Impoverished women and girls are pressured, rented, bartered, traded, and sold to unimpoverished men the world over. The direction of the trade is from the lower or poor social classes to the upper or rich social classes, from the poor countries to the wealthier countries, from the dominated peoples to the dominating peoples. The directions of trade vary over time, but are most obvious from Latin America to Southern Europe and the Middle East, from Southeast Asia to the Middle East and Central and Northern Europe, from Eastern Europe to Western Europe. So far, it is more difficult to trace the shipment flow of the so-called 'missing' American women and girls, females who are not just missing, but who have been kidnapped. Kidnapping in the US is the way our guy Moreno got caught; he got connected to some sloppy kidnappings. His men were caught buying the victims. One of his child catchers talked to the Feds to protect himself."

Burt tried to be nonchalant about all this. He smiled at Andrea. She couldn't possibly sense Burt's deeper involvement in this business, that he was more than merely defending these people because they happened to walk into his office seeking legal representation, that he was working on a lifelong project, the top secret hidden cities movement, filling them with carefully screened women and girls, motivating these females *any way necessary* – to get them to behave well there. And if they did not cooperate, they were offed, that was all. Poof.

"Don't worry," Burt told Andrea smoothly, "you would never be mistaken for one of those women. Anyway, they can't have you." Burt got up, moved behind Andrea, and began to rub Andrea's forehead. "Because I have you, you're mine," he told her.

Andrea shuddered at the parallel Burt was drawing. Men could be so simple-minded about women. But, maybe, Burt, without knowing it, had a point. Andrea mused that no matter how far away a woman has come from a more primitive status, from being chattel -- men's property -- a woman is still, on some level, expected to play out that role. It is especially difficult to see this among highly educated, successful career women. These women are making great progress in the working world. But follow some of these women home, into the hidden corners of their private lives, where take place the most basic, most intimate, most simple transactions between even the high-powered woman and the man she loves, lives with, marries, and or sleeps with. There, behind closed doors, between the lines, it is clear that some of the links in the centuries-long chain of enslavement remain. Sometimes these links are so subtle they are entirely overlooked. Many times these links are dressed up to appear to be the opposite, to appear to be progress in the liberation of women, women's lib. But it was not so long ago that modern women were still property, and it will not be hard to turn history back on this.

"What did you say?" Burt interrupted her thoughts. "You're talking to yourself again."

"I said 'yours?' I'm yours? You said 'yours'." Andrea forced a smile. She wanted him to want her and their baby, but she didn't want to be -- even vaguely, implicitly -- his property. How could she tell him all this?

"Just a figure of speech, Andrea. Words can mean all kinds of things. Should we take a break? Then I'll show you exactly what I mean." He looked at Andrea with bedroom eyes.

"I bet you will." She smiled for real this time. He was virtually irresistible. But then she caught herself and she said, "Maybe in a few minutes. First I want to decide if I can go on with this."

"With us?" Burt looked suddenly alert.

"No, with this work, Burt. What do you think I've been trying to say?"

"What on earth are you talking about?" he asked her as if he had no idea.

Andrea waved at the papers they had been working on. "This case, Burt. I think I'm starting to feel too dirty. Maybe I should turn it over to someone else."

"Andrea, why?"

"I don't think I want to help these people, no matter how well it pays. They stand for everything I became a lawyer to fight: things like the transnational sexploitation of women, I call it that, but you can call it what you want. The international sex business is not going away, it's growing. It has become an illicit but nevertheless multinational business, one that is linked to other more legitimate businesses, to major sources of investment, and to governments everywhere either by contact or by blackmail. Do not think women's liberation has saved women from all enslavement. It has just driven the enslavement and the economy of this enslavement underground. I won't be part of this. I won't help Moreno or anyone like him."

"Andrea, wait. You aren't helping him. You're just helping his little girlfriend. That's not these people. It's just a girl who got caught up in a game that was too big for her to play." Burt stopped. His face went from kind and loving to stern and tight. He swallowed hard. "And, Andrea, if you quit now, after you know so much about their underground business, you're taking a very big risk."

"Risk." Andrea repeated the word as if it had no meaning to her.

"You become a leak." Burt informed her, "A potential loose canon."

"What?" she said, untouched.

"Andrea," Burt turned her head to face his by grabbing her chin and moving it. "Leaks get plugged, loose canons dismantled."

Andrea pulled his hand off her face. She understood Burt's words to be a warning. Was she actually in danger or was he just trying to scare her? What kind of man was her irresistible mentor and lover? Did she actually finally wonder?

49.

GOODMAN RESIDENCE….

One day, some weeks later, when both Burt and Carla had left their house and gone their own directions for at least the day if not the night, their missing daughter, Sheila, broke in. It was not actually a break in, as the old key was still hidden under the planter in the back yard. Sheila had not expected to find it there, but when she had looked, it was there. Upon finding the key, Sheila had imagined a sad picture of her mother secretly checking to be certain it was still there, week after week, just in case Sheila would come home while they were out.

Sheila went in, and, out of habit, went straight to the refrigerator. Sure enough, the same kind of milk was in it. And then she opened the cabinet. The same kind of peanut butter gingerbread cookies were in the jar. Was Mom still baking them even though Sheila was the only one who liked them?

So Sheila had milk and cookies, just the way she did almost everyday after school for many years. All the bombs, all the guns, all the smuggling of weapons, all the kidnappings and killings dropped out of her mind for a while. Why think about work when you can eat milk and mom's cookies at the kitchen table?

After a while, when Sheila had eaten almost enough of these cookies, she walked around the house. She peeked into the closets, the scrapbooks, and yes, even into her mother's secret box. Not much had changed. It was as if time had stopped.

She went to her father's desk and went through papers, as she had planned. Then she found herself at her mother's desk, which she opened after only a few moments' hesitation. On the right side, in the bottom drawer, were some scribbled notes.

Sheila put down the remainder of the cookie she was eating and started to read her mother's handwriting:

> *Butter melts in the sun. Sugar dissolves in water. But mediocrity is stubborn, unbudging, powerfully resistant to change or erosion.*
>
> *It is the most mundane ones who are the most powerful, the most adept at pulling the veil, the deceptive shroud of mediocre reality down over our eyes. These are the Usual people. I bow to them.*
>
> *The other of us, the UNusual people, are therefore not as capable as the Usual ones. UNusual people can grab only on to the edges of the veil, of the false shroud of constructed, invented, reality, the threadbare ends of the fabric of lies where actual truth about reality is already so tattered. An unnerving truth leaks into the hearts of the UNusual: they cannot manage to pull the shroud of mediocre reality over their eyes, they do not have the ability to do so. For these UNusual people, this thing called*

"life" wears thin. They can't live in it. They can't bear it. They want to die out of even the edges of it.

"God Mom, are you depressed or what?" Sheila whispered, ghast, and then read on:

Most unusual people do not know they are unusual. They just think that they do not fit in, that they are not successful at living.

The mediocre illusion of mediocre reality is being fed to and believed by an ever larger number of people. This is all we are seeming to bring about, the spread of mediocrity.

The wealth, well it is in the power to define the truth. The truth about power.

And all this is happening to men and women in an especially sad way. Warehouses full of high school yearbooks store the faces of cadres of old Maxwell House wives, one of our greatest products. Even the women's movement has done little to deny the lift-and-separate-shape-your-heart mentality. Nowadays, female attorneys, doctors, professors, and the like are still, deep down inside, Maxwell House-ized. They will deny it, but they just live the lie better than the old housewives of times decades past.

Are we drugged into numbness or into our forced stupidity? Are we brainwashed into half-personhood, robot-hood, mental slavery? We surely do not know the difference either way. It is safer not to ask large questions of this kind.

Sheila laughed. Was this a draft of an article? A piece of a book? At least mother was still writing. Or writing again. But now, a brand new tone had crept into her work. A kind of political thinking was appearing. Could it be? Was her mother waking up?

Was the irony in her mother's words her mother's way of expressing her disappointment with her self and her life? Or with the world's secret and unbudging true hierarchy?

Now Sheila caught a glimpse of her own face in the mirror. She was oddly relieved. Well, that's one thing she herself could never be accused of, being a Maxwell House wife. Not then, not now.

Sheila heard a car pull up. She jumped. She stuffed the papers back into the desk drawer. She grabbed her glass of milk, stuffed the rest of the cookie into her mouth, and went out the back door. Fortunately, Sheila had already rearranged the remaining cookies so none would appear missing. She had covered her tracks as she had moved through the house, leaving everything in the home as it was, and putting the house key back under the planter before coming in. Sheila looked at her watch as she slinked across the back yard. She had somewhere else to go. She crept over the fence and snuck out of the neighborhood still carrying the glass of milk which she would get rid of elsewhere.

No one but the bird on the telephone wire recognized the tall, gangly young woman with short cropped hair and sunglasses. She looked like a man at first glance anyway.

50.

GOODMAN RESIDENCE….

Carla thought maybe someone had moved her secret box. But no, it was just her imagination. She wanted to find some more things she could leave Sheila, things she had not thought to include before the first suicide attempt. In shuffling through old letters, Carla found a note she had written Burt years ago. He had tossed this note into the waste basket without reading it and Carla had taken it out of the waste basket, uncrumpled it, and saved it:

Burt,

You are trashing me. Your disrespect for me and devaluing of everything I do is unfair and ridiculous. You are completely wrong about me. You don't know me at all. I wonder if you even care to know me. You don't seem to want to change your dead set impressions of me. You seem to need to see me the way you do.

Sure, you tell everyone, even me, you adore me. But many of your actions and even most of your words completely undermine the façade of this lie. That is, unless you call your intense mental cruelty "love."

And then, quite regularly, I get a lecture from you about how I should once in a while at least let you do a, b, or c sexually with me. When you lecture me, your voice is severe, the tone is one of complaint, the sound is punitive. Your message that our sex life, while the best thing we have going for us, needs some spicing up, feels like pressure. You expect me to automatically want to do these things and to do them like an obedient machine even if I happen to need something with feeling, with an emotion such as love, accompanying it. I never had trouble with sex until I spent most of my adult life with you. Now, I feel alternately sexually criticized, rejected, and manipulated. There are indeed times when things go right. But it seems to me that you forget these times. You never bring them up unless I remember them. And, even then, you don't find them significant.

Around here, most of the air time goes to how <u>I</u> don't come through for <u>you</u>. Well, I think that <u>you</u> are actually very fortunate to have <u>me</u> in your life. If you can't see that, then forget it.

You want an automaton, a blow up doll, a servant, a robot, not a true wife. You want another cup of coffee guaranteed. DAMN you. I have given you deep love. I have lived a life which aimed to flow in the direction <u>you</u> wanted our family and your career to be and to go. I have surrendered my will to your life. You have consumed my energy, my life force, and my intelligence, like a hungry parasite -- not a symbiotic life form, perhaps what a good husband is, but a parasite. And then you say that everything we have is all yours!

If I don't watch out, I'll be that joke -- when <u>I</u> jump off the bridge, <u>your</u> entire life will pass before <u>my</u> eyes. You do know that joke, don't you? Well, we, you and I, are that joke.

But <u>I</u> am watching out. Even if you give me no help getting out of a major down point in my life, I <u>will</u> get out. I will not have you to thank for being out. But I don't need you.

Most of your comments to me concern my failures with respect to wifehood. For example:

- *Something is either wrong or entirely wrong with about 80% of the dinners I cook for you. What I do around here is either reduced to failure and remembered forever as that or reduced to meaninglessness and then forgotten immediately.*
- *I don't do stuff around here that you want done, or the way you want it done. When I try to do something, it has to be done your way or it's not good. IF IT HAS TO BE DONE <u>YOUR</u> WAY, ONLY <u>YOU</u> CAN REALLY PLEASE <u>YOU</u>. DO NOT EXPECT SOMEONE ELSE TO COME THROUGH <u>PRECISELY</u> WITH YOUR TASTE, YOUR JUDGMENT, YOUR DECISIONS. i.e.: Me: Let's not switch to that new gardener you wanted, he's too expensive. You: NO. i.e.: Me: Let's whitewash or paint the door, instead of spending the money to replace it. You: NO. i.e.: Me: Let's move to a moderately priced house, have me fix it up and sell it for a profit eventually. You: NO. i.e.: Me: Let's support me while I have another baby and give me a guarantee of a future sense of ownership in what we share. You: NO.*

You are making a big mistake dumping your merde onto me. If you want my participation around here, you can't get it with me forever backed into a corner about to be checkmated into death -- soul death -- by you.

Your problems with me are things that you have manufactured as a way to have someone to direct all your unhappiness with your self on to.

Your elaborate mental cruelty is so complex, so Machiavellian, that it is difficult to point to. But I see it. You siphon from me, for your own use, all my energy and then return no energy except your own fame and your own choice of lifestyle. And I am supposed to thank you. And to thank you while you regularly beat me.

You are consuming me and then, as I am being used up, running me out of your life while saying that you are not. You are attempting to break me into nothing while saying that you are not. You are putting me down on a daily basis with your continuous disapproval and disregard, while saying that you are not.

You are, in the final analysis, hurting yourself. You won't get what you want from me by beating me verbally, emotionally, and physically. ***You are basically beating exactly what you want from me right out of me.***

You will, in the end, have it all your way. You will run me out, or do me in. But you won't have me. And the way your life looks, that will be the single greatest easily avoidable error you will ever make. But you will move on and find a new woman's soul, brain and body to use as fuel for your continued advancement, and expect her to thank you all the while.

I would say that I love you, or that I have loved you, but I suppose that is irrelevant at this point. It was sure pretty stupid of me. Anyway, I have loved you and I have, in your eyes, failed you.

OK, tyrant of the household -- king of the land of lies -- take your domain and wallow in the horrible dungeon of reality you are creating for your self, one in which your cruelties are always justified in your own, the only, eyes.

Carla

Carla stopped reading. She crumpled up the old note and aimed to toss it into the wastebasket. She stopped herself and uncrumpled the note. She folded it very neatly and put it back into her box. She should leave all this in this box for Sheila, or better yet, have "Uncle" John save it for her.

51.

GOODMAN RESIDENCE….

Carla's thoughts turned to her daughter. Carla knew, with the sort of certainty one can only feel from deep in the heart, that Sheila was not dead. No matter what anyone told her, Carla knew that Sheila was somewhere on the planet, and very much alive. But, how could Sheila stay away for so long? Was something very wrong, was Sheila hurt or imprisoned, or did Sheila simply hate her parents so much that she never wanted to see them again?

Maybe, and Carla feared this possibility more than anything else in the world, maybe, it was that Sheila felt betrayed by her mother's failed life, so deeply betrayed that she could not bear to be around the woman from whose womb she had come.

A dark wave of shame and misery washed through Carla. She chastised herself: To fail as a mother was the worst failure imaginable. To fail as a model for a daughter was to be worth nothing. Carla's great career had fizzled even before it had begun, her marriage had disintegrated leaving only a façade of itself, she had lost all respect for herself. But, worse, she had failed as a mother. This went right to the core of her being. The shame and self-disgust welled up in her gut, in what remained of her aging womb.

Giving birth and mothering a child was the only good thing Carla had done with her life and she had done that wrong too. She could never fix this for Sheila, but she could get out of her daughter's way, out of her daughter's world. What young woman needed a hopeless middle age mother lurking in the wings of an otherwise wonderful world? ***Who are the daughters of we women who have lived as mere puppets, women who, even in this age of liberation, have not fulfilled that drive for liberation?***

Carla should get out of Sheila's way. So, the next time Carla would attempt suicide, she should succeed. All she needed to do first was to be sure Sheila would understand that Carla very much wanted to leave this life. Carla wanted Sheila to know that her mother's suicide was the strongest, bravest, most independent thing that her mother had ever done in her life. Carla wanted Sheila to finally be proud of her mother and not to believe what people who do not understand say about suicide.

Carla therefore decided to write another note to Sheila, another note to add to the collection of notes and items stored in her safe deposit box:

My dear, dear Sheila,

You already know I have left the world. You already know I died peacefully. Maybe you have already seen the other notes and things I left for you in this box. This note is more important than anything else I have left you. It tells you that I feel that I have not only made the right decision, but that it is a good decision. I feel good that I am able to take such strong action.

I am certain that you know that I would never have left you when you were younger and still needed a mother. I have waited until I felt that you no longer needed a mother.

Of course you may be saddened by my choice to kill myself. (It sounds so extreme: "kill myself," but "commit suicide" sounds so impersonal and antiseptic.) I do not want to deny your sorrow, but I do want to suggest that you also try to feel a little of what I feel about my choice to kill myself.

First of all, I have been killing myself for a long time. Being your father's wife has been a kind of death sentence for my soul. In fact, many days I wake up dead, (even before this suicide -- hah, hah!), dead at heart. My life has felt increasingly empty, meaningless, valueless and futile.

While you still needed me, I could distract myself from the creeping sense of pointlessness I was feeling. But as you grew more independent and older, I could see, with each new day, that my importance in the world was diminishing. And, this is, in terms of motherhood, how it should be. A mother should be proud of her child's successful development from infancy to independence. And you know, I know you've never questioned this: I am very, very proud of you. A mother should never hang on to her child in order to avoid life's major issues.

Second, I feel good about having the guts to leave this world. I feel good about doing something entirely my own, that no one, not even your father, can take away from me.

Third, and most important, you need to know that I am quite rational about this. I see my killing myself as a very special flesh trade. I am trading my body away for my freedom. I am finished with this life in this body. If there is no life after death, then my suffering will be over because I won't exist in any form. If there is, and I tend to believe there is life after death, then it will be a life where I do not feel the tremendous accumulation of inescapable humiliation, failure, and pain that I am feeling and have been feeling for years.

Do not blame your father for this. You do not need to spend your life hating him because I killed myself. The police may blame him for a while, but when you show them this letter, they will drop the case. I have made this decision to commit suicide on my own. I was not coerced or conned into it.

This does not mean your father is blameless. He surely has been committing slow wife murder over the years. But this is not against the law. No one really cares about such hidden abuse and cruelty, not when it is abuse of a wife who seems to know enough to get out. But your father did not out and out murder me. I do very much believe that, no matter what he says and how he acts publicly, he thinks of women as lesser people, as a sort of underclass of beings, and that his way of thinking is only revealed in a close, long-term personal relationship. But I also believe that this is the challenge faced by all women at this time in history -- to really see what perceptions hold them back from their own full power.

And how we are inadvertent accomplices to our oppressors, my dear. We just don't fight back hard enough. Or at least I didn't. Until now. Yes, I finally do understand this aspect of the story. But I have damaged so much of my life not getting this, that now I feel it is too late to take my life back. I have given up, that is all.

I have found myself without power, for many reasons, some of which are Burt's, some of which are mine, some of which are the world's. But the only way I can finally have some power is to make this decision for myself. Women today are starting to know about this, but I have lived lost in the stupidities of previous generations. Or in the deprivation of them.

I have made my choice, to take my power back in this way, by trading my flesh, my life in this body, away for my freedom. Now I have found my power.

By the time you read this, I will no longer be a slave to the confusion of old sex roles -- roles which appear to be crumbling in public yet which can be ever more rigid and denigrating to women in private, even in the privacy of their own minds and intellects.

I love you. Please learn from my experiences. I know you will. That's what you are like. In fact, you probably already have.

Your mother forever.

Carla found one tear at the corner of her eye. Just one. This letter did not say it all. It certainly did not express the immensity of her love for Sheila. It definitely did not detail the domineering, manipulative cruelty of Burt, Sheila's father. But it said enough. Sheila knew, both directly and through her intuition, everything she needed to know about her father, Burt. No further legacy of misery need be left.

Carla put the letter in an envelope and sealed it, wrote Sheila's name on it, and put it in her purse. She would put it in the safe deposit box like a message waiting in the limbo of time. John would be sure Sheila would receive it.

John. She had refused to see him or take his calls since her failed suicide attempt. "John."

52.

JOHN'S HOME….

Carla knocked at John's door. He opened the door, saw bruises under make-up again, and immediately his face grew agitated and worried. He usually prepared himself for this pain, for knowing that she had been beaten. But today, he hadn't been expecting her. Furthermore, his new, temporary daughter was across the street at the mission. If she came back, how would John explain? It was such a strange story. A girl in a coffin….

Carla stood in the doorway. "Hi John. I have something else I need you to put in my safe deposit box," Carla said as if nothing had happened.

John pulled her inside and closed the door. "Me?" John locked his door and put the chain on. He would hear if anyone wanted to come in. Advance warning, he figured.

"Yeah. I can't go down there."

"Why?"

"Too tired."

"That's not why, is it?" John scrutinized Carla's face, neck and hands. "You've been hit again, haven't you? You don't want anyone to know." Now John felt sick, disgusted and sick. Desperate.

"No I haven't, John. Just stay out of it, OK? Be a friend and mind your own business," Carla begged him.

"Carla, can't you let me take you away from here? What are you doing to yourself? What is he doing to you? I'll call the police if he touches you again."

"Mind your own business, John," Carla warned, "or our friendship is over for good."

"Carla, I just want to help."

"No one can help," she answered stiffly.

"I can't understand why you've turned away from the possibilities of joy and love in your life and stayed with Burt. What sort of self-destructive tendencies are these? What kind of hold does he have on you? What?"

"Come on, John, don't you go analyzing me too. I can't stand it anymore. Everyone thinks they see what's going on with me and everyone is wrong. Just plain wrong."

"Or maybe you are wrong. You are wrong about yourself, Carla."

"Fine, take their side and not mine. Some friend you are," Carla glared at John.

John sat down on the couch and motioned for Carla to join him. She remained standing. John went on, looking up at her,

"That's not what this is about. I *am* your friend. But as your good friend, I have to be straight with you."

"So, be straight with me. Be straight about your motives, John. Tell me what it is *you* really want," she challenged him. "Be direct."

John was a bit taken aback by Carla's turning the tables, but he met her challenge with honesty. "Carla, I've waited years for you to leave Burt. You know I've always wanted you. You've been the only one for me since we first got together. I want you, of course I do."

"Well, you really blew that, John. You had your chance a long long time ago and you blew it. So why all this now?"

Tears welled up in his eyes, but he refrained from crying. "I'm sorry if I hurt you, Carla. I was so young and naive. I couldn't, for the life of me, figure out what to do about the baby. But I never meant to lose you, Carla. I wish I could do it all over again. I'd marry you and have as many children as you wanted." He motioned for her to sit next to him on the couch.

"John," Carla remained standing, "I'm not blaming you. I said it wrong. But that was then and this is now. You've kept your whole life on hold waiting for me. Don't you think I see that? Of course I can tell. You never married. You have no children. You are a success, but at what? You come from family. You believe in family. You want family, but look at your life. Where is family? Don't you think I feel funny knowing this? Do you think I wanted you to put your entire life on hold hoping I'd come to you someday?"

"No. But we love each other. We still do. We always have, Carla. And *we're* family."

Carla shook her head no. "Look, family or not, love changes over time. Things are different now. It isn't the way it was with us back then."

"I don't have any illusions about that, Carla. I'm not that out of it. But I think that the best kind of marriage is one where both parties know each other very well and know what to expect. So marry me."

For a moment, Carla looked as if she would laugh. "Marriage?" she asked.

"Yes."

Carla made a face full of sarcasm. "Marry *you? Me?*"

John was undaunted by her reaction. "Yes," he shrugged, "you. Me."

Carla dropped the tough facade and softened. She went to the couch and sat down next to him. She touched his hand. "Oh John, that's so nice. I love you so much for saying that, but I can't marry you."

"Why not?"

"Well for one thing, I'm married." Carla smiled gently.

"The marriage from hell. A paper marriage, that's all. A death warrant disguised as a marriage license. Get out of it. Save your life. Now. Now or he'll really kill you one of these days."

Carla didn't like John's forcefulness. "What if I don't want to save my life?"

"I want you to, Carla, please. If not for yourself, for me for God sakes."

"It's *my* life. If you love me, you have to let me go. Find someone else. You're a good man and I know all kinds of women who are after you. Let me give you their phone numbers, please."

"What is it with you, Carla? I may not be the best catch, but I'm probably your best friend."

She agreed, "Yes, you probably are."

John looked down at the floor and muttered, "And we make very good lovers, great lovers."

Carla grimaced with exasperation. "*Made* great lovers. That was a long, long time ago, John. We were kids. Stop it, John. Just stop."

"We can still have a baby if you want. Let me be the father of one of your children. It'll be wonderful." John was as sincere as anyone could be.

She was touched; however, the intimacy of the offer was too profound for Carla, it reached too deep. Carla resorted to the wall of sarcasm again. "If that's part of the deal, I'm definitely saying no."

"OK, let's skip that. I just thought maybe you still wanted that. Let's just have a warm, cozy life together." He put his arm around her.

She pushed him away, saying, “How trite. John, sometimes you sound like the back of a cereal box.”

John was hurt and jumped up. He started to pace, and raised his voice. “Trite? Trite is being savagely beaten by your narcissistic bullshit husband on a regular basis and then acting as if it never happens. Trite is walking around bruised and cut and broken inside and not leaving the source of your pain! Trite is make-up covering over truth!” He stopped moving and scanned Carla’s neck for bruises. “This has to end now,” he said. He started to pace again.

“John! Stop! *I* am the source of *my* pain. No one else.”

John froze in his tracks. “I can’t believe that Burt’s got you believing that all this is your fault.”

“Don’t you get it, John? Whether I believe that or not, the fact that I’m still in it *is* my fault.”

John narrowed his eyes. “Don’t you get it? I hate what he’s doing to you so much that, if you wanted me to, I would kill him for you, Carla.”

Carla tried to hide her extreme discomfort with this thought. She came on tough as a result. “John, don’t ever let me hear you talk like that. That’s not like you. I *need* you to *stay out of it*. I need you to stay clean and steer clear. If anything ever happens to me --”

“Carla! That’s exactly what I’m trying to prevent! I want to be certain that one of you, either you or Burt, doesn’t kill you!”

"It's not your fate to interfere with. It's *my* fate. But I was saying something more important --"

John was still standing. He crossed his arms stubbornly. "There is nothing more important."

"Just wait a minute, John," Carla stood up and put her hands on his arms. I *need* to count on you for help. I really do. Can I? Please?"

"Of course, that's why I'm here. But you have to *let* me help you, Carla."

"Then help me this way, my way." Carla took his hands in hers and looked him in the eye. "My daughter *will* come back. I know she will. I can feel it. And, if something happens to me --"

"Carla --"

"Wait, John, let me finish. If something happens to me or to Burt and to me, then Sheila will need someone to help out with things, legal affairs, personal affairs, family affairs, and all the papers and things I left in the safe deposit box that I gave you the key to. I need you to stay out of what's going on so that you can be available for Sheila, no matter what happens. Please. Please promise me this. Please, I beg you."

John agreed with a nod. Now he put his hands on Carla's shoulders. "Of course, you know I'll do anything for you, but what do you mean by 'what's going on'? Please, explain this. It scares me," he told her with serious eyes.

"No. I can't tell you right now. I will some time, maybe. Or maybe not. But certainly not now." Carla pulled away and sat down again. She was lying.

John sat down next to Carla. He put his arm around her again.

She looked him in the eye and said, "John, I never loved anyone the way I once loved you. But that was young love, coming at a time in life when ideals dominate and reality hasn't set in. Still, even now, you're a wonderful man. But maybe you wouldn't have loved me anymore by now if we'd stayed together. Burt says that I --"

"Burt is a God awful liar, a self-aggrandizing, narcissistic socio-psychopath," John interrupted sternly. "Burt says what Burt needs to say to control everything and everyone he can. Burt has brainwashed you. He's taken over your mind. You are the number one member of the cult of Burt. I DON'T CARE WHAT BURT SAYS!!! Stop letting him kill you!"

Both Carla and John had tears in their eyes now. John grabbed her hands. "Just promise me that you *will* consider it. That you *will* spend five minutes or whatever, a little time, thinking about the possibility that you and I could be happy together. Think about it after you leave today. Think and then let me know. *Please*."

John abruptly took Carla's face in his hands and kissed her. At first she held back, but then she embraced him. He continued to kiss her. She let him.

"Make love with me, Carla."

"Not now, John."

"I want you, Carla. I still want you. Come on. Live, don't die, live with a man who loves you."

Carla could feel her inner chemistry shift abruptly as if she had just turned a corner. "I want you too," she said, expecting that she would do no more than say the words. But she longed for John now, quite desperately.

"Then let's. Even if it's just once. Even if you decide it's the last time. Just once if that's all you want. I still love you," John told her as he ran his finger over her lips, "even if it's the last time we ever let ourselves touch each other."

The passion got the best of Carla and she acquiesced, knowing that it would indeed be the last time, because she was definitely on her way out of this life. This was a sort of futile farewell celebration. A bittersweet wind swept through Carla along with the waves of her desperate, starving for love, sexuality.

John, on the other hand, was overjoyed. Finally, he had the love of his life back. And, more important than that, he felt that this was the only chance he had to bring her back to the world, to keep her from killing herself. He knew this. He knew it and he put his whole self, every bit of his soul, into loving her. Could he turn the tide? Oh, could he?

53.

GOODMAN RESIDENCE….

Burt was home in time for dinner, but Carla hadn't made any. He made a phone call and ordered burritos from a local Mexican restaurant. After they were delivered, Burt and Carla ate together at the kitchen table. Carla was in her bath robe, which had become typical of her since she came home from the hospital.

"Didn't you feel well enough to go out today?" Burt asked coldly, wondering why she could not have bothered to buy some food when she had so few responsibilities.

"No," she lied. She had been out to see John. What a bad Maxwell House wife she was, she told herself.

"Still tired?" He tried to make conversation but sounded cold, angry and volatile. Each of his words pierced her like a long pin.

"The tranquilizers are getting to me, I guess." Carla made an excuse for herself.

"At least you aren't stockpiling them."

"Now, why would I do that, Burt?" Carla smothered her sarcasm with robotic blandness. Burt glared at her. Carla paused and then added, "If I decide to kill myself, you'll be informed. Shortly thereafter. And if I don't kill myself, I'll write a great book about how a woman could manage not to kill herself after being with you for so many years. You're a great real-life model for a fictional terrible man. You are one."

"Well, if you use me in the book, if you quote me, the book is half mine," Burt told her threateningly, "I own half the profits."

"Sure, community property." Carla wanted to vomit all over him. "Like I own half of everything you've made, Burt."

"This would be different, because I'd actually be the source of, the star of, the story." As usual, Burt saw himself as the star. And, as usual, he had to remain in control of whatever Carla might do. Even if it was Carla only thinking about doing something, Burt took over.

But Carla had a response. "No. I'm the story and the source of the story. Me, Burt. But, if, and I doubt I will, but if I ever manage to want to live and to write that book, the man who plays the suicidal woman's husband will be portrayed as corrupt, cruel, selfish, self-centered, domineering, manipulative, threatening, and terribly violent: everything you are. But it would destroy you to admit it, to admit to even some of the things you've done which I'd use in the book. So if you ever try to claim that you are the lead male character, let alone that the book is half yours because it's about you, you'll probably spend the rest of your life in jail. Now why would you want to admit that you are as horrible as you truly are?" Carla was surprised that she had dared to say this. Where had this come from? Why now? Was it because she had so little to lose at this point, at least in her mind?

Burt felt somewhat outwitted here. He didn't like it. "You think you're a genius, don't you? Well, Carla, if you're so smart, than why don't you have any money, any career, anything to show for your life, any desire to live? Why don't you have a man who loves you sitting here? Answer that!"

The tension was so thick that, to recoin a well-used phrase, you could cut it with a knife. Carla squinted her eyes at the burrito and stabbed it with her knife.

"Not hungry?" Burt asked. He sounded to Carla like a Gestapo. Would he punish her for not eating? Of for having a brilliant answer to his takeover of her old now useless dream of writing a book?

"Not much." She dropped the knife and pushed the plate away. Life just kept going on, didn't it? Empty anguish filled each numb minute to the brim until it spilled over into the next. More, and then more, of the same. Where were the Maxwell House wives now? Couldn't Carla's imaginary Maxwell woman's army rescue her from this? Imaginary?

Burt shrugged. "Oh well, thought you liked burritos."

"Thanks anyway," she said. "For the burrito, I mean."

Burt stopped eating. "Carla, was the maid here yet this week?"

"No, it's Tuesday, she comes on Thursday. You know that. Why do you ask?" Carla wondered what he was after. She also wondered why he would bother a woman who was recovering from a suicide attempt with such trivial details.

"I don't know," he answered. "I think someone's been digging through my desk."

"Why would the maid do that?" she wondered. Is he actually accusing his wife and not his maid?

"She wouldn't I guess. I don't think she ever has," Burt answered. "But then, she hasn't been here since Thursday, which is the last time I sat at my desk."

"Burt," Carla raised an eyebrow at him. "Are you suggesting that *I* went through your desk?" Of all things, now this? How dare he?

"No. But did you?" He put the question on the table, like the next course of dinner.

"No." Of course not, you jerk, Carla said in her mind. I hate you. I hate you.

"I didn't think so. It's not like you." Burt went on eating.

"What *is* like me, Burt?"

"Oh come on, Carla. It's just that I left some highly confidential, worse -- some extremely dangerous information -- sitting there. My mistake. But, the problem is, it seems as if it's been reshuffled. It would have to have happened sometime in the past two days."

Carla tried to think about who could have been at Burt's desk. No one came to her mind. "I didn't go out today," she lied again. "But I did yesterday."

"Did you lock the house when you went out, Carla?"

"I always do, Burt."

"OK, well then, we have no explanation." Burt finished his burrito. "Maybe I'm just imagining the whole thing."

"Overly paranoid," Carla tried to agree, but it came out wrong.

"Or understandably concerned," he said defensively, trying hard to sound hurt, to be the victim here. "Can I eat the rest of your burrito?" Burt took Carla's plate from the center of the table before she answered him.

"Sure. Eat it. Take it all. It's yours, just like everything else," she said.

Burt's mouth was full. "Don't start on that now, Carla. We're having a nice dinner."

"Nice?" Carla asked. "You just happened to drop by to order in take out and ask me if I've been through your papers?"

"Carla, if my clients, you know, Moreno and company, get any sense that any one beside me has seen the stuff --"

"They'll what, Burt, kill us?" she said facetiously.

"Yes, actually," he answered. He meant it.

"*Yes*? It's that serious? Then why bring it home and risk *my* life?" Carla was angry.

"Oh, I suppose only you are allowed to do that?" Burt was mad too.

"Yes. That's right. It's *my* life, Burt. *Mine*."

Burt shoved Carla's plate back across the table. Only, he shoved it a little too hard and it went right off the edge into her lap. He stood up and went to the sink to wash his hands.

Carla removed the food from her lap. She stood up and collected the plates. She was heading toward the sink with the plates when Burt wheeled around and knocked them out of her hand unintentionally. "Shit," he muttered.

They each automatically knelt down to clean up the mess. Burt looked at Carla as they both were kneeling there on the floor. He put his hand on hers to get her attention. "You may not believe this, but I love you very much. Those guys *are* dangerous. I may be in over my head. I wouldn't want anyone to hurt you."

"Anyone but you." She stared at him trying to hold back tears.

"What does that mean, Carla?" For the first time in as many years as he could remember, Burt found that he cared about what Carla thought of him.

"Anyone but you to hurt me. You're the only one with that privilege." Carla picked up the rest of the mess. She had stopped herself from crying.

Burt stood up, looked down at her, now irritated. He narrowed his eyes. "Really, there is no room for bullshit on this. I'm very serious. Life and death serious. You have to believe me no matter how much you hate me. These guys will kill *anyone* who crosses them. They're big players in an international syndicate built on illegal and powerful criminal business. They've got their fingers in everything, governments and corporations all over the world, and many branches of government even here in the US, such as IRS, CIA, FBI, including local law enforcement."

Carla went and put everything into the garbage.

Uncertain as to what he was really feeling about Carla's cleaning up the mess, Burt watched awkwardly but did not help Carla. He could not figure out how he felt about her. His emotions here were all over the map. He loved her. He hated her. He wanted to protect her. He felt like beating her senseless.

Carla turned and looked Burt square in the eye. "If all this is true, if it is, then get off the case, Burt. Don't take any more of their money. I don't know how much you've taken or how long you've been taking it. You haven't told me anything about this case. Ever. You hired other people to work with you on it, unlike most of the rest of the cases where you used me as your cheap Harvard Law School educated lackey. Where could you ever get someone so good free? So I don't know what this is all about, but I insist you give whatever they've paid you back and take no more. Just give it all back."

"I'm afraid a lot of it's spent," Burt sighed, gesturing as if to say it had been spent on their multimillion dollar house. Maybe he would feel better if he told her some of the truth. He sighed and sat down on the floor. "Carla, it's pretty bad, I have to tell you.

This is putting it mildly. It goes back a long way, too long. I've been on retainer, a big retainer, with them for years. They even put me through law school."

Carla was stunned. Who was this man she had just spent a couple of decades of her life with? "And I had no right to know? You've been endangering our lives for years -- Sheila's life as well -- and I haven't been told?" she asked, hating herself for her own blindness. How could she have not picked up on any of this? She remembered the locked file cabinet she had found early in their relationship, the one she was told never to ask about. Damn it, she should have asked long ago. She would ask right now: "Well, I *demand* to know *now,* Burt. What business are they in? I insist on knowing."

He looked at this woman he had called his wife for so long. Had he ever let her know him? Had he ever gotten to know her? Where was her new assertiveness coming from? Suddenly, he saw that she had indeed turned some kind of corner. He felt a little something shift between them. She was demanding truth. Maybe this was healthy for her, a sign she wouldn't be suicidal again. But this particular truth was dangerous. Knowing it could kill her.

Burt cared deeply about Carla – for a second. But then the next moment, Burt felt a rush of anger rise. How dare she suddenly insist on knowing what had for so long been his private business? Then the next moment, Burt felt his feelings jumble. Now he was feeling, at the same time, both angry at her and sorry for all this.

So he told her more.

Time for truth. "International flesh trade – human trading companies -- *woman trafficking*, Carla. Trafficking with a destination, with a plan, with a global goal." Burt told her, slipping and saying a bit too much, but knowing the global part of it would make no sense to Carla so it would not matter, that she would be shocked by the woman trafficking itself, and be put off by Burt's sounding defensive but defiant as he disclosed this to her.

Carla was speechless. What?

Burt felt his rage rising again. What in the hell was he trying to tell her? Why? He wanted no questions. He turned suddenly and left the house as quickly as possible in order to avoid her reaction. As he drove away, despite the danger to both himself and Carla, he felt a great sense of relief, as if he had just ended a dangerous lie that had spanned two plus decades. His burden of deceit had lifted. He felt better than he had in twenty-some years, better, until he realized that someone was following him, weaving in and out of traffic as a way of hiding.

Burt's tension flooded back into his body, now a thousand times stronger than it had ever been. "No relief for the wicked," he whispered to himself and chuckled nervously. He was beginning to despise himself, at least a little.

This was, for Burt, a whole new sensation.

He artfully left his pursuer, or thought he had….

54.

GOODMAN RESIDENCE….

The final blow. It came when she was least expecting it.

Burt walked into the house, after being gone all night, just as Carla was putting the envelope addressed to Sheila, the one John did not want to take to the bank, into her purse. Carla was on her way to the her safe deposit box for the last time. She was ready for her suicide, this time more carefully planned. She felt, clear, focused, and in a detached way, quite good. This state of mind, including this illusion of hyper-rationality she was experiencing, was new. In a strange way, she was proud of herself, a sensation she was not questioning.

Burt seemed in a hurry. He went straight to his desk. And then he shouted for Carla: "Carla? Carla!"

At first Carla did not respond, but when he shouted her name again, she thought she had better act as if nothing unusual was about to happen. She decided to stay calm, no matter what, calm and detached. She could hear that certain kind of anger in the tone of his voice, the kind that could get out of control. She didn't need his weird unpredictable madness, his rage-aholism, right now. She went into the den, obediently.

"What Burt? You don't have to shout. I'm not deaf. I can hear you."

"Carla, you said you weren't in my papers!" Burt demanded.

"I wasn't," she defended, her sublime detachment wavering.

"But you say no one was here?" he interrogated her.

"No one," she cringed thinking here she was, even now, attached again. Involved in it all again. Attached to the ongoing cycle of abuse and pain she called her marriage.

In the next instant, Burt leapt up and stood next to Carla. He shouted down into her face: "Then explain how someone out there knows what no one can know -- what was in one of those documents. How can I be hearing that there has been a leak? How could this leak?"

Carla looked up into his eyes, fiercely. "*You* explain, you bastard. Maybe all your corrupt crap, your years of questionable ethics, your endangering your wife and daughter, is coming back at you, Burt. I hate you, Burt, you're killing me with all this. Just let me die in peace."

Burt missed Carla's subtle reference to another suicide attempt, or maybe he just did not care. He raised his voice even more. "You *had* to be the one. What did you do, *sell* the information? What are you trying to do, get us both killed? Do you understand how dangerous all this is?"

"No, but it's a good idea," Carla said, shoving Burt away from her body with more force than she had ever shown him. Right now, she had something more important to do than listen to him: she had to kill herself to get out of ever hearing his voice again, to get out of the miserable pattern of their relationship.

Burt was surprised that she had shoved him so hard. He grabbed her arm and shook her viciously. "Don't you *dare* touch me, Carla. I talked to a divorce lawyer and he said that once our voices are raised in anger, if you so much as touch me, that's an act of violence."

"Leave it to you to find a legal excuse for beating me, you bastard." She pushed him away again. He slapped her face, punched her in the stomach, and then grabbed her by the neck with both his hands and shook her, his thumbs pressing in on her wind pipe.

Carla tried to free herself, hitting his sides. Burt laughed at her and let go. Carla turned to leave the room. But then Burt kicked her, hitting her tail bone with his knee. She fell onto a carton of papers, cutting the side of her leg. As she was falling, she reached out to grab something to stop the fall and snagged her arm on the corner of a tall metal sculpture. The sculpture then fell, hitting her on the forehead and knocking her unconscious.

The phone rang. Burt looked at it, did not answer. He grabbed some papers, and ran out of the house, whispering, "You bitch," and then shouting from the door, "go ahead, kill yourself, but don't take me down with you."

Carla came to when Burt slammed the door. She found herself full of blood. She pushed the sculpture away and tried to stand, but fell over. After several minutes of struggling, she was on her feet, trembling.

The phone stopped ringing.

Forgetting entirely about her trip to the bank, Carla went right to her bed, and reached under the mattress. Without hesitating, she pulled out three bottles of pills and a plastic bag containing some kind of powder. She sat down and emptied the bag into one of the two tall glasses of water she already had sitting there by the bed. She dropped two sugar cubes into that glass of water. She stirred it with her finger. While she waited for the sugar cubes to dissolve, she put handful after handful of pills into her mouth. She swallowed them with the water in the other glass until all the pills in all three bottles were gone. Next she drank the water with the sugar cubes and powder in it. Then she laid down and cried herself to sleep, softly and with a strong wish for immediate, intense, and very permanent relief.

Time to go. Now the tears will stop.

Now.

Part Three

This Moment to Be Free

55.

CARLA'S HOSPITAL ROOM….

She was in a coma by the time the cleaning lady found her. Alas, Carla had been in such a hurry to leave the filthy world of pain that she had forgotten that the cleaning lady was coming.

Carla had not intended to make such a foolish mistake. This time, she had meticulously and intelligently planned the perfect and foolproof time to end her life. However, when she planned this, she had not expected to become so very upset so close to the time she had planned to kill herself. Carla had intended to commit a very calm, premeditated, rational, even serene, act. Unfortunately, or fortunately, depending on how you see it, she failed.

Or she may have failed. Now her life was hanging in limbo. She was in the hospital in a coma, hearing only the sound of a lone bird's flying wings.

56.

BURT GOODMAN LAW OFFICE….

They walked into the elegant reception area of the famous law office and asked for Mr. Burt Goodman. The secretary told them that he was in a meeting and could not be disturbed. But, just then, Burt came out of his office in a rush to be somewhere and they stopped him.

"Mr. Goodman, may we see you alone?" They showed him their official I.D.s.

Burt glanced at them and looked apologetic but distracted. He looked at his watch. "No, I am quite late for a critical meeting."

"Mr. Goodman, we must see you in your office now. I think you would prefer that."

Burt snapped at them, "I would prefer to be on time for a very important client. Make an appointment please." He turned to rush out.

"Well then, if you insist, Mr. Goodman, you are under arrest."

Burt stopped, his back to them, and said in a cool voice, "Arrest?"

"For attempted homicide. You have the right --"

Burt turned around. "You have *got* to be *kidding me*."

The secretary dropped her pen and gaped at the scene.

"Attempted homicide or murder one, if Mrs. Goodman dies." Detective Stanger was being quite matter-of-fact.

Burt felt as if the floor had just rushed upward and crushed him against the ceiling. They took him in and booked him. Of course, as is typical in the case of a man of Burt's stature and connections, bail was arranged immediately. He got out. He went back to work.

57.

MISSION CONVENT IN CENTRAL AMERICAN JUNGLE….

By now, the most recently rescued girls had been taken to join the others in the convent nestled deep somewhere in a mountainous Central American jungle. They were bathed, fed, dressed in clean clothes, checked on by medics, and given bunks in the old colonial dormitories. Each girl was shown the hidden access to the underground hiding area and taught the signal that meant an evacuation to that yet more hidden place was required immediately.

These dormitories housed several hundred young women. At first glance, this appeared to be a school for girls, which in fact, it was. Most of the girls who were housed there had been rescued much the same way that these newcomers had, by members of the same liberation army, the IUWM. Some of the convents' other guests were members of that army. In fact, the Central American headquarters of this army was based in a large underground hall directly beneath this Mission Assisi church. The entry to this hall was impossible to find and impossible to open -- for anyone who had not been trained to find and open it.

Indeed, most of the women dressed as nuns were members of the WWLF, the World Women's Liberation Front. Among those IUWM-WWLF women, unbeknownst to most of them, were a few female members of the American CIA, and the American NSA, National Security Agency. These women had infiltrated. They were actually double agents seeking to assess the extent of the ever-growing secret gender war, at least that is what they called it. Gender war? Or simply an effort to ensure the freedom of women now and in the times to come?

58.

CARLA'S MIND….

Carla found herself lurking somewhere deep within the recesses of her mortal mind. She was but a tiny speck of consciousness, hanging in limbo between life and death, but alas, woe to be, she was not gone. Yet.

She heard her own voice coming from a far corner of her own brain: This can't be happening. I'm alive *again*. Not again. What kind of cruel joke is this? How wretched.

God, let me out! Let me out of this damn world! Kill me! Kill!

She tried to scream in mortal anguish but no sound came out of her. This limbo was a new improved hell, one from which only one's own murder would provide an escape. Burt, just kill me outright! You're doing it too slowly, too cruelly, why not just get it all done now?

Carla continued on, unconscious, a bird singing a song of silence in the dead of her own personal night.

59.

BURT GOODMAN LAW OFFICE….

Andrea walked into Burt's office and shut the door. Desperate for comfort, Burt rushed to her to hug her. Andrea pushed him back coldly.

"Burt. I just came to say I want out. Out of any of our work together. Out of our relationship. Out of your life. You out of mine."

"But," Burt had sudden tears in his eyes, "you can't mean that." He wilted inside. Why this now? He suddenly felt so sorry for himself.

Andrea was unmoved. "Yes, I can," she said.

Burt grabbed her and hugged her, pressing hard against her body. He was breathing in gulps, almost sobbing.

She tried to unloose his grip on her, but could not. "Stay away from me. Let go. Now."

Burt did not let go. Instead he squeezed harder and started to sob. “You can’t abandon me now. We have a good thing together. You know I’m innocent. You know it, Andrea.”

“Stay away from me.” Andrea shoved him away.

He was stunned. He sat down. “Why? Why this treatment? How can you do this to me, Andrea?”

But Andrea had an impenetrable wall around her heart now. “You just forget me, Burt. Leave my name out of every discussion you ever have. Don’t ever let me find out that you ever said anything about me with regard to our affair, our work, our whatever. Stay away or you will pay.”

Burt stood up in order to gain some kind of power in this conflict of hearts and wills. “Are *you* threatening *me*?” He was the one who sounded threatening.

“If I have to,” Andrea responded, unfazed by the threat buried in his question. “You decide, Burt. I have lots of options. I can call the FBI, I can blackmail you, I can lead Moreno to believe you’re telling the feds, I can kill you. You can choose. I prefer allowing us both the dignity of my very civil, very to the point request: Get out of my life. Now. Or else.”

Andrea turned and left without waiting for a response.

Burt was stunned.

60.

SAME HOSPITAL ROOM….

John had been informed Carla had emerged from her coma. “Carla?”

“Go away, John,” she whispered in a faint lifeless voice from the land of the would-be dead.

John felt as if his heart was being torn apart, piece by bloody piece, at the sight of Carla back in a hospital bed, but in far more critical condition this time. “No. I won’t go away,” he told her and sat down.

“John, go or I’ll buzz the nurses’ station and have you thrown out,” she whispered again.

John leapt up to stop her from searching the sheets for the buzzer. “Carla, wait, wait, don’t, I’ll be brief, I promise.” He rested his hand on hers.

“Well, be brief then. And don’t get emotional,” Carla murmured hoarsely. “I hate feelings.”

"I won't get emotional, but I am emotional. The woman I love, the love of my life, almost died and I --"

"John, that's emotional. Stop. Or I will have you thrown out."

"OK, Carla. I'll stop. But tell me this. Just tell me one thing. Did Burt do this to you?"

John was waiting, as if hanging on the edge of a disintegrating cliff, for confirmation of what he feared and yet believed was the horrendous truth: Burt had tried to murder Carla.

Twice now. The police had just told him so.

Carla shut her eyes and turned away. She said nothing. John sat down next to the bed. He felt himself grieving as much as if Carla had died. Maybe even more so, he thought to himself. "Because if he did, I'll kill him, Carla."

John could see Carla's eyelids press themselves shut even tighter than they already were. Why wouldn't she look at him? Why should she protect Burt after this? "I'll kill him before he kills you, Carla."

Carla held her breath and tried to will herself dead. A tear escaped from one tightly shut eye. But the dead don't cry.

"Carla," John took a rose from one of the bouquets in the room. He placed it across her chest with the bloom over her heart. "Carla, don't let this happen to you. Don't waste yourself on this pain. Don't let Burt get away with this. He's got some kind of crazy hold on you. Why? Is it sex? Is it money? Is it some kind of sick dependence? Has he hypnotized you? Are you hooked on this cyclic violence?"

Carla still refused to speak. Her eyelids ached as she squeezed them closed ever more tightly. Shut this world out. Go away, reality. Go.

"Carla! Don't go on like this. Carla, listen, please. I can give you whatever you need to make the break from Burt. You can have my money, my time, my legal work, my friendship, my house, my car, my love -- take all or any part of it -- no strings attached -- take me or leave me -- but let me help you break out of this sick cycle. Really, no strings attached."

John felt he had to get through to her for once and for all or Burt would finish the job. Why would such a beautiful woman allow a man to brutalize her this way?

Carla still refused to speak or even to open her eyes. Having John see her like this was too humiliating. She simply refused to deal with his presence, let alone what he was saying.

"Carla, the police don't have a case against Burt without your testimony. Thank God you lived to tell the story. You've *got* to talk. You've got to help put Burt away, for once and for all."

Carla opened her eyes, avoided looking at John, reached out abruptly and, in anxious desperation, buzzed for the nurse.

She held the buzzer tightly and shut her eyes again.

"OK, Carla. I'll leave. But Burt won't get away with this. It's time he pays for his cruel manipulation of you. For his crimes.

Look what he’s done to you! I’ll make him pay. You can bet I’ll make him pay.”

John almost collided with the nurse on his way out the door.

61.

SAME HOSPITAL ROOM….

Some number of hours passed by like a slow-flowing river of suffocating mud.

And then, another intrusion: "Carla, we have to talk. Quick, before they find me here. Please."

She opened her eyes from a dream in which she was a bird. Burt? Could it be Burt? How dare he come here? "Burt? ... Burt, go ... Burt, I really don't want to talk about anything ... with anyone ... right now." Carla closed her aching eyes. World go away. Burt be gone. Death be.

Burt stood at Carla's bedside and took her icy hand. He waited there a long time, wishing for her to look at him. When she finally opened her eyes, he saw such an empty woman, a woman who very much wanted to leave herself, to abandon herself, forever. This frightened him. How long had his wife been in such great pain? He had absolutely no idea. This realization frightened him even more. He held her hand tightly and tried to make real eye contact with her, pouring into her eyes with his will. She continued staring right at him, with her eyes making no contact.

"Please, Carla, please see me, please. We don't have much time." Burt was not used to feeling this way about Carla. So he told himself he was not certain he cared so much. But, damn it, he was feeling as if he truly did. Furthermore, if she died, he could be in big trouble. Maybe this was his real concern.

Carla blinked. See me? What was Burt asking for? She actually looked at him for a moment. And then she looked away. Burt did not release her hand.

Carla turned back and washed Burt in her iciness. "Just ... leave me ... alone right now," Carla warned, in a muffled voice, trying to sound irritated. She turned away.

Burt, in desperation, giving way to his urgent need to communicate, pulled her toward him by yanking forcefully on her hand, disturbing the wires running around, on and into her body. "*Carla* --"

"Let go of me!" Carla sat up as best she could, tugging on her I.V., trying to move it back into place. "I don't want to be pushed around *ever again*."

He let go. "But Carla." Burt, his eyes cast downward in apparent shame, was suddenly speaking in a softer tone, "Carla, you've got it all wrong. You've got me all wrong. I don't want to push you around. I love you, I --"

"Oh shut up, Burt. You're a walking lie. A river of lies. An ocean of bullshit." Carla glared into his soul with truth. "You wouldn't know the truth even if it slammed you in the face. You've been beating me violently for years and you know it."

Shocked at Carla's atypical spurt of ferocity, Burt looked at her as if he were a hurt and cowering child. Could the truth have just hit him in the face? Now, for the first time ever, Burt's voice became meek. He practically whimpered, "Please listen, Carla. Just listen for a minute, a few minutes. Just give me a fair hearing," he pleaded. "I know I've been mean, very mean for years, but please, please."

Carla was a bit surprised by Burt's newly submissive behavior, and his (probably bogus) admission of abuse, and she did not trust it. Was he manipulating her as usual? He was, after all, the king of manipulators. But what for? Why manipulate her now? Burt had tears in his eyes. Carla told herself she had never seen Burt really cry honest tears, or maybe even cry at all, not once in all their years together. And now tears? Tears for her? Or tears for himself?

"Carla, I'm not here to bother you, I'm here to *beg* you, to *beg* you to listen to me." Burt gazed at her with pleading eyes. Perhaps he was being sincere. But why?

Carla sat up a little taller. She had something he wanted. "Whatever, Burt. Just don't bullshit me. I can barely believe you, so don't think anything you say or do will sound like truth to me."

"Thanks, Carla. . . ." Burt seemed to be groping for words. He sat down. "I just want to say first that I don't think, I don't believe, that you told the police I tried to kill you." He scanned her eyes for some kind of reaction to his words. “You didn’t say I tried to kill you, did you?”

Carla took a deep breath. Oh, this is what he’s here about: himself. “Burt,” she whispered slowly, “I will answer this question once and only once, and I will tell you the truth: No. No, I did not say anything of the sort to the police.” I said it to the Gods, but not the police. And it was another form of wife-killing I was referring to, Carla said to herself.

Burt went on. “Carla, did you --”

“I said I would answer only once, Burt.”

“I know, but I’m on a different question now,” Burt moaned, trying to remain calm.

“Oh, I’m being cross-examined now, Burt?” Carla strained to find out what he wanted now, here and now.

“No, Carla, I am trying to find out what’s happening to me, what possibly could have rendered me suspected of attempted murder.”

“Nothing I said.” Carla winced inside. She was not lying, but she did feel guilty. After all, it was something she had thought. Be careful what you wish for. And then her guilt disappeared. She felt angry. “What about you, Burt? Maybe you did something to implicate yourself.”

“What do you mean?” Burt looked sincerely scared and confused. Actually, he was terrified. His name, his fame, his reputation as a wonderful man, his bar license, his career, his life, were all in jeopardy.

"Well, I don't mean that you did something people would see or hear." Carla paused, trying to find words to explain this sense that she had that Burt was indeed involved in her killing, albeit invisibly, and perhaps subconsciously. Or maybe consciously on some level.

"Carla, you're losing me. I'm not getting it," he looked honestly perplexed for a moment.

Carla realized that this honesty, itself, was a new look in Burt's face.

"Well, think about it, Burt," Carla was cool here. But even after all that had happened between them, even in her worn and weakened state, for some reason incomprehensible to her, she was somewhat caring. "Just think without arguing back for a moment. Just this time."

Burt knew exactly what Carla meant. He always had a viewpoint that differed from hers and he always argued against whatever she said, as a matter of course. He decided not to this time.

Carla noticed that Burt had made this decision. She went on. "Burt, on some level you *have* been killing me, or at least trying to kill me for a long time."

"What?" Burt looked sincerely appalled. "You really think I would do anything like that? How could you think I would kill the love of my life, which you are even if I've messed it all up."

"You're arguing back, aren't you? . . . Oh, maybe not. This 'love of my life' stuff has to stop. It's bullshit. … But anyway, no, you wouldn't murder me in any conventional way -- and not in any way the police or the courts would ever find you guilty of."

"Then what are you saying?" Was Burt actually trying to understand her, or was he just feigning it?

Carla tried to pull the shreds of herself together, barely, just enough to let Burt know what she meant: "I am saying that most of my life with you, which was really not a life, has been a life in which there was a person around me, a person very close in to me, posing as my husband, who was, for the most part, largely and intensely disappointed with me. There was nothing I could contribute, accomplish, or achieve, even in your name – which it always was – you always took credit for it all – nothing I did was ever good enough. And the level of this disappointment was so high for so long that it wore me down, chiseled me away to just about nothing."

Carla felt her collected pain, amassed over many years, rising. Behind the pain, a distant voice was calling. What was it saying? Something about the unspoken agreement she and Burt had somehow made, the one saying all was for BURT.

"But, that's not murder. That's not attempted murder." Burt was baffled, but not argumentative.

"Then what is it?" Carla asked him.

Without realizing that he was admitting that he had been acting largely and intensely disappointed with Carla for many years, he said, "That's just a person disliking another person's approach to life or --" Burt felt a wave of intense honesty, something new to him, sweep over him, "Maybe it's just a person belittling someone he's close to, to avoid belittling himself. Maybe he hates himself so very very much that he has to direct it at her."

Carla swallowed. She was startled by this unexpected admission, albeit small. Still, she told herself, be careful, he isn't really admitting anything at all. I shouldn't think for one moment that he is sincere in any way here. He never is truly sincere. What had made her think he was sincere now? "You sure water it down when you describe it like that. It's much more vicious than you're admitting here," she said. "You beat me violently whenever you want to. And in between physical abuse, there is a stream of emotional abuse."

It took more energy than she had, but Carla managed to glare fiercely at Burt.

Burt did not want to alienate her, not now. He needed her help. And her emotional support. "What do you want me to say, Carla? I'm deeply, immensely, sorry?" Burt wondered whether he actually was sorry. For a moment, he wondered why he had such a hard time getting in touch with his feelings about Carla. His real feelings. What were they? He didn't know. He was so far away from himself, he didn't know anything about anything at this point. He hadn't known for years….

"I want you to say -- no not just to say -- to understand -- that the way you have treated me for many many years has been controlling, cruel, abusive, manipulative -- and profoundly damaging. You trashed me, my life."

"But that's not murder." He said it more forcefully this time. He very much wanted to be sure she got his point here.

"You hit me so many many times, Burt," she said coldly.

"I *beat* you so many times, Carla." Burt paused and gulped hearing himself admit this. He looked around to be sure no one was listening. "I did … but that's still not murder."

"You beat me even when you weren't hitting me, Burt. It all sure has felt like murder, death, to me. A slow kind of torturous death, but death. ... You've been killing me for a long time, Burt. Killing my will, my self-esteem, my hope, my life, stealing my energy and then beating me for reserving the last miserable bit of myself for myself."

"Oh, Carla, that's not what I wanted to be doing. I wanted, I wanted --" Burt began to sob. Crocodile tears, or real ones, he was unsure, flowed from of his eyes. Burt had for so long been a façade of himself that even now he did not know who he was or what he felt, not for sure.

Burt sobbed. The sobbing seemed sincere, it did. However, in Carla's eyes, these sobs were Burt's sobs for Burt, not for Carla. He felt pain for himself. Carla's resentment mounted, a pot about to finally boil over, but she managed to hold it in. "What, for God's sake, could you have been wanting?" she said tightly. "To rob me of myself? What was the benefit of that? Slave labor?"

Burt blinked several times. "I --" Burt had more tears in his eyes. He cried for several minutes until he could speak again. "Is it too late to say I'm sorry, I am really, really sorry?"

"Yes. It's far too late. Don't even go there. The damage has been done, Burt. I'm already broken -- damaged and long gone. I'm already dead."

"Carla," Burt was speaking from his heart now. He really thought he was. "I was just fumbling my way through life, like everyone does. Making mistakes, some horrible mistakes."

"And I was one of them?"

"No, Carla, you weren't a mistake. I loved you. I really loved you. I wanted so much for us, for you and for me. You weren't a mistake. You were the golden girl, the trophy girl at Harvard Law School. You were no mistake."

"You sure treated me like one."

"You weren't a mistake, but the way I treated you was one. I wanted to have you, to take you over, to own you -- and if I couldn't have all that, and I couldn't, then I had to crush you. I needed all your energy for me, your brains for me, and none of your energy and brains for you. I don't know why, but I actually wanted to crush you from the very beginning. To get you out of the way. At first I didn't realize it. I just felt like I wanted to race you and win. But, when I look back, I wanted to crush you because I couldn't stand that you were smarter and better than I was. I wanted whatever fueled you for myself."

Carla sat up straight, stronger now. "I still remember that, when you first asked me out, you said, 'If you can't beat 'em, join 'em!' " Carla told him in an accusing tone.

"But you said yes to me, Carla. You could have said no."

She agreed. “Yes, in the beginning, I could have said no. I made a mistake too. I didn’t see you for what you were: a predator, an energy predator. I surely made a big mistake letting you consume my life, and my body, and my brains, and everything I had. I never knew what to do about you. We hadn’t been together long before you started threatening me with all kinds of horrible things if I even so much as thought a second about leaving you. … And now, well now, if I were to decide to live on, I’d write something about the whole process, something to help other women caught in this sort of relationship.”

“Wait, you said, ‘if you were to *decide* to live on --’ ” Burt’s eyes widened.

“Yes, if *I* decide.” Carla emphasized the “I”. “I have no desire to go on like this, but who knows? If *I* do somehow go on, you can read about why in my book. I’m sure you will know which character you are, Burt. You’ll be easy to spot. Real easy.”

Burt was uncomfortable about this. Burt wanted to get back to the subject at hand. “Still, none of this is evidence that I attempted to murder you.”

“No, Burt?”

“No, Carla.”

“Burt, it may not be evidence in the courts, but if we took our story before a jury of the heart, a place where only full honesty could be heard, what do you think they would hear? What would be their ruling? You yourself have admitted that you wanted to crush me. In fact, you were crushing me, a very slow killing of me.

… So, I may be guilty of my own suicide, but you are guilty of my true murder -- of killing my life. We are partners in this crime. You did it to me. I was here for it to happen to me. I fulfilled your wishes."

Burt was sobbing yet more heavily, still more convincingly, now. Something about this concept must have gotten to him. He put his hands over his face and mumbled, "So, you are saying that I deserve what's happening to me? That I deserve to be brought up on charges in the here and now, because, on some level, even if it's a very hidden level, I am very, very guilty…."

"Yes, I am saying something like that. I'm saying that maybe this *is* justice. A divine sort of justice, Burt."

"Then I'll be destroyed for sure."

Carla looked at Burt crouched in a hovel on the chair by her bed. At this moment, when she held *his* future in *her* hands, when she could dictate *his* destiny with *her* decision to or not to claim that Burt forced her suicide, Carla was overpowered by a sudden awareness. She realized that she did not want to hurt the man who had hurt her for so long. She did not want to destroy him. She really did not. She just wanted to be no part of *him* any more.

"No, you won't be destroyed. At least not by my hand," she said softly. "They have no case if I won't testify. You know that. But, if I do testify, and I might have to, well then, if you do admit to all your violence against me, then I will tell the truth, that you have beaten me, abused me, for years, decades, but that you never forced me to suicide. You never tried to kill me and make it look like suicide. I tried to kill me and it was suicide, a suicide attempt on my part. The actual suicide attempts were my doing. Without me, they can never prove you forced me to attempt suicide. And, Burt, as much as you have violated me, as much as you have wronged me, I will not lie to wrong you back. I am not the kind of person you are. I never will be."

The two of them sat quietly for a while, just crying and looking at each other. Their tears flowed freely, the first equal exchange of energy ever made between them. The dead may not cry, but Carla was not one of the dead. Not now. If she had ever been one, then, as of that very moment, she had come back to life, at least for the moment. Speaking one's truth can have this effect.

Finally, Burt spoke up, almost in a whisper. "Carla, thanks. Really. I mean it. Thanks. I know my fate is most definitely in your hands." He had to be sure she would not change her mind.

Some strange sort of power shift had taken place. Carla could feel it. "Not really Burt," Carla said, "I can't fix what you have to go through, the living with yourself part of this. I can't fix what you are going to see when you look at yourself in the mirror every morning. And if you don't let yourself see yourself, then no one can do anything for you – nothing for you when you burn yourself out trying to fool yourself, spending so much of your energy lying to yourself about what kind of man you are, what kind of husband you've been, what kind of father you were. Your fate is in *your* hands, just like my fate is in *mine*. And I have to deal with myself just as much in that I have allowed myself to live as a half person, a person of sub-human status, your sad wife, all these years."

They were quiet again. The silence was long and thick; it was a blanket of meaning and, maybe, just maybe, a blanket of some new, softer kind of love. Did either of them recognize this for what it was: The love of truth; no matter how faint its presence, no matter what its consequences, they both felt it now.

Burt was the first to speak again, and he asked her a question she could not answer. "Carla, will I ever have you back, have your love again? Will you ever even be my friend?"

Carla took an incredibly long and deep breath. It filled her. It was the first breath she had taken in years. She was quiet for a while longer. She looked away from Burt so that he would not see the many emotions, including love, in her eyes. When she pulled herself together, she spoke. "I don't know. I just don't know. … I don't think so."

Burt looked frightened. "Carla, you don't mean that you'd try to kill yourself again?"

"They say the third time's a charm, Burt. But this was at least the third, so where's the charm?"

"Carla, please, please. Let's get some help. Let's find a way to prevent you doing that. Please! I don't want to lose you. I really don't." Burt's tears were falling freely like rain after a drought.

"But, Burt, you have already lost me."

"What? Why?"

"Because," Carla was resolute, "the Carla you think you are talking to is dead, gone. One way or the other, I am getting rid of that me. I don't want to be Mrs. Burt Goodman, Maxwell House Wife number 5,864,328, factory flawed, alpha female broken, sucked dry, any more. I either die totally or change my life entirely."

Burt was stunned by her certainty. Had she ever sounded like this? Ever? He realized that now, for the first time, that at this moment, he wanted what was best for Carla. "I want you, Carla. I want you in my life, to be my wife. But, if you're going to kill yourself staying married to me, then I want you to do whatever you need to do."

"Why, Burt, why do you want me? So you won't appear guilty of murder? Or attempted murder? For appearances' sake? Do you think I'm an idiot? Don't you think I know that you have someone else? Another woman?"

Burt looked thoroughly startled, and grabbed the arms of his chair. For a moment, Carla thought he was going to jump up and run out the door.

But he stayed still. He momentarily considered denying the whole thing, but then thought that if indeed Carla knew about Andrea, he would be lying to her again. This was hard for him, telling the truth here. "OK, so you know. … I didn't think you knew that there was someone else. There was. It lasted for a short while. But there isn't anyone any more. It's over. Very over. And I never stopped wanting you. It's just that, that --"

Carla's eyes flared with indignation. "Burt, how could you have insulted me that way, and have done it in such a way that the entire community has to have been talking about it? Burt, how can you run us both through the mud like that?"

"It's over, Carla. Another mistake, a horrible mistake on my part. Can you forgive me?"

"I don't know. People don't change as quickly as you say you suddenly have. … Anyway, forgiving you is only part of it," she told him. "Ever trusting you again is another. Without trust, what is there? Not much."

"Carla," Burt was rubbing his forehead. "I'll do whatever it takes. I don't want you to leave me. I don't want you to kill yourself. I don't want to crush you. I don't want to hurt you anymore. How can we fix this? Please, please tell me how?"

"I don't have any answers, Burt. Right now, I just want to take care of myself. I may kill myself or I may not. You're going to have to help me with the 5150 thing. I mean if they want to lock me up because I am a threat to myself, then I may as well tell them you tried to kill me, not me. So, as I see it, you have to make sure I am not 5150'd. Get me?"

Burt's eyebrows rose almost off the top of his forehead as he nodded yes. *This was the deal she wanted?* He got her. He'd get the best attorneys in on her case. She was not crazy, he would make sure they knew this.

"Burt, whatever I actually do is my business. I may go away a while. I may go away for good. And, since you're here, you should know that I may take whatever I need to do so. Don't worry, I won't take much. I don't want any part of any money you made related to this horrendous defending of women traffickers thing. I want no part of that flesh trade money. But half of all we have which came to us legally, for good work, was mine, is mine. I know you think it's all yours and that I have no right --"

Suddenly, Burt stood up. "Never speak of trafficking matters. Ever again. God, please never. Not just for me, for your own sake." Burt decided he could not tell Carla just how deeply involved he really was, too dangerous. The hidden cities project was too secret and too dangerous for anyone to know about.

Carla stared at Burt blankly. She was about to respond when Burt waved his hand weakly, hoping to stop her from continuing.

"Carla, please, don't, don't rub my nose in it. Take whatever you need. You earned at least half of it. For God sakes, you and I both know I couldn't have won all those cases without you. The earnings are yours as well as mine. Take half or take it all. Stay and take it. Leave and take it. But don't leave without making it clear that I didn't try to kill you and to then make it look like your suicide. And, please leave the trafficking stuff out. And please, please don't leave without telling me how to find you."

Carla made it clear that the answer to that last request was no. "That's not part of the deal, Burt. I leave and let you know where I am if and when I chose to. I take whatever I take without making you any deals, except that you aren't charged with my murder so long as you leave me alone, never look for me or come around me unless and if I invite you. And keep me from being 5150'd. And admit to abusing me if I have to testify. … So, you open the coffers so I can take what I need. Trust me to be more than fair to you. More fair than you've ever been to me."

"But, Carla, it's not fair to me if you leave and I don't know where to find you. You're the love of my life." Burt was surprised not only to hear himself talk this way but to maybe even mean this as well. Too little too late, he told himself. Yet it felt good for him to know he loved her.

"Burt, you sound ridiculous. It's too late to say this. I really had no idea that you would ever act like this if I told you I was leaving." Carla was trying to look into his soul. She couldn't trust him ever again, but he seemed to mean what he was saying here, maybe. Still, even if it was the truth, it was coming to her far too late. "I had no idea that you would be upset about my leaving you. I'm really surprised and even touched, touched to the heart, but I can't make up my mind based on you, even if you are being honest, which I cannot know for sure. I can't let you decide my fate. That's what I've done for most of my adulthood. I'm practically a non-person as a result. I just can't make up my mind based on what you say or what you say you want."

Burt was in tears again. Carla was virtually certain that those tears were real now. It was amazing to see this man cry real tears, not the fake ones he was so good at. "OK. Whatever you decide, Carla, I'll be here for you. I'll wait."

"Burt, I only wish we'd been able to get some help with all your violence. I only wish you could've stopped hitting me long ago. I only wish we'd been able to find each other and connect years ago, before Sheila left us and, and --"

Now Carla was in tears. And Burt was still crying. The river of their lives flooded with a simple kind of wordless truth. They both had suffered when their daughter had left them. They both had been deeply and, quite possibly, irreversibly wounded by her disappearance.

Would she ever return? Did she hate them this much? They shared these unspoken fears in unspoken pain.

62.

ANDREA'S APARTMENT….

Dressed in faded, tattered army fatigues and a black turtle neck, looking more out of place than an ordinary burglar, Sheila was caught going through drawers. Someone came in and gasped.

Shocked, Sheila turned to the intruder, frowned, and whispered, "What are *you* doing here?"

"What are *you* doing here?" Andrea answered indignantly.

"You're not my sister, are you?" Sheila inquired.

"Your *what*?" Andrea demanded

Sheila scrutinized Andrea's face. "No, you're not that young. Maybe the right race, but probably the wrong age. We're fourteen years apart, she's fourteen years older than I am, or something like that. How old are you?" Sheila studied Andrea.

"I said *what are you doing here?*" Andrea demanded again.

"I came to see *my father*," Sheila snapped.

"Your father? ... Oh my ... no ... you're not the one he thinks is dead?"

Sheila looked at Andrea as if she were out of her mind. "Do I look dead?"

"No," Andrea replied, "but you haven't answered my question. What are you doing *here?"*

"Yes, I did answer your question. I said I came to see my father. So now, if you aren't my sister, you'd better tell *me* what *you* are doing here," Sheila looked somewhat threatening.

"Actually ... this is *my* apartment," Andrea said somewhat hesitantly.

Sheila's face turned red. "*Yours*? I thought it was *his*. My *father's*." Sheila shifted to an apologetic stance for a moment. "Ugh. I'm sorry. I broke in thinking this place was his."

"Now, why would you think that?" Andrea was a bit distrustful.

"Because I've been watching him for a week, and he comes and goes from here a lot. I thought, uh ... I ... oh, now I *know*. I get it. You're his *girlfriend*." Sheila looked Andrea up and down, now with disgust. Something more threatening, a new and very violent, very bloody, look, appeared in the corner of one of Sheila's eyes.

The two women eyed each other, their mutual hostility emerging. Andrea was caught off balance by all this, but, finally she answered with a hint of defensiveness in her voice. "I'm not. But, what makes you say that?"

"I can just tell," Carla explained harshly. "I'm trained to notice details. Slight shifts in body language and vocal tone."

"Trained?" Andrea laughed a little, as if she thought Sheila was kidding. "Are you a detective?"

"No, I'm a secret agent in a secret army," Sheila retorted.

Andrea laughed again. "Sure. And I'm an alien space being."

"Think whatever you want," Sheila told her, making sure to reveal no more.

"What do you spy on, then -- who do you agent for?" Andrea asked a little more seriously now.

"That's classified." Sheila sat on the edge of the nearby desk in her tomboyish manner.

Now Andrea was uneasy.

They were silent for a moment. Then, Andrea seemed to decide to make things right. "Look, we got off to a bad start. Why don't you sit on a chair and make yourself more comfortable?"

"Sure, I was just about to." Sheila got off the desk and headed for a chair. In the process, she took off her jacket, revealing a pistol in a holster.

"My God," Andrea was on alert now. "What's that?"

"A pistol. Or did you think it was my handbag?" Sheila made herself comfortable as Andrea had suggested a few moments ago.

Andrea swallowed. Was this girl, this young woman, dangerous? Crazy? "Oh," was all Andrea could bring herself to say.

"Don't worry, I won't shoot you. Won't waste the bullets." Sheila tapped her gun. "Just tell me where my father lives."

"With your mother. At his house."

"*His* house?" Sheila was upset. "He still calls it that? As if it's not hers too."

"What *are* you talking about?" Andrea asked.

"Look, I should warn you, my slick, sweet-talking, super actor, falsely empathic, shady dad is a woman-hater. Get away from him while you can," Sheila warned.

"You sound mad," Andrea said. Mad, as in wildly insane, or, mad, as in just a little angry, Andrea wondered to herself.

"Mad is mild." Sheila leaned forward. "Don't you know he tried to kill my mother and make it look like she killed herself? And he had the gall to try it more than once?"

"Do you really believe that?" Andrea's ears burned. She wasn't sure she wanted to be discussing this. Just talking about it could implicate her in some bizarre way.

"I know what you think," Sheila guessed. "You think I'm saying this because I want you to stop seeing my father, so my mother can have him all to herself. You couldn't be more wrong." Sheila's indignance was obvious. "I don't know you, so I don't really care much about you. I really don't care what he does to you. But I love my mother dearly. I can't stand what he's done to *her*. I want him *out* of her life. Way out."

"You really think your father is that bad? He seems like a wonderful man who gives a lot," Andrea asked with the facade of sincerity.

"Yep, lady. My father is a wonderful man if you don't scratch the surface. He's wonderful to his public. But, to be so supposedly wonderful, he needs to focus all his hate on a small, very private, bull's eye in his life. He needs to prove his manhood -- to act out all of his tyrannical power trip stuff -- somewhere where it won't affect his reputation or his much applauded work. My mother has been the perfect target for many years. A sitting duck. Hopefully he'll shift to you before he kills her. Watch out, he's smooth. He's deceptive. He reels you in 'til you're completely hooked; then, when you don't see it coming, he sucks you dry, he takes all you have to give. He destroys you."

Andrea was silent for a while. "Do you really think he'd try to kill her? That's murder."

"Yes, I do," Sheila responded confidently. "But I am surprised that he's a suspect. I am amazed that he'd be stupid enough to get caught. Maybe his sickness is leaking out a bit. Maybe he can no longer contain his pathological, diabolical, secret self. I hope he's finally doing himself in, undoing his crafty facade and letting his true and disgusting nature show through."

Andrea thought she had better stay on the good side of the angry and armed young woman in military fatigues. Maybe sympathy would work. "I feel sorry for you, hating your father so much."

"Feel sorry for my mother," Sheila went on stridently. "He took a young brilliant woman with a wonderful life ahead of her and put her light out the way a smoker rubs out his cigarette with the bottom of his shoe. Complete and total disregard. Identity theft, hah! Energy theft. Life stealing."

"But this is a free country. She could have left him. Why did she stay with him all these years?" Andrea made certain she asked this in a gentle voice.

"Me," Sheila said. "Me. He told her again and again that if she left, she would never be able to leave with me." A trace of guilt whipped across the face of this militant young female. It looked as if there were tons of anguish stored behind it. However she knew non of that was her fault. Still….

"Is that really a reason?" Andrea tried to stay calm. Would this volatile young woman go crazy right here? "You can't blame yourself for your mother's problems, can you?"

But, right or wrong, she did blame herself. Now, with unintentional force, Sheila cut right into Andrea's heart. "Have *you* ever had a baby? Do *you* have any children?"

"No," Andrea gulped. She was glad her pregnancy did not show yet.

"Well then, maybe you shouldn't be questioning a woman's reason for staying with the father of her child."

"But I still wonder why she stayed with him all these years...."

Sheila turned the tables. "Why do *you* stay with him?"

"I don't."

"Don't think you can fool me. Listen instead. You just don't see him taking you over until you're almost gone. And then it's pretty much too late. You should think about it. I watched him alternately charm and rip my mother to shreds bit by bit 'til I couldn't watch anymore. You're still a whole person. Or is it too late for you already? Has he already nabbed you?"

Andrea was silent. She forced herself not to answer. She wanted to tell this young woman, Sheila, this seemingly semi-psychotic armed trespasser, that she was already pregnant with Burt's child, with Sheila's half sister -- Andrea was certain this would be a girl. Andrea wanted to talk about it with *someone,* even if it was this crazy someone, of all people, to choose. But Andrea would tell no one. There were sharp tears stinging her eyes as she told Sheila, "Thanks for caring. And whatever connection your father and I had is already over. But thank you anyway."

This gratitude ruffled Sheila. The hairs on her arms stood on end. "Why should *I* care about *you*?" she asked Andrea. "That's not what this is about. It's nothing personal. It's just that women should stick together, not allow men like my dad to divide them and to produce angry daughters like me." Sheila patted her gun.

Sheila was finished with Andrea. She stood up, put on her jacket, and walked out, saying, "Take care of yourself while you still have a self."

Once the door was closed, Andrea sighed with immense relief.

63.

GOODMAN RESIDENCE….

Carla had been home from the hospital now for three days. Home and left alone rather than institutionalized or having someone hovering over her 24-7. Maybe Burt had managed to work this out for her as it was part of the deal. And, of course, maybe he wanted her home alone so that she would try suicide again and succeed, she told herself. She was not sure but did not care. Burt was a man of many personalities and plans. Devious, two-faced, scheming, even when trying not to be.

She hadn't been answering the telephone, which had been constantly ringing. Now the phone rang again. Why she answered it this time, she would never know. It sounded different for some reason.

A voice waited and then said simply, "Mom?"

Absolute silence.

Carla said nothing. Could it really be Sheila? Was this a cruel joke? People could be so cruel.

"Mom. I know it's you. Please answer. It's important. You don't have to forgive me for being out of touch for so long. You don't have to be nice to me. Just talk to me a bit."

Yes, it *was* Sheila. Carla, instantly whipped out of her depression, felt new life, a new adrenalin, race through her veins. She wanted to climb right into the telephone. "My God, Sheila? Where are you?"

"Nearby. Can I come over, Mom?"

Carla practically danced with joy. "*Can you come over*? When? How soon?"

"Later today."

"Later? No! Right now! Please." Carla realized she sounded desperate. She thought she had better sound more like her old self, who ever that had been, so she said, "Come home right now, young lady," in a trumped up, stern voice. "You've been gone far too long."

"Still as funny as ever, Mom."

"Well, seriously, I couldn't stand the wait. Please don't tease me like this."

"Mom, you'll have to stand the wait. You've waited a few years --"

"At least. It seems like forever, Sheila."

"So you can wait half a day longer, Mom."

"What choice do I have?" Carla asked her long lost daughter.

"None, Mom. See you then. Could you get some cookies?" Sheila did not want to ask her mother to bake them. But they both knew that Carla would.

Carla was actually happy to have the time to buy the cookie ingredients. She grabbed her purse. On the way out the door, she caught a glimpse of herself in the mirror. "Oh God, look at me. In my robe and all. I can't let her see me like this," Carla mumbled aloud. With that, Carla turned another corner. She finally wanted a new face.

Some minutes later, when she left for the store, Carla looked absolutely stunning. Pale, a ghost of herself, but hauntingly stunning in a porcelain doll sort of way.

64.

GOODMAN RESIDENCE….

Carla drove home to prepare for Sheila and to bake those cookies. As soon as she pulled into her driveway, the detective, watching from down the street, jumped out of his car and headed over. When Carla got out of her car and picked up her two bags of groceries, he was right there and reached out to help her carry them.

"Here, let me help." And then he saw how very well she looked. "Well, well, Mrs. Goodman, you look good, very good. So, how are you?"

"Oh, it's you again. I can carry these just fine, thanks," Carla responded coldly.

And then, as one bag began to fall, the detective grabbed it and said, "I'm sure you can, but so can I."

"Very cute," she said unsmilingly and headed for the house.

He followed her to the door. Carla did not want to let him in. "I've got other things to do right now. I have company coming later and I have to bake something. What else do we have to say to each other anyway?"

"Just one thing, Carla. I know you are determined to claim that you attempted suicide more than once, each time of your own free will, and that your husband did not coerce you and was in no way involved."

"That's not one thing, Mr. Stanger."

"One other thing, *Carla*," he said, emphasizing the fact that he was using her first name by saying it slightly flirtatiously, "If you are protecting Mr. Goodman, you are also in the wrong, as either an accessory to the crime or an accessory to its cover-up."

"Yeah, right. Now I'm an accessory in my own murder."

"Attempted murder," the detective corrected her. "You're not dead, are you?"

"Good question," Carla was wondering this herself. She actually felt more alive than she had in years. "Listen, Dan, that is your name isn't it, go home and go back to sleep, or go back to school and get an education, but don't work your naiveté or your stupidity out on me." She hoped this insult would drive him away.

She turned to go inside. Dan followed her with the bag he was carrying. Carla put her bag down on the table. Dan was about to put his bag down next to it when Carla turned to Dan to make yet another curt comment. She turned without realizing how close behind her he was standing, bumped right into him, lost her balance, and knocked the bag out of his hand. Dan reached out with both hands to keep Carla from falling and caught her. Carla caught the bag.

They ended up face to face, eyeing each other warily and then laughing. Their faces were very close together. "OK, Carla," Dan said awkwardly, "have it your way, tell me the truth or don't tell me the truth, and --"

"Thank you for the permission," Carla interrupted him.

Leaning over the bag she was holding, he moved half an inch closer to her. "And I'll --" Their lips were almost touching. "I'll leave you alone," he finished, raising his eyebrows involuntarily.

Carla spoke slowly without pulling away. "Thank you."

They touched lips and froze in that position. In the next instant, under other very different circumstances, they could have become wildly passionate. It was something that both of them, even Carla, despite her resistance to the absurd idea, wanted – at least in the moment.

But neither was prepared to acknowledge let alone act upon such a surge of irrational desire, especially not there in that house. Dan stepped back. He looked at her affectionately. "It's just that -- you're such a beautiful woman, I can't stop thinking about you and hoping you'll be all right, and uh…." Dan shook his head and laughed at himself. He headed for the door.

"A cliffhanger?" Carla asked.

He looked back at her. "No, a door knobber." He cleared his throat. "I think -- I have fallen in love with you."

"Perhaps you mean in lust, detective." Carla watched his face. "Love takes more time, more knowing."

Dan looked her face and then her body over. "I guess I admit lust is certainly part of it." His eyes went back to hers. "But it certainly isn't all of it. All this has let me know you in a special way. It's let me feel you, see you -- see who you are. You're an incredible soul. ... Oh, geeze, I should go. I'm a fool. Call me, you have my card."

Carla nodded. "Maybe next life."

"You let me know," he said as he tripped out the door like a smitten schoolboy.

Carla rolled her eyes. She has more important things to think about right now.

65.

GOODMAN RESIDENCE….

All the time in the world passed as one lost woman waited for one found daughter. It seemed to be forever before Sheila was there at the door.

At first, although Carla was stunned by Sheila's weathered appearance and her short, cropped hair, it was pretty much like Sheila had never been gone. Then, there were shouts and blamings. Then, there were tears and hugs. Then, there were only two women, one who had once lived inside the other and come from her womb. The mother and daughter settled into conversation.

In the hours that followed, after Carla promised never to tell, Sheila told her mother why she had left West Point to become a guerilla, an underground soldier.

"But you had a wonderful future ahead of you," Carla had interrupted.

"Mom, Mother, Carla, whoever you are, let me explain," Sheila had expected to explain this.

"Of course I will, Sheila, but I only am wondering why a girl --"

Sheila interrupted. "Do I look like a little girl?"

"You'll always be my little girl," Carla sighed, "but I stand corrected. Why a woman would get, would earn, such a rare and prestigious opportunity and then dump it."

"Mom, you're the one who dumped opportunity, not me. You came out of Harvard Law School with all the brains and looks anyone could ever want and then you settled into this particular wifehood."

"I had you," Carla smiled wistfully and yet proudly, "which is the best thing I could have ever done."

Sheila did not find this pleasing. "Oh, thanks a lot, Mom, Mother. So I'm the one that ruined your life, not you."

"I didn't say that, dear," Carla explained. "I'm responsible for my own mistakes."

"So I'm a mistake?" Sheila responded quickly.

"Oh no, of course not, Sheila. I swear, you are the single best thing that ever happened to me."

"It's not enough, Mom," Sheila reprimanded. "It's not enough for me to see my mother shipwrecked, all washed up, with me as the only part of her life she feels anything positive about. How do you think I felt growing up, watching you let Dad hit you and treat you like garbage?"

"OK, OK, I know what all went on. I should've left him, but I couldn't, I just didn't know how to break away safely -- and with you safely with me too -- not back then," Carla said. "He was threatening me left and right, for years, whenever he thought I might be thinking of trying to get out. So I stayed. But that is not your fault, that is your parents' fault. … But, what does this have to do with you leaving West Point?"

"I need *my* life to mean something, Mom," Sheila insisted. "I need to feel like *I* am making a difference."

"And being a mercenary soldier who disappears for years at a time, makes her poor parents think she is dead, does this for you? I just don't get it, Sheila."

"Mercenary soldier is just a euphemism," Sheila answered, "a relatively nice-sounding phrase, for some very important, very underground, very controversial, and very dirty work."

"I still don't get it," Carla said. "Doing dirty work for money makes you feel like you're accomplishing something?"

"Mom, you must just be playing dumb, because you aren't stupid. You know I'm not so base or so simple-minded."

Carla was uncomfortable. She felt unfairly criticized, but, at the same time, somehow caught in the act of doing something wrong, something of which she was only vaguely aware. She giggled as if she were a teenage girl trying to sound wicked.

"Cut the silly giggle, Mom. I don't have time to bother with trivia. I have to get out of this town and out of this country before my cover is blown."

"Cover?" Carla wanted to grab her daughter and beg her to stay. Carla felt desperate at the thought of Sheila leaving again. But

Carla restrained herself and managed to recover quickly. "OK -- You're in a hurry. Then don't beat around the bush, Sheila, and just tell me why you threw West Point out the window after all you did to get in and all I did to raise a daughter who had the confidence and strength to do more with her life than I did with mine."

"I left West Point because something better, far far better, came along." Sheila paused.

Carla raised her eyebrows and motioned an etcetera with her hand, meaning for Sheila to go on, to tell her what better could have come along.

"I was *recruited out* of West Point, Mom."

Carla nodded and waved her daughter on again. "And so?"

"I was invited to join an international army, a kind of undercover police force."

Carla was surprised. "Who invited you?"

"Scouts. They had been watching me at West Point and before. In fact, it was one of them that gave me the idea to apply to West Point in the first place." Sheila proceeded to remind her mother of the many athletic competitions she had attended during junior high and high school. Carla remembered them well. Sheila was almost always a winner.

"Do you remember me telling you about scouts, scouts from colleges around the country?" Sheila asked.

"Well, yes."

"Well," Sheila continued, "a few were from military academies, trying to recruit female applicants. More than once, some people from West Point talked to me. Actually, I sort of laughed them off. I told them, 'Me? In the Army? I don't know if I'd fit in.' But, I remember, they thoroughly assured me that I was made of the right stuff."

"So you applied."

"No, Mom. That wasn't the reason. It was after that, the time I went to the big international high school field and track meet, when I won first in so many of the events."

Carla remembered it well. "You were fantastic. I was so proud."

"Between races, some women came up to me. They invited me to go out, after the races that day, to a very fancy lunch. They said it was about colleges. Later, at lunch, they told me I was the type of young woman the WWLF, and its action arm, the IUWM, needed. Of course, they didn't name those organizations that day."

"The WW-- and IU-- what?" What was all that, Carla wondered. Maybe indeed this was a cult.

"That's what I said. WWLF, World Women's Liberation Front. IUWM, International Underground Women's Militia. Let's just say it's the GIA, not the CIA. The Global Intelligence Agency, which it is, but you can never ever discuss this agency or its name or any of these names with anyone, including not Dad -- not that I think you will, right Mom? You swear to secrecy, right, Mom? I need your solemn promise."

"Sure, whatever you want."

"Mom --"

"Sure, uh, right, I swear to secrecy, total and absolute secrecy, but really I have no idea what you are talking about anyway."

"Good. I believe and trust you with my life. And it could come to that."

Carla shuddered but Sheila went on before her mother could speak. "Anyway, they told me the WWLF was a branch of the military – of someone's military anyway -- which served people around the world -- people whose freedom was in jeopardy -- especially women and girls. And that the GIA was their international information arm. And then there was their militia. They told me more. I am still not at liberty to repeat it all. Although they were vague with me, I was interested. I asked them how I could join, just in case I decided to. They said that the first requirement was that I tell no one that I had talked to them. The second was that I get admitted to a top cut military academy, such as West Point. The third was that I excel there. The fourth was that I not look for them. Ever. They told me that if I continued to shine both academically and athletically, and did what they had asked, they would contact me about half way through college."

"And they did?" Carla was uncomfortable with all this. How could total strangers have interfered with her daughter's life without the parent knowing? "They contacted you?"

"They did."

"Did your father know about this?"

Sheila's voice turned hard. "Absolutely not."

Sheila reached into a carton she saw sitting on the floor near her feet. Suddenly Sheila's voice became girlish. "Mom, what's this?"

"Just some stuff I pulled out of the basement." Carla had been digging through some cartons of old things.

"Oh, look Mom, it's my baby book! And look," Sheila pulled out another scrapbook, "you saved every ribbon and newspaper clipping from every competition!"

The conversation softened and took on a nostalgic flavor for a while. But then Carla wanted more information about Sheila's work. "So, dear, tell me more."

Sheila went on reluctantly. "I've already said far too much, Mom. I shouldn't even be here."

"Why not?"

"I've gone completely underground. As it was, I had to sneak back into the country in a coffin to see how you were doing. I'm not really here. But I had to see you. I could feel that something was really wrong. And I sure was right." Sheila's eyes scanned her mother's face.

"A coffin? What does that mean?" Carla was appalled at the thought. This had to be a joke or something.

Shelia didn't want to scare her mother too much. "I mean a box, sort of. Just a way to get into the country under the radar, that's what I mean. Look, all I'm saying is that it is dangerous for both of us that I am here, but I had to see you."

"At least you came back to see us." Carla leaned back in her chair, not thinking she had just said "us". "Thank goodness," she sighed with the greatest relief in all the universe.

"I came back to see *you,* Mom. I just came back for *you*. To save your life. I have a place where I've stored money for you. I have a way for you to find me by getting me a message in a certain way. Memorize it, when I give it to you. Don't keep it written down, Don't. I have suggestions about where you should live. And, I even have a job for you, if you want it. I'm here to save your life."

Carla was shocked but tried to sound nonchalant. "Seems like everyone's on that kick right now. Trying to save me. Why can't everyone just let me be?" She did not mention the situation around her suicide attempts.

But Sheila's checking around had revealed at least parts of this sad story to her. "Mom, *I won't let dad kill you.* I happen to know they're trying to get him on attempted murder, but if he gets off, he'll probably try again --" Sheila lectured her mother.

Carla flushed with shame. So Sheila knew what had been going on, or at least some of it. "Sheila, let's get one thing straight. *I* tried to kill *myself,* more than once, and I honestly am not sure how many times over the past few years. Your father *did not* help me or force me to take the pills or the poison."

Sheila felt chills ripple through her system at the thought of her mother committing suicide, however, she tried to stay somewhat calm and with the conversation so as not to shut her down. “Please, mom, stop defending him. You’ve been doing that as long as I can remember. For a while, I hated you for it. Now, I pity you. But don’t lie to me. Please don’t.” Sheila was begging and threatening at the same time.

“I’m not. If Burt had attempted to murder me, I’d tell you right here right now .” Carla wanted to get off the topic. “So let’s get back to your work, now. Tell me --”

“No,” Sheila cut her off, “let’s get back to your life.”

“First your work, then my life,” Carla insisted. “I’m still your mother, so you should let me tell you what to do every once in a while.”

“Well, Mom, sometimes I think my work is, in a strange way, about your life.” Sheila laughed uncomfortably under her breath.

“So now you’re blaming me for *your* mistakes,” Carla noted.

“No. I haven’t made any mistakes, Mom. I save lives, women’s and girl’s lives. Maybe I act out a wish to save yours, I don’t know.”

“Or your own,” Carla clipped. Then she wanted to know more. “You save lives? Does this have anything to do with that last letter I got from you? The last one before you disappeared?” Tears came to Carla’s eyes but she did not cry.

Sheila was silent a while. She finally decided to answer her mother. “OK Mom, I’m going to tell you something. But I’ll tell you because I believe that you can help us, not because I’m your daughter. I’m going to say it once and never again. And, you have to promise to tell no one.”

“Of course I promise,” Carla said, “But why? Why the secrecy?”

“Because if you say one word, you will kill me.” Sheila meant it. “I mean it.”

But Carla did not believe her. “Oh come on, Sheila.” Carla did not want to believe her.

“I mean it, Mom. Unless you promise to say nothing about this to anyone, not even my father, unless you promise right now, I’m out of here, out of your life for good. That is, if I live to get out after you talk about this to anyone at all.”

The mother and daughter looked at each other, wading with their hearts through the years of being who they had been to each other, trying to find themselves in time, trying to find who they were to each other now. Finally, Carla sighed, “OK, OK, dear, I swear I’ll say nothing.”

“Mother. There are girls, young girls, in many countries, who support their whole families with the money they make doing forced sex-work. These girls, many of whom were destined at birth to be forced into such work by their parents, often bring in money doing such work even while they are still children. And even more girls, other girls, are sold, or kidnapped, or just taken off the streets, and made slaves."

Carla did not get the point. "But what does this terrible reality have to do with us? With you?"

"Mother. There is an extensive international underground slave trade, which, especially in the case of the sex slave trade, the flesh trade, is minimized, ignored and even denied by governments and many international agencies."

Being so overwhelmed by Sheila's presence and her revelation, Carla did not connect this with the confession Burt had recently made to her regarding his long-term involvement in women trafficking. Instead, at the moment, being so engaged with Sheila, Carla remembered only that she knew a little about this, not much but that she knew it was true. "I've seen numbers on this in magazines."

"But Mom, those official estimates are major underestimates," Sheila went on. "They are curtains designed to distract us from the massiveness of the human trafficking business. Everyday, women and girls, and boys, are either traded, sold, harassed, lured, or kidnapped into slavery. Sometimes they know exactly what is happening but feel they have absolutely no alternatives. Other times, especially in the case of the young ones, they have no idea what's going on. Along the way, they are bribed or threatened or beaten or raped. Eventually, they get the point. They cooperate or die. And that's just the tip of the iceberg, I've just discovered. There is --"

"I know all this is important, Sheila. I'm proud that you care about social issues, Sheila, but I can't help being more interested in you than I am in these poor women and girls at this moment."

"This *is* about *me*, Mom. And *about you*."

"I have no idea what you're trying to tell me, Sheila."

"You live in a bubble, Mom. You think your troubled life has nothing to do with the lives of women around the world."

"Sheila, please, don't be offended. I just want to talk about --"

"Mom, violence against women is not decreasing. Even in the US, with all the efforts to stop this violence, and all the government's efforts to say that all the money it is spending to stop it is working, it's still going on. Around the world, (and you *are* part of the world, Mother), the number of victimized women is actually increasing. And the age span of the victims keeps expanding to include younger and younger girls, and older and older women. Rape, forced prostitution and woman trafficking is on the rise."

"But, what for Pete's sake, is the point, Sheila?" Carla was pressed to the limits of her awareness. She wanted to cry out and beg Sheila not to go away again -- not to go risk her life doing something so vague, so unreasonable. Yet, right then, at about that moment in the discussion, Carla suddenly remembered Burt's admission about his years of entanglement with the flesh trade. How could she have forgotten this when it had made her so mad?

Sheila noticed the look of sudden and anxious interest in her mother's face. It was as if her mother had just woken up. "Mother, the connection between all this and me is that I am part of an international underground army dedicated to the freeing of women and girls from all kinds of oppression. And working to keep them from being taken for good, sometimes taken to places we've never heard of, hidden cities, forced into slavery and forced harem-like situations for life. Do you get it now, Mom? Even a bit?" Sheila asked impatiently.

"Is that why you have a gun under your jacket, Sheila?" Carla had seen it.

"Yes, Mom, that's why the guns, the bombs, the --"

Carla balked with revulsion. "Bombs? Sheila, are you a terrorist?" Bombs had killed Carla's parents.

"Call me whatever you like," Sheila folded her arms. "I prefer to say I'm a freedom fighter. But since you will never discuss this with anyone, not even my father, you can call me whatever you like in your mind."

Carla nodded sullenly. How could it be that Sheila, her dear, dear daughter, had ended up working against the same filthy thing that Burt, her husband, had been secretly participating in, profiting by, and indirectly defending?

"I don't think you understand what the flesh trade is, Mom."

"Maybe I don't have the whole picture," Carla agreed.

Sheila then described to her mother what she had seen in her travels, the exploitation and the empty faces of the exploited – girls, girls often even as young as five and six, and women who have become living dead -- empty but abused vessels. The buying and selling of human bodies and human lives as if they were commodities. The more Sheila said, the more her mother looked as if she were waking up from a life-long sleep. What Sheila had to say was something too many people were avoiding knowing. And then, there was something virtually no one knew about – the hidden cities project and its long range goals.

What Sheila did not talk about was her own bout of captivity and how close she herself had come to being shipped, sold, to a hidden city for good.

66.

FEDERAL OFFICE IN UNDISCLOSED U.S. LOCATION….

The government men met with Detective Stanger for two hours, with little progress. In fact, by the time the meeting concluded, they had decided that there was really no case. Although the cover of police detective had served Agent Stanger well, it had given him no opportunity to collect evidence that Burt Goodman had tried to kill his wife.

“It’s too bad. That would have been the best way to discredit him, to take him down, professionally,” one of the men said, “maybe even to put him away for good.”

“You’d think she’d want to help us out on this, that she’d want to put him away,” another one of the men said.

“So now what? How do we get him out of this sort of work, this bullshit legal defense of international syndicate crooks? Soon, they will all be going to him and he’ll be getting them all off.”

“We’ll just have to talk to him. He’s not so far gone that he won’t listen to reason. The guys he’s defending are the worst.

We're lucky that some of them made mistakes here and broke some American laws. Gives us a slim chance to put 'em away here. But what this is really about is that this Goodman is getting them off here, getting rich doing it, and then they all go back to big-time international crime. Including Goodman in his white collar bow tie sort of way. And, if we don't watch out, they'll soon have Goodman as their invisible secret hidden cities project man in the US Senate. Their planning on running him for Senate."

Dan, Agent Stanger, could not stand defeat. "I just can't believe that he could set this up, make it look like she wanted to kill herself, force her to make it look like suicide, and then get her cooperation. I just can't believe it."

"Dan, listen," his boss said, "maybe you'd better not believe it. Maybe you were wrong. Maybe it was just suicide."

"Attempted suicide. Carla's not dead," Stanger clipped.

The boss was outraged. "*Carla*? Now you're calling Mrs. Goodman *Carla*? What was that we warned all of you about last summer -- not getting too close to the women involved?"

"I'm not too close," Stanger retorted. "It's just that something doesn't fit the picture. Why would a wonderful, beautiful woman like that be trying to kill herself?"

"Whatever the answer to that question, the portion of the case on Mr. Burt Goodman which concerns his wife's suicide attempts is now officially closed. We no longer have an interest in his wife's behavior or her welfare. Do you understand me, Stanger?"

"But I still think --" Stanger tried.

"It doesn't matter, Stanger, what you think, the case is closed. No more investigation of the possibility of attempted murder. And stay away from this -- this – *Carla*, if that's her name."

The meeting ended. However, agent Stanger had a difficult time taking himself off the case. For the next several days, he watched Burt Goodman, quietly. Secretly, he followed Goodman everywhere. He wanted to get this man.

Or did he want to have this man's wife?

67.

GOODMAN RESIDENCE….

Sheila was giving her mother a quick lesson in the global reality, to quickly help her feel her own connection to it, despite her lack of awareness of the plight of women and girls everywhere.

"Mom, just let me talk to you for another minute. Just sit back and take in what I'm trying to tell you, because I don't have much time."

Carla tried to object, but Sheila just put up her hand to signal "halt" and shushed her, "Shhhh."

Reluctantly, Carla nodded a silent yes. She felt she had no choice. And yet, she actually found herself wanting to know about what was driving her precious daughter.

"OK, so let's see, let me start by saying this: The problem I am talking about is going on all over the world, anywhere a large number of women and girls live in poverty, including in Central and South America where I have been working recently, and in places where there is less poverty too. Basically everywhere. Including around here."

"Central America? South America? You should have told me, I mean –"

"Yes, I mean no, but wait, Mom. Men from wealthier countries, where at least on paper sex with children is illegal, travel to places where they can buy sexual favors, sometimes from very very young girls, cheaply. Children living in poverty sell themselves to support themselves and their families, Mom. And often, they are sold because this is a big business. Selling sex with women and girls, and also boys, is a very big business, Mom. Big. People have no idea what a large gross national product, I mean gross international product, the human trafficking and flesh trade business is. No idea." Sheila paused and stared at her mother, wondering if she had any idea how much of what Burt brought home came out of protecting that industry's leaders.

"What? Why are you staring at me? I'm listening, aren't I?" Carla felt there was a point Sheila was trying to make here, but Carla did not want to get the point. She thought she would let her daughter tell her some of this. She would show some interest instead of saying anything more for a while. At least this would keep Sheila there with her a bit longer.

"Just wondering if you were listening, Mom, really listening. … OK, so, people think none of this is happening, or that it isn't happening anymore if it ever did. But things are actually getting worse, and more hidden. And the new forced conception, and forced egg and organ donation, businesses are huge and growing. Anyway, we could start with almost any country, but let's pick India. … In some regions of India, Mom, teenage girls are still, and more than ever, but more discreetly, being sold by their relatives to brothel owners who are based in the big cities there. This sort of thing is such big business in so many countries that girls are disappearing. For example, many Nepalese villages have no teenage girls left. In those places, no girl is safe from the traffickers, especially once she is about twelve years old. People in many regions of the world are so poor that the sale of a few daughters is frequently the only form of relief, even temporary and slight relief, from poverty. Daughters are bought and sold like property!

"Of course, it is now illegal for families in many parts of the world, such as Nepalese families, to sell their daughters. But it still happens all over. In fact, now this sort of thing is protected by corporations and big monies, giving it new forms of cover. Some families have no idea what they are doing when they take money for their female offspring. They don't, they really don't. … They just think they are being paid by someone hiring their daughters for domestic work and such. Or at least that's what they tell themselves, we cannot know for sure. But many feel they have no choice, the poverty is so extreme. And, all over the world, not all of the girls who serve the flesh trade are sold into the business. Some of the girls actually volunteer, having no real idea what they're doing. Others are kidnapped. But no matter how they come to the business, once they arrive at the brothels, they are frequently raped, tortured and beaten into submission, and or operated upon against their wills, or even mutilated."

Carla's face changed. She looked horrified, confused and worried, as if she could not sort out her emotions. "This is a horrible thing you are telling me. It is so sad that I cannot --"

"There's more. In Malaysia, Mother, as elsewhere, in many countries, authorities hardly monitor the flesh trade because they insist that it is hardly taking place: "negligible" as they call it. But, what is truly negligible is their treatment of it. Teenage girls are forced to give their bodies to ten, twenty, and often more men a day. When they are paid, it is a tiny percent of what the rental of their bodies for sex earns their pimps. These young women, many really still just girls, and when I say girls I mean they can be as young as five and six or younger, are beaten if they refuse to 'work' and are beaten if they bring in less money than expected. *Many attempt suicide,* Mother, seeing this as the only escape. They most commonly drink rat poison...."

"Oh God."

"By the way, this is happening to young boys too. ... Let's see, um, how can I summarize all these examples I know of quickly to give you a real picture of what is really going on. ... Oh, here is another sad fact: in recent years, as happens in many places, several hundred thousand women have been secretly smuggled from one particular country I won't name right now into other counties. These women were smuggled like drugs, treated like farm animals at best, for flesh and slave trade purposes. This sort of thing is not uncommon. In fact, it happens every day. Oh, here are some countries I can name: large numbers of women are have been brought into various countries such as Pakistan, from Sri Lanka, Burma, the Philippines, and Afghanistan. Pakistani girls are also for sale in the Pakistani flesh market. Which countries are the center of all this shifts back and forth, but this trade does not go away. And now the organ and baby trades are also added in.

"Mom, really, you have to get it: women have been bought and sold throughout history. These sales have been conducted privately and publically in different places in different times. It varies. Even these days, woman sales are sometimes conducted openly, just in ways undecipherable to naïve onlookers. Of course, actual open sale of women and girls is going on in many many places. I know. I've seen this first hand several times, and not long ago in South America. Women are examined at flesh markets like cattle, bought and sold like farm animals."

Carla looked at her daughter in disbelief. This was too terrible to imagine.

Sheila chose not to tell her mother about her own recent time in a captivity, from which, had she not escaped, she would have been sold into slavery of some sort herself. "Well, its true, I've seen it firsthand. … Anyway, in many of the countries where many Afghani women have been bought and put to work, such as Pakistan, virginity has been and still is publicly valued to a great degree. Again the countries of focus shift, but the business stays the same. Flesh trade slaves, most of all the ones that were virgins before being placed in this business, do not dare report to the authorities of these countries that they have been brought in and are being forced to work as prostitutes, because the consequences are extreme. Being a social outcast at home or in a foreign land, which these women become because they are not virgins, or because they were prostitutes – no matter whether they were forced or not -- is so very degrading that private humiliation, even physical torture, is preferred. And they really are tortured."

"Stop, please. I can't bear to hear anymore. I got it. This is the work you do, dealing with this, but the whole thing is so so sad." Carla eyes were full of tears.

"Mom, I know it's hard, but just listen a bit longer, please, I need you to. Many poorly educated and economically deprived women of Indonesia, for example, are being sent as so-called 'domestic helpers' to the Middle-East, and also to many Asian countries such as Singapore, Malaysia and Hong Kong, and also to other parts of the world. Hundreds of thousands of Indonesian women are working under this label in the Middle East and Asia. The Indonesian government, as well as the governments of the countries where these women work, know full well that many of these women are physically and sexually abused by their employers, but no significant action is being taken. Every month, *many of these women, and girls, mom, little girls, kill themselves* rather than face further harassment, rape and torture."

Carla was sobbing now.

Sheila continued, wanting to keep her mother's attention solely on this issue for a while longer. "In areas of Korea, for example Mother, women are required to remain chaste, untouched, virginal, yet they are constantly regarded as sexual objects. While women's sexuality is strictly controlled, it is also used for economic, political and military purposes. The old tradition of 'Jungshindae', (a word which refers to women serving as so-called 'volunteer comforters') involves the forcing of women to sexually serve soldiers, either those of their own nation or those of the nation that has conquered and occupied them as Japan had done with Korea for several decades in the first half of the 1900's. And be sure that Jungshindae is far from dead, no matter what they say or call it now. And this isn't restricted to one or two countries. Just check out the prostitutes collected around military bases the world over. What is happening today stems from a long tradition, maintained in many cultures, where women's bodies are used in the so-called national interest in times of warfare or military occupation. Even though more and more women are serving in militaries, this other use of women continues, less overtly but still very present."

Carla hid her face in her hands, the tears flowing like rivers now. She was not sure what she was crying more about – the sad story she was hearing, the sad fact that Sheila had seen such things, or the sad fact that she, Carla felt so powerless to help change this mess, and hated this fact. Or the sad fact that only a little while ago, ***Carla had felt sorrier for herself than anyone else in the***

world. Carla did not know what made her saddest. But she was shifting inside, waking up….

"And don't even get me started on Africa or on the Americas, Mom. I was just in several parts of Central and South America, and the extreme degree of this problem, against the backdrop of the poverty there, like elsewhere where there are so many poor, is almost indescribable. Really. Girls living in poverty sell themselves to tourists. Homeless girls, lots of them, living in the streets, are kidnapped, just taken off the streets, collected like animals and then bought and sold to flesh merchants, slave traders, organ collectors. And baby-producing farms.

"These girls are taken places where they are abused, used, impregnated, raped, beaten, prostituted, cut up, whatever the people who pay the best price for them want. And many times, women and girls are sold in bunches like cattle, and are bought by people who take them to places, places where they will never be found, never be freed, saved, or protected, and where their abuse, extreme molestation, rape, cutting to take organs, forced impregnation to produce babies for sale, and more will never be stopped. Hidden places, off the grid so to speak, islands and places not detected or places protected by very big money, are everywhere. These secret societies are places where women and girls are enslaved and treated like cattle openly."

Now even Sheila, trained to remain unmoved emotionally so that she could conduct her work, had tears in her eyes. Something about describing all this to her mother hurt so much.

"Don't think this is only happening in a few places, Mom. Parts of the organ, baby, slave, and flesh trade are everywhere. Even in countries where prostitution is formally illegal, governments look the other way with regard to what people call sex tourism, because it brings sizable revenues into hungry countries. Sex tour guides take tourists on visits to bars, hotels and brothels, guaranteeing their touring men that they will meet the most beautiful and exotic young native women, and that these women, unlike the women these men left home, will be cooperative and do anything they are asked."

Oddly, now Carla started to laugh. Sheila was surprised by her mother's odd response to the truth.

Carla realized that she was laughing inappropriately and stopped herself. "I just think it's humorous, it's astoundingly funny, that men away from home are marketed to – marketed to with the offer that women elsewhere will be more submissive than women back in their own homes. Don't you think this is humorous?"

"Mom, those women and girls are being *beaten* into submission; they aren't just choosing submission as one of their several options. They have no choice."

Carla was silent a while. "Isn't there always a choice?"

"No!"

"You're right, of course not."

"Mother ... you know what being beaten into submission is like, I know you do."

"What do you mean, Sheila?"

"Come on, Mom. I'm not stupid. I'm not blind. And I'm not deaf. You've been letting dad beat you into submission for years and years. Don't you think I knew how bad it was -- that I saw and heard most of it?"

Carla's head hung in mortal shame. Had she disgusted her daughter forever? Could she ever rise again, come back, in her daughter's esteem?

Sheila seemed to know what Carla was wondering. There was a way. "You want my respect, Mom? Then get out of this house. Get away from Burt Goodman. Do something to help other women. Maybe even work with me. Then you'll be helping yourself. Then you'll be using what's happened in your life and making what you've been through a kind of training program. With so many women being trapped and forced into submission all over the world, yes even in this OK-now-women-are-liberated era, the women who have a choice, who can leave submission, must. And must do it all the way. Totally. *That's you, Mom, even you.*"

Carla loved her little girl. God, she loved this child! She asked herself: Could her own child be saving her life? Carla could feel Sheila's love and her power. "OK, OK. This is a lot for me to take in all at once. I will consider it very seriously. I *am* going to leave here. I know this already. But I need some time to find myself -- time to know where I really should be going. And then I'll let you know."

Sheila understood. She wrote down the address of the mail drop in Washington D.C., an anonymous box through which Sheila could receive a note. “Memorize this and burn it right away.” Sheila had to leave before she was found in this country. A transport box that appeared to be a coffin awaited her.

The mother and daughter hugged and parted. There were absolutely no tears now. It had to be this way. They both knew this now. A mother and daughter meeting on new terms and parting in a cleaner way.

68.

SAME DIRT TRACK IN SOUTH AMERICAN JUNGLE….

The lumbering medical truck had again come and gone, again meeting the guerillas at the appointed time to take yet another injured girl away. She had lost a lot of blood, but they expected they could save her.

The guerillas had moved far ahead of the so-called cargo truck by taking their jeep out onto main roads and racing ahead full speed, and then cutting back into this hidden roadway to meet the meds. Now, three armed women, members of the secret liberation army, remained behind, in hope of ambushing the truck loaded full of young women for sale. They were about to give up when they heard a truck approaching.

"Listen! I think this may be it!" one of their voices whispered.

"Sounds like one of their trucks," one of the others answered.

"OK, then, you know the drill. We come at it from three points, you from there, you from there, and me from here. Got it?"

"Yes."

"Yep."

"OK, then, I'll wait until they've unloaded the girls to let them pee. I'll go in and get the one or ones guarding them. Cover me. Then jump and get the rest. Got that?"

"Yes."

"Yep."

"Don't let them get away with that truck, we need it."

They were silent as the truck pulled up to the turnout. One man jumped out of the truck cab and opened its back doors. Sure enough, the truck was loaded with the young women who were now being taken, still tied together, out to the bushes to relieve themselves. They were listless and exhausted. Only one armed man followed them. Two others remained in the truck, smoking, laughing garrulously, and telling jokes in slang-ridden Spanish.

The armed man charged with watching the young women had little concern that they would escape. They were hungry and thirsty and sick. The young women attempted to shield each other from the armed man's view as they did what they needed to do in the bushes. There was little if any conversation among them. The older ones helped the younger ones, who sobbed softly now and then.

No one saw the approach of a female soldier or the butt of her rifle hit the armed man in the back of the head. He collapsed and went down, blacking out, unaware that he was at gunpoint. The young women tied together had not noticed yet. In efficient haste, the woman soldier who knocked him out took his gun, searched him for other weapons such as pistols and knives, which she took from his body, and handcuffed him, stuffing a handkerchief in his mouth to keep him silent if and when he came to. She dragged him behind a boulder.

One of the other liberation army members took her hat off and let her hair down so the young women would realize that she was also a female when she approached them. She went to the young woman at the end of the line, and said, "Shhhhhh!!!"

Startled, the girl almost yelled but caught herself. She whispered to the next girl and then the message traveled quickly down the line. They quietly moved behind the liberation soldier and headed for a place where they could hide not far away. Absolute silence was essential and the girls understood.

Now the first liberation soldier and the third headed for the truck. What they had to do was make some noise, away from the girls, to lure the men from the truck. Once on the other side of the truck, they picked up handfuls of stones and threw them onto the ground in the direction of the truck.

Both men sitting in the cab of the truck stopped talking and leapt out, pulling their guns, ready to shoot at anything that moved. There was little time for the soldiers to consider non-violent means of taking these men. Instead, the two of them gestured to each other regarding which man each of them would shoot, and then did so in unison. Both men went down. One downed man began shooting. One of the female soldiers fired several more shots until he stopped. They went to the men, searched them for weapons, handcuffed them and left them to either die or be rescued, whatever the gods might have in store for them.

The young women, now free of the rope that tied them together, ran hand in hand to the truck as they were waved to do by the soldier who had freed them. They climbed in and stared back out, their newly hopeful eyes wide and alert. One of the other soldiers had already climbed into the cab and started the truck. The other dragged the men they had shot into the bushes. Then she headed back and asked her armed partner, "You riding with them or am I?"

"I'll start, then when we stop, we switch. Watch our backs from the jeep, for sure. But let's get them some water first."

"Of course."

"Hey."

"What?"

"We did it."

"Of course. Celebrate later. We have to make it all the way out first and get the girls to the safe house."

"Set the captives free."

"Set the captives free."

The soldier riding with the girls climbed in with flashlights and bottles of water. The truck doors were closed behind her. The soldier manning the jeep ran up to the truck cab and said, "All good. All done. Ready to go. We'll hurry."

"OK, set the captives free then."

"Yes, set the captives free."

They were off, the truck full of young women guarded by a soldier and driven by another, followed by the third in the rusty jeep.

They had set at least these captives free.

For now.

69.

GOODMAN RESIDENCE….

"Hello?"

"Hello."

The distance between these two women who had never met was reduced to a series of electronic signals parading through the telephone line.

"Is this Mrs. Goodman?"

"Who is this please?"

"My name is Andrea."

Carla wondered if this was someone she should know, someone she had met and could not remember. But no, there was something different in the caller's voice, a kind of hesitation, a sort of fear.

"Andrea Villayorona."

Villayorona? Where had she heard that name? Where had she read that name? "Villayorona?" Carla asked.

"Yes, Villayorona. You may have heard my name, or read it in the papers, I --"

"I think I have," Carla said hesitantly. What did this woman want? "I don't remember where right now, but I'm not sure what you want with me."

"I am, I *was*, the co-counsel on the Moreno-Milmar case with your husband," the voice explained.

"Oh, yes. I remember. But he's not here. He's probably at his office. Try there."

"Yes, he *is* at the office. He has a meeting there all day," this Villayorona woman said. "That's why I'm calling you now."

"Why?"

"I need to see you, to talk to you, alone," the voice said.

Carla felt, for some reason, very nervous. She wanted to hang up. Maybe it was her ongoing discomfort with Burt's willingness to defend certain criminals. "I never get involved in Burt's cases." Carla lied here, but she did not lie about the fact that she had never gotten involved in Burt's defense of flesh trade moguls, criminals. This was the truth. Burt had never asked her to, and she had never wanted to.

"That's OK," Andrea Villayorona said, "I'm not going to involve you in any confidential legal matters. Anyway, I resigned from the team a while back."

"You did?" Carla was somewhat surprised by this note, but not enough to want to know more. So what? "Well, thanks for the information, but I am too busy for visitors these days. Maybe some other time."

"There will be no other time, Mrs. Goodman. I am about to leave town for good," Andrea said. "You need to know what I know, and now."

Carla got it. There would be no other time, and this might be important. Nevertheless, she said, "Well, good luck in your future ventures. I have to get going now," Carla tried to rush off.

"Wait, Mrs. Goodman, wait, please," Andrea practically begged, "Your daughter came to see me --"

Carla's heart skipped a beat. In fact it seemed to halt entirely. "My *daughter*?"

"Yes, your daughter, Sheila."

How could this voice know Sheila's name? Carla did not like this, but now she could not let go of it. She was hooked. "Sheila? You? Why?"

"We must talk in person. Can I come by in ten minutes? Please?" Andrea pleaded.

Carla shrugged. She tried to sound dispassionate. Perhaps she should have wondered why Andrea knew where she lived, as Andrea had never been there so far as she knew. Yet Carla did not wonder. "Alright, but make it quick. I do have other appointments today," she lied.

It seemed but a few minutes before Andrea knocked at her door. Carla, having never met her and having only seen a small photo of her in the paper sometime ago, was surprised by Andrea's dark beauty. Carla greeted Andrea stiffly and showed her in.

Andrea sat down, awestruck by Carla's classic beauty and the great deal of intelligence in her eyes. Could this be the woman Burt had been complaining bitterly about? Cheating on? Why in the world? What could he possibly have seen in me after this incredible woman, Andrea asked herself silently. As she did, she straightened her collar, and groped for a way to begin. How do you tell a woman that you are -- *were* -- her husband's lover? Especially a woman who has recently tried to commit suicide? Especially this woman? How do you tell and why?

The eternal perfect hostess by habit, Carla showed Andrea into the living room and beckoned her to sit down.

Andrea spoke first: "Sheila is a wonderful young woman."

Carla did not receive this compliment well. She acted as if she had not heard it. Why would Sheila spend her brief time in the area with this woman rather than her mother? Why would Sheila do this on a short visit back to this town after being gone so long?

Andrea tried again. "As I said, Sheila came to see me."

"I don't believe you," Carla replied. "Why would she do that? Why you? She doesn't know you."

"No, she doesn't know me. But now she has met me."

"My Sheila doesn't have time for trivial conversations, Mrs. Villayorona." Carla recoiled at her use of the word "my" in front of Sheila's name. Was she feeling possessive? Why?

"Miss. It's Miss. But Andrea's better, just call me Andrea, Mrs. Goodman."

As much as Carla hated being called Mrs. Goodman, she did not offer her first name in return.

"Sheila couldn't have visited you." Carla continued to reject the information. "Why would you come in here and push this lie on me?"

"I'm not pushing a lie on you. If anything, I came to push a little truth." Andrea looked Carla dead in the eye.

A cutting chill raced up Carla's spine. More fear. Why? Truth? What did this woman mean by truth? "You're an attorney -- is my daughter in some kind of trouble?" Carla asked nervously.

"Well, I don't know. However, she is very angry."

"Is she in trouble, I said," Carla pressed, anxious, angry, alert, and exhausted at the same time.

"If she continues to break into people's apartments while carrying firearms, I'm afraid she will be, Mrs. Goodman."

"What?" Carla sat up very straight. "What are you trying to tell me? Sheila wouldn't do that."

Andrea tried to be gentle. "She did," Andrea's voice was strained. "I found her in *my* apartment. She was carrying *a gun*."

"You must be mistaken," was all Carla had to say. Not Sheila. But she did have a gun, of all things, Carla told herself.

"No, she told me who she was. I know she's your daughter."

"My daughter does not steal, Miss Villayorona."

"She wasn't there to steal," Andrea answered patiently, "She was there looking for something. I suspect it's something she can never have: a different set of parents, mainly a different father."

Carla was taken aback by what Andrea seemed to know as well as by this insult directed at the Goodman family. "But, if you are telling the truth, which I still doubt, why was she in your apartment? Are you here to make trouble for us? For our family? Really, we have enough already. You maybe know this. Or are you here to tell stories, to lie to me about my daughter?"

Andrea swallowed hard. "Your daughter, Mrs. Goodman, was looking for her father. She thought she was in *his* apartment."

"His?" It took only a moment for all the fragments of information to form a whole picture in Carla's mind. This Andrea, she was Burt's lover! This in-her-face truth felt like a cold fist crushing her heart and then beating it into a pile of shredded flesh. A dead heart. Another death for Carla. But I already knew something was going on, and anyway, why should I care anymore what Burt does, Carla wondered. Carla was surprised at the intensity of her shock and pain. Still, she pulled herself together quickly. "So it's you?" she said coldly. The moment of truth. Or one of such moments.

"Was," Andrea corrected Carla.

"Was?" Why would this Andrea try to make it past tense? She thinks I'm a real fool.

"It's over. I am deeply sorry, truly sorry for both of us, for you and for me, that I let it happen, Mrs. Goodman."

Carla felt suddenly furious. "You knew he was a married man, the whole community knows he is a married man. So your behavior was dishonorable and that is that. So, don't come in here and relieve yourself of your guilt by dumping your confession on me."

"That's not why I'm here," Andrea said quietly, her heavy shame apparent. "I came to tell you that Burt is not an honorable man and --"

Carla raised her voice, her vocal cords tight. "You think you're giving me news? I don't need it. I know more about him than you'll ever know!"

"But his dabbling in the dark side may be endangering his life --" Andrea stopped short.

"So what?" Carla was quite loud now. "Should I care?"

"*And yours* --" Andrea said more forcefully.

"So what?" Carla echoed her previous question.

Andrea gulped. "And your daughter's."

"Why would you bring my daughter into this?"

"I'm not bringing her in. She's in. I have the strange feeling she knows about her father's dealings. Don't ask me why. And just knowing is already very dangerous. You have to tell her to get out of here, go far away."

Carla was stunned by her realization that Sheila could be quite aware that Burt was defending some of the people the GIA, or IUWM, or whatever they were called, were fighting. “Miss Villayorona, I don’t have any reason to believe anything you say,” Carla blurted out harshly. “You are lowlife to me, you’ve dishonored your womanhood.”

“Yes, I have, I know, and I know, more than I can say that you are right. But, Mrs. Goodman, please believe me. You don’t have to like me. I would probably hate my guts if I were you, but you should know that Burt has made some very powerful and very dangerous people very angry -- people who, I suspect, have been paying Burt a massive annual retainer over many years. Burt has not kept certain promises, perhaps because he knows the FBI, and now the CIA, are hovering. Or maybe because he’s having second thoughts, a crisis of conscience, which I doubt. Whatever explains Burt’s decisions now, you might want – you must try -- to protect yourself. Stay away from your husband, get your daughter out of here, protect yourselves. I’m off the case and I’m leaving town for good, today. I’ll leave now.”

Andrea stood. Out of professional habit, Andrea almost reached out to shake Carla’s hand, but caught herself, realizing it was a foolish gesture. Andrea thought maybe she should stay to be certain Carla would not try anything crazy, like suicide. Again. “Uh -- will you be all right?”

Carla had to laugh. “What a ridiculous question. You come in here. You tell me you’ve been my husband’s lover and that my life, and worse, my daughter’s life, are in danger. Then you ask if I will be OK? Perhaps I should wonder whether you’re OK, or whether you're certifiably insane? You have to find a way to live with yourself, but I don't have to help you. I'm OK enough to want you out of my house and to tell you forcefully: Get out!"

Andrea hated herself for upsetting this poor Mrs. Goodman. Maybe she had done the wrong thing. She rushed out the door.

At least she hadn't gone too far and mentioned her pregnancy, she told herself. That likely would have killed Mrs. Goodman.

70.

JOHN'S HOME….

For years, John had known that one day his unchanging sad life of waiting for Carla would shift. He just didn't have the will to shift it on his own. Now, the series of recent, virtually earth-shaking, events had rattled him to the very stubborn foundations upon which he had build his very predictable and lonely life. All that was gone now. Entirely gone.

Carla's repeated suicide attempts, if this is what they were, ripping John to shreds, revelations about the real depth of Burt's involvement in human trafficking, and finding a girl-become-temporary daughter in a coffin: all this had now totally changed John's world view. And then, of course, the tales of Revuelta, the soldada de los muertes, revealing the perilous rescue from her owners, who had been about to sell her off to a hidden place from which she would never return, forced a sort of wake-up call onto John. He would never be the same. And he would do something to help Revuelta and the other girls she had told him about. He had to, *a moral imperative had knocked on his door*. He didn't know what he would do, but he would.

Having Revuelta around, even though John knew it was temporary, was a whole new thing. On the one hand, she was the daughter, the family, he'd never had. On the other, she was a mercenary soldier – *of all things*. Or so she had confessed to John and Enrico with their promise of total secrecy even from the FBI and CIA – *of all things,* and she had been smuggled into the US (by now John figured maybe she was smuggled in on a mission) in a coffin – *OF ALL THINGS*! Try being a rather quiet, dull, lovelorn guy and having all this happen.

Minute to minute, John did not know what might be happening next. Reveulta, who gladly called him "Papa", came and went to and from who knew where at will. Already she had disappeared several times for several days at a time, something the CIA would not be happy to know about.

But she had returned this morning and asked whether she might make lunch, there at John's, for some friends. Happy about her return, John had said, "Please let me take care of lunch, how many?"

Revuelta had thanked him profusely, told him twenty-nine girls, and then had raced across the street to the mission. Like a kid, but not like a kid.

Twenty-nine girls? Where had Revuelta already made twenty-nine friends, John asked himself as he ordered ten extra large pizzas and raced out to pick up thirty-some cans of juice, soda, plus paper plates, napkins, plus six freshly baked pies.

But then Revuelta did not come back from the mission across the street. Frustrated, John waited thirty minutes and then called Enrico and asked him for help transporting the food across the street.

Revuelta was no where to be seen, so John asked Enrico to watch the food a moment while he looked around for someone, anyone, who would know anything about twenty-nine girls.

John saw no one. But a nun wearing a habit the wrong way and hiding from view was watching him.

John was going to give up and send the pizzas away with Enrico when he heard a noise behind a door across the courtyard. He approached the door and heard hushed voices speaking in a rapid Spanish. What he saw when he opened the door topped all the other shocks of late.

John rubbed his eyes, hoping to better focus. What happened next happened very quickly and all at once, but seemed to be taking place in slow motion.

"***SHEILA!!!???!!!???***" he shouted.

There was Sheila, long gone, missing, likely dead, Sheila, surrounded by quite a few seated girls ranging in age from about eight to eighteen!

Revuelta, who John had not seen among the girls, leapt up and took John's hand, introducing him to the girls as, "Mi Papa! Mi Papa Americano!"

"Uncle John?" Sheila shouted at the same moment, then turned to Revuelta saying, "Mi Tio!" My uncle. Not really my uncle, Sheila said to herself, but close.

Silence all around. There could be no quick explanation. There could only be an instant connecting of all the dots. A siren blared somewhere down the street.

Then there was a lot of commotion as all the girls suddenly decided to hide. When John looked again, Sheila was gone.

71.

GOODMAN RESIDENCE….

After Andrea left, a sullen kind of shock crept through Carla. Here was the moment, she knew it, here was the moment that could tip her over the edge. But now there was Sheila, here and alive.

Carla sat perched on the edge of her final extinction, truly wavering for the first time. At first she did not notice this real change in herself. Instead, the heavy misery engulfed her. Still, very slowly, the change she was undergoing became clear to her. She started to see her life in a different way:

For too long, I have allowed myself to be controlled by my own sense of powerlessness. This sense led me to want to die, to want to commit suicide. However, because I am not truly powerless, my decision to kill myself was not to the point. When I feel powerless, I am not feeling my power, I am not feeling myself. So if I kill myself out of a sense of powerlessness, it is not that I am killing myself, it is that I am killing my powerlessness. The only problem is that my self, at least my physical self, gets killed along with my powerlessness....

A force which is not me, the force of powerlessness, has been murdering me. If I choose to die, let me instead do so from a place of confidence, strength, and my own power; do not let powerlessness decide. Then and only then will it be my own choice. In the mean time, let me live.

72.

ANDREA'S APARTMENT….

Andrea packed up what she needed and put it into her car. Everything else was already in boxes. She was surprised at how quickly she'd been able to pack. Of course, the moving service had been willing to send three staff over to work all night at double time pay.

She locked the door behind her, knowing that the service would load the truck in the wee hours of the morning and take everything to her uncle's farm. Tio Mario, her father's brother, was expecting her. Well, not her, but her things.

Andrea was not certain where she was going. She was just going. She just had to get as far from this woman-trafficking case as she could. She even had to hide. Burt was right about one thing, she knew too much about these clients to quit them. But she was quitting. She had to. She detested them for the business they were in, and refused to defend them, no matter what. She wondered why

Burt did not just refuse them as clients in the first place. Most likely because they had too much on him.

First, she would look up an old friend in the next state who had become an M.D. He would help her get an abortion. There was no question in Andrea's mind. She repeated to herself over and over that she was doing the right thing. She had to exorcise Burt and all his extensions into her. This meant the baby they had conceived as well.

While Andrea had grown up a Catholic and had never imagined that she would be a woman who would even consider an abortion, she now told herself fretfully that there can be reasons that women who would never do such a thing would do such a thing.

Something about the look in Carla's eyes, and also about the look in the eyes of Carla's daughter, Sheila, told Andrea more than either of the Goodman women had said or could have said about Burt. There was something about the atmosphere around Burt. Something about the subtle but domineering control over a vulnerable, shaky, lost woman, control of a woman and her daughter, control of them by a man. Well, maybe not the daughter now, today, armed and angry, but the daughter growing up.

Well, Andrea told herself, it was not that long ago in history that women and children were men's property, chattel. We think it is all over, that we have come a long way, but we should not be so surprised when we find that there are remnants, little invisible threads of attitude, unraveling from the past into the now and weaving themselves insidiously into the future. And into the future that wants to rebuild -- to fortify and guarantee its continuing on -- the patriarchy, the rule of men over women, even the age old ownership of women by men.

There is nothing wrong with equality, but this equality is being resisted on so many levels. Andrea said to herself that maybe this thing that many but not all men still have, this desire for male power and control despite the progress women have made, maybe it's just a message they carry in their DNA. No matter how much difference the women's movement has made in many corners of life, maybe history will prove that the men in charge will, in the end, when it looks like women are gaining way too much power, do whatever it takes to stay in power. The historically imprinted dominance of men will, in the final analysis, strive to persevere. Even if we did not start out that way, and even if we think we are finally leaving that way behind, we may all be trapped by that old way.

We women may be programmed into an ultimate sort of subconscious submission, no matter how much we change, no matter how much we accomplish, no matter how much we think we change it. We may be bound by DNA, by the biological coding inherited by all living things from their ancestors. We may be biologically coded, bound and programmed, for ultimate male control of all major social interactions. And if they see the power of the patriarchy truly slipping away, the men in control, the global power brokers, will take action. And these men are already taking action, quietly, all over the world. These are not all bad men, they are just victims of their coding.

Andrea shook her head at herself, wondering if she was right. How could she have come to this conclusion? What kind of thinking was this?

A kind of peace came over Andrea as she turned onto the highway. The road was so nice when it was empty. So clean. Almost pure.

But she wanted this baby girl.

73.

BURT'S PRIVATE OFFICE....

That night, Burt told himself he absolutely had to catch up on this work. In the short time since Andrea had quit working with him, Burt had fallen embarrassingly behind. He was rustling through the chaos on his desk when a strange envelope appeared. "What's this?" he said aloud, jumping a bit when he heard his own voice.

Burt opened the envelope and found an unsigned typed message:

> *This is a case where the facts can kill ---*
> *YOU.*
> *Silence is the best policy ---*
> *LIFE INSURANCE.*
> *Think of those you care about if not yourself.*
> *OR ARE THERE ANY PEOPLE WHO FIT THIS CATEGORY?*

Distraught but undaunted, Burt crumpled the note and threw it across the room, missing the waste basket by several yards. And then he looked up and tried to see into the night through his window.

Nervous about something, something indefinable, feeling that he might be being watched, Burt got up as casually as possible and closed the shades. Then he sat himself back down and went to work.

He decided he had to block out the nagging whimper of fear tugging at the corner of his soul. And it was fear, but of what? He was so very good at numbing himself to his feelings, including his fear, that he felt nothing when suddenly there was actually a sound at the door. He did not even look up. But Burt did not have himself entirely fooled. He did stop writing a moment and freeze, staring down at his desk. Where was his pistol hidden, he asked himself, which drawer?

The door opened.

"Burt," someone said.

He did not look up.

"Burt," someone said again. It was a woman's voice.

Burt slowly raised his head. And then his eyes became very wide. "Who are you?" His stomach snapped into a tight knot.

"Who am I?" she repeated his question.

"*Sheila?*" Burt could not believe what he was seeing. "*Sheila is that you?*"

"Yes," she said.

"You?"

"Yes," she said again. Sheila closed the door and stood before him.

Burt could see her angry eyes. He wanted to stand and hug her, to cry the tears he had been holding back for so long, all the tears he had not really allowed himself to cry, the tears for his missing and most likely dead daughter. "You're back," was all he said, "Thank goodness. Thank God."

"No, I am not back. I just came to settle a few things, and then leave," Sheila informed her father curtly.

"Settle a few things?" he asked.

"That's what I said."

"You have to see your mother. It'll change her life, save her life, to know you're alive, Sheila. She needs to know you're alive."

"I have seen her." Sheila glared at him.

"Well, why didn't she --"

Sheila stopped Burt from finishing his sentence. "Because I told her not to."

"Well, why would you do that?" Burt honestly did not understand.

"I have something to say to you," Sheila shifted her weight from one foot to another.

"It doesn't sound like anything very nice, Sheila. Why don't you sit down first?"

She did not sit. "Nice?"

"Nice," Burt answered.

"Nice? *You* dare talk to *me* about nice, *now?"*

"Sheila, you're my daughter. I've missed you more than you can know. I thought we lost you."

"You have lost me," Sheila informed him. "I am out of your life. I am no longer your daughter. Disown me. I am disowning you."

"Sheila," Burt responded slowly, feeling as if he had just stepped into a pit of quicksand, "sit down and slow down. Let's stop this. We just got off on the wrong foot."

Still Sheila did not sit. "The wrong life, Burt."

"Burt? What's this Burt stuff? Call me Dad. Remember me, your Dad?"

"Dad?" Sheila asked sarcastically. "Burt, I have some business to settle with you."

Burt shrugged. "OK, shoot, kid."

"I'd like to."

"What?" Burt did not yet know Sheila had a gun.

"Let me put it this way." Sheila had blood in her eyes. "Do not try to kill my mother again."

"What? You too? You can't possibly think that I would do such a thing. Who's been talking to you? Your mother didn't --"

"No. She claims you didn't. That's what she says, anyway. She still protects you. But I've been watching and listening. I know what you're up to. I know you've been seeing someone. You'd be just as glad to get rid of Mom."

He played dumb. "Seeing someone?"

"Andrea, you know, your girlfriend, Andrea?" Sheila quizzed.

Burt stood up, moved around his desk, and reached for Sheila. He wanted to hug her, to tell her he loved her, to promise that everything would be all right.

But, in that instant, Sheila took a quick step back and pulled the gun.

Burt froze. "Sheila," he whispered, "What in the hell are you doing?"

Sheila had moved into an attack pose. "Stay away from me. And stay away from my mother."

Burt stepped away cautiously. "Do you hate me so much?"

"I don't hate you. I hate what you do to women. I hate what you do and I want you to stop. And don't you dare kill my mother."

Burt's voice cracked as he spoke. "Sheila, what are you doing? I'm your *father*, remember?"

"Father? Father in name. Father in biology. But not father in heart. I have no father. You are dead as far as I'm concerned." Sheila waved the gun ever so slightly.

Burt hardly breathed. He tried not to move even a cell of his body. Would this young woman, could this young woman, this thing his daughter had become, kill him? Was she capable of that?

Burt summoned some words. "Why are you doing this? Whatever I have done --"

"What do you mean *whatever?* You know what you've done." Sheila looked at Burt from over her gun as if he were a target.

"What? What have I done?"

"You have beaten the life out of my mother. Did you really hate her so much? Did you really want to take her life over and ruin her and leave her with no hope, no self, no life? Did you hate *me* so much?"

"No," Burt could barely reply. His jaws were clenching. His throat was closing tight. Would Sheila kill him? Had she gone crazy?

"Then why, why did you unravel her spirit and leave her for dead?" Sheila was furious. "Then why did you use her, use her up, and then throw her away, you bastard?"

Burt put a hand over his mouth. He did not know whether to cry or say kill me. He wanted to defend himself. "Sheila, you are old enough to know that it always takes two."

"Don't feed me that bull. You might be able to convince my mother, and your girlfriend, and everyone around you of that, even your doting sycophant public, but you and I both know how you chiseled away at her over the years, how you checkmated her when she was down and then kept her there, holding your advantage as if it was a game that you had to win. It was all a game to you. Sure it takes two. The victim has to stick around, or be threatened into sticking around, for the abuse. But this does not excuse the abuser."

Burt took a deep breath. Sheila was, after all, somewhat right. Or maybe very right "I can't excuse it, Sheila. I can't quite explain it. I can't quite admit it, because I don't know exactly what I did, but, I'm beginning to get a general picture, to have a general feel for the overall process."

"What garbage. A stream of meaningless words. Typical of you," Sheila said through clenched teeth. "The politician."

Burt hoped he could reason with his daughter, talk her out of her fury. But she was still aiming her gun at him. How to proceed? "It isn't garbage, sweetie," he tried, "it's a feeling I have -- I sense that I have gone very very wrong. And, even though I don't think I'm that different from many other men --"

"Many other men don't physically and psychologically abuse their wives and daughters as much as you have."

Burt wanted to say "oh yes they do," but thought the better of it and instead asked, "Daughters?"

"Me, the daughter. Any assault on my mother is an assault on me. A daughter can't help but feel a part of her mother. You almost ruined me too. But I got out. And I got strong. And I saw right through your controlling manipulations. And I've been able to shoot many men in my work."

Burt recoiled. Sheila seemed to be proud of this. Burt wondered what work this might be, but dared not ask. "So, now what?" he asked timidly.

Sheila looked at the gun and then at her father. She shrugged and started to put the gun away. When he saw this, Burt stood up and moved toward her to try to hug her again. Sheila lunged forward, pushing the gun into this gut. “NO!”

Burt moved back. “This is sick,” he said.

“No, this is healthy. I feel better than I have ever felt. I like seeing you this way. Although dead would be even better.”

Burt leaned back against the wall. His eyes filled with tears. “What? What do you want from me?”

“For one, I want you to keep your hands off of my mother. To get out of her life.”

“Don’t you think that’s up to her?” Burt said.

“If she had had the strength to break away from your bizarre control, she would have.” Tension rippled throughout the room. Even the molecules of air were locked up tight. “She’s weak. She’s broken. You broke her. You found her, you lured her. You trapped her. You used her. You built your reputation on her brains and ingenuity. Yes you are smart, but she is brilliant and you have known this all along. Your wore her down. You broke her. Big time. You were going to kill her one way or the other.”

“But, do you think she’d put it that way, Sheila?”

“Why else would she try to kill herself in the prime of her life?”

“The prime?” Burt had always thought a woman’s prime hit much earlier than middle age.

Sheila was still aiming the gun at her father. “It should be the prime. But you robbed her of that.”

"Sheila," Burt tried to argue calmly, "doesn't your mother have any responsibility for her plight? Is it really all my fault?"

"You are the one who should accept responsibility," Sheila insisted, still pointing the gun at him. "The refusal to make room for her is, and has always been, yours. She tried to make room for herself without leaving you, to make room within the boundaries of our family, but there was no room."

"Why didn't she leave me?" Burt still wanted Sheila to rethink her indictment of him.

"Because, while I was growing up, she didn't want to deprive me of a parent, although I would have done better without you. When I finally left home, I figured she would leave you. But then I realized that she was too far gone to leave you, that she was too broken to feel confident enough to go. It's like a person who's been kidnapped and held captive, the person comes to love the kidnapper because that is all she knows. Stockholm syndrome."

"You hate me," Burt whispered.

Sheila pushed the gun a few inches closer to him. "Yes, and I hate what you do to women."

"We've come full circle. So, now what?" Burt tried feebly to take control of this scene.

"Stop killing mother. Do not try in any way to trigger *or force* another suicide attempt. Keep your hands off of her. If she can't stop you, I will." She released the trigger lock on the pistol to emphasize her point. The click was loud.

Burt gasped and froze.

Sheila looked at her father. He looked much smaller than she had remembered him. Older. And far less handsome. For the first time in her life, he looked vincible. She hoped that he had heard her. Because she meant what she said.

"And, there's more: back out of that project, now."

"What? What project?"

"Hidden cities."

Burt inhaled sharply. "Hidden what?"

"Yeah, right, like you don't know what I'm talking about."

Silent.

"We both know the ultimate mission, which by the way, I will kill to stop."

Burt swallowed. Now what? How on earth could Sheila know about this most top secret business?

"Your work with that creep Moreno and his people will be your undoing. All of it, all you're up to, will eat up all of you if you go on. You can't go through life feeding the darkness without answering to the light."

Sheila glared at her father, and aimed her gun at him as if about to shoot. The two of them froze there for a minute. Then she turned and headed out.

"Wait, please wait," Burt begged. "Please, please, Sheila."

But she did not turn around. Instead she said something he could not quite make out, something like "set the captives free."

Burt sat down shaking. What did those words mean? And, how could his daughter know that he was defending an underworld flesh trafficker? How did she get Moreno's name? And how on earth did she know about the hidden cities project? He stared at his papers without touching them or thinking about them until the wee hours of the morning. Then he turned out the lights and left. He made his way home through the fog, through the fog in the streets and the overwhelming gloom in his heart.

For some reason, all he wanted was breakfast. He focused on the idea of an omelet as it were a life raft.

74.

GOODMAN RESIDENCE….

There are things that can shake even a cruel and dishonest, usually untouchable, man to his core. Of all of them, perhaps coming face to face with himself has to be the most unnerving, threatening, shattering.

Burt did not want to see his dark side. But it was following him around now, like his shadow. Only the shadow had grown bigger than he was.

He went home and tried to make an omelet. When he found the door mat a little bit out of place, he didn't think twice about it. When he found some papers on the floor, he figured the wind had blown them off his desk. He was too world weary, too beaten down by life, to notice that there was not one window open. There could not have been any wind in the house.

Carla was not there. He would cook for himself. Of course, he dropped the entire carton of eggs on the floor. This infuriated him. He was very hungry. He cleaned up the eggs in a hurry, not very thoroughly, which is typical of a person who has a cleaning lady coming in the next morning, and a spouse cleaning most everyday. He stomped out the back door to the other end of the back yard, beyond the shed, to dump the whole dripping mess into the garbage can. Some animal had knocked over one of the cans, so he found himself on his hands and knees picking up his old garbage.

Some would call this a mixed blessing. However, the turn of events was cast when Burt dropped the eggs in the kitchen: this mess saved Burt's life. It was at the very moment when Burt was out at the garbage cans picking up old garbage that the bomb which had been planted in Burt's house exploded.

Burt froze, stunned, cowering behind the shed….

It was several minutes before he came back to himself. And then he realized that someone had just tried to kill him.

He immediately realized that the only way to save his life was to let whoever it was think that he was dead. He needed protection, maybe even the police. Suddenly, being arrested for his wife's murder seemed like a good option. Maybe he should turn himself in for murder. Carla would defend him and get him released. But, what if Carla tried to kill herself again? What if she died in some other way? Or what if they killed her? Then the truth would die with Carla. Then he was a dead man, either way.

So, no police. Burt knew he had to get away immediately, far away, unseen, undetected. Everyone should think him dead.

It was dark now. Burt still had his suit on. His wallet, containing the hundreds of dollars in cash he typically carried with him, and his bank and credit cards, was in his pocket.

The terrified man left town.

75.

SHEILA ON THE ROAD….

Her heartstrings were tugging on her, calling her home, but her orders were to go. She was a key member of the IUWM and she had to go on with her work for GIA, with the fight to free women and girls around the globe, and to stop the hidden cities movement before it grew too powerful. Once you join an organization like this, once you pledge your highest allegiance to it, there can be no turning back. Ever.

Especially in Sheila's case, her resignation from the IUWM would mean her death. The death of a traitor to the World Women's Liberation Front, the WWLF, was, in Sheila's estimation, entirely appropriate. Sheila knew that she knew too much already, and had been part of too much already, to ever walk away and not be seen as a threat to the organization's master plan, which she now understood: stop, squelch, the hidden cities global takeover plan.

Sheila blindly told herself, as she had been taught: The world gender war was already on. And only some could see it taking place yet.

And furthermore, she was rapidly climbing the ranks of the WWLF. Sheila would be well-situated in the coming years, well-situated for instatement into a position of high power in the most elite of the global female elite -- star one leader of the World Women's Liberation Front.

76.

JOHN'S HOME OFFICE….

A knock came on John's door.

"CIA," a woman's voice announced.

John let the agent in, knowing she was coming for Revuelta and knowing Revuelta was long gone.

77.

CARLA ON THE ROAD….

Racing down the open highway, Carla was already several days into her new journey. And still she was almost breathless with the realization that she had spent twenty some years on a detour away from herself. Rather than hating herself for wasting so much time, she was proud that she could finally see this.

Maybe she would be able to show others what she was finally seeing.

Yes, she would do so. She would use her own realization to help others detect the illusions, the traps, the false realities which they come to live in and believe to be real. She would teach people, especially women, that *the only way they will not be controlled is for them to take control of themselves*. And, this was going to have to be the next wave, a bigger shift than even feminism had brought about. Of course, Carla had pretty much missed the modern women's movements, even though she lived out those decades. But now she would leap frog to the next level.

Her life was going to mean something, to her, and to women in general. One way or another, she would show herself and therefore other women how to recognize the false realities, the traps of life's illusions – show women how to know when what they are doing is generating their own power for their own use, and when it is merely feeding their own power, their precious power, to someone or something else, sometimes even in the name of women's liberation. Carla was rapidly coming to feel this was not so much about women versus men, but more about women and men working together in the name of human rights.

She would, indeed, finish that book she had told Burt about. But it would have a different conclusion than the one she had originally imagined: it would have life! Carla pulled over onto the shoulder of the road and made a few quick notes:

> *If you are riding your emotions roughly, like a roller coaster, or even calmly, like a Ferris wheel, and never seem to get beyond them for long, then someone or some thing else is feeding off of the energy produced by your emotions. Someone or something else has a vested interest in holding you in this pattern, keeping you stuck.*
>
> *Reclaim your energy. Take back the energy you generate. It belongs to you. You have created it.*

Carla stuffed the notes into her briefcase which lay open on the seat next to her. She drove on, marveling at the way she had left her old life. She had simply packed a few things and thrown them into her car. And that was all. She had taken the money she needed, cashed out several accounts, and re-deposited the funds somewhere else. Burt could have the house. She had gotten into her car and driven herself away. No suicide needed. No good-byes. No regrets. She thought she saw some Maxwell House wives following her, looking for leadership. But she knew this was all in her mind….

The road promised a fresh start. She had all she needed. Secret accounts somewhere else. And a suitcase full of cash. A good supply of clothes. Her most important papers (except those left in the safe deposit box with John), tucked away somewhere, several bottles of pills -- enough to do herself in any time she wanted – just so she knew she was in control. And the gun Sheila had given her. Bullets as well. Just in case she needed it. Funny how Carla had finally given herself permission to feel strong, to be strong.

Carla knew now that it would be a long time, if ever, before she would again want to end her life. She was just beginning it. Now she was filled with a special kind of hope, a kind of light, a light beginning like a glimmer and expanding throughout the universe. She had finally made the real trade -- she had let her old life die, trading it for a new, more authentic one.

The road seemed to know this about her and released her from the drudgery typical of car travel. The hours and miles sped by as she traveled what seemed like light years in what seemed like no time at all. Aha, so *this* is death, she smiled.

78.

HIGHWAY SERVICE STATION….

In a highway service station not more than an hour from the town the Goodmans had lived in, another bomb exploded. And the explosion triggered a dangerous gasoline-based fire. By the time authorities finally managed to sift through the scalding and toxic wreckage, it was clear someone had been killed there. However, the explosion and fire had ripped the body to bits and incinerated these bits, making any form of identification impossible.

Terrorism specialists were called in. This was war.

79.

UNDISCLOSED WWLF MEETING LOCATION IN US....

"Seventy-seven knows. She's bright, tough and dedicated."

"And she's figured it out," General Dame told the CIA agent.

"Well, you were going to tell her anyway. Can't promote her without her knowing the bigger picture," the agent replied.

"And I'll say she sure is plucky. Not many would have made it through that time in the box, in captivity, which is where she found out about the hidden cities project."

"She passes all tests, I know. There's just this thing about her father."

"Yes, but it's why we recruited her years ago, in the first place."

"She's connected, motivated -- driven, talented, and stubborn as hell."

"So what do we do, do we tell her here in the US, or when she gets back to headquarters?"

“The proof would be in the pudding, test being that she does return this time, after seeing her parents for the first time in years.”

“You know?”

“Yes, and you know?”

“Keeping tabs on her while she was here.”

“Same here.”

“On the other hand, we would ensure her return, cement it in, by telling her about her promotion here.”

“Here then. Find her and tell her.”

“Here then, if I can find her. She slipped away recently. And if she is on her way back, then we tell her there.”

“Yes.”

“Yes.”

“Set the captives free.”

“Set the captives free.”

They parted.

80.

IN ANOTHER STATE….

In another state, some months later, a baby girl was born. Her mother, having absolutely no concerns and no shame about being unmarried at the time of her daughter's birth, gave the baby the Villayorona family name, a name of which she was very proud, but as an undeclared middle name. She found a way to make Smith the last name, to protect her. Although she had thought of seeking the safety of the federal witness protection program, she knew that this would not really protect her or her child. She knew too much, even more than Burt knew she knew. More than anyone wanted her to know.

The mother decided that the baby's first name would have to be Cara-Sheila, almost like the baby's sister's name. And the baby's sister's mother's name. In a sense, Sheila and Cara-Sheila were the same child, separated only by years and by the choices their mothers had made. In a sense, they were the same daughters, offspring of mothers very much alike except for the changing face of hope that two slightly different decades in history offered them.

Time cradled this mother and daughter for the duration of this birth passage. But time knew what its inhabitants did not: Although Burt, Sheila, Carla, and Andrea had departed in different directions on different paths, their fates were irrevocably intertwined.

Destiny does as destiny wants, authoring the higher purposes of people's lives and lies.

When Cara-Sheila Villayorona first laid eyes on her mother, she cried. And her mother did just the same.

81.

AN OFFICE….

“Funny, listening to you, sitting here with you pointing a gun at me, all I can think about is the meaning of what you are telling me. I mean, one minute the world and history looks as it always does, the next minute an angry young woman tells it like it is, while she is deciding not to shoot you.”

“One minute the world and history looks like it always does, the next, the very next, you see it, you see it all.” Sheila rested the gun on her leg, hand still on it.

“OK, fine, I get it. So it hasn’t been very long since the US guaranteed women the right to vote. Not long at all. And it’s even less time since the modern women’s liberation movement came on…..”

“Good, you are listening. And then the backlash,” Sheila prompted him.

“And then the backlash.”

"The backlash. When it becomes clear that, in a world of limited opportunity, limited money, limited access to power, when women gain more, men give up some. And then the backlash."

"Hmm."

"And then the backlash, say it."

"And then the backlash."

"Right. At the same time as all that progress, the hidden wave repossessing women's freedom's in steps, steps most people don't see or take seriously if they do see. People just don't see what's happening all over the world. And yet, from one moment to the next, if we don't watch out, things could change very quickly, we could move way back in time, or worse -- to a whole new treatment of women. As a global slave population."

"So you are fighting the ultimate gender war in advance then?"

"Something like that. Freeing those who are already losing it right now, this is the place to start. This and getting the people, the men and women, of the world to see, to admit, what is happening. People don't get it."

"Guess they don't."

"Do you?" She put then gun down and opened the door, letting him go.

Stanger shrugged and looked at Sheila. "What if I do, what does that make me?"

"An ally, a man who knows the truth. See ya', Uncle John…."

EPILOG

WHERE….

A crumpled note blew along the side of a road, a road somewhere. A woman walking by picked it up and uncrumpled it. She read with great curiousity:

Blood and Trade:

Mother dear,

This story is far from over. Every new generation of women carries the torch farther. The flame of freedom -- of freedom from the most visible and freedom from the most invisible forms of slavery -- must burn.

We've come a long way. Yet, unbeknownst to us, now the flame wavers, with darkness fighting to engulf it. The darkness is both within us and in the world around us.

There is an increasingly large and increasingly poor underclass of women around the world. We might like to think that we have for once and for all reversed this trend, and that the women's movement has eliminated the possibility of all types of female enslavement. However, we are quite naive to think so. The poverty of the female underclass and of their families feeds the flesh trade and related businesses.

Moreover, prostitution can be forced or it can be voluntary. Unfortunately, most voluntary prostitution is being forced by social, economic, political, and spiritual conditions. Prostitution takes many forms, and is a big business everywhere. There is sex tourism, which makes it possible for men who aren't earning large incomes to travel to foreign countries and have affordable and memorable exotic, erotic experiences. There is the mail-order bride business, in which women are bought and sold through catalogues and other marketing tools.

And there is the new surrogacy business, which brokers women for breeding. Watch for the greater emergence of this activity. As the surrogacy business builds, many of the women and girls who have been bought and sold for use in forced prostitution will be bought and sold for use in forced child-bearing. These women are being engulfed by a global state of mind, one which says that it is acceptable to use, abuse, buy and sell the powerless people.

So the flame does waver. Still, it continues to burn. At one time, a minor flame was all that remained as a reminder of a far gone era, a time when women ruled the earth, when Gaia, the earth spirit, was strong. Now this flame, which has been nursed and fanned and whetted with the hope and perseverance of women through the ages, rises, again.

Now the one flame has become many flames. Fires are beginning to rage everywhere. They blaze into the dark with vigilance. They seek to enlighten the global state of mind. Is there such a flame in your heart? If so, if there is even a flicker there, you know who you are. You are a soldier in the real army of women's and the earth's liberation. Neither women nor Mother Earth should say yes to any form of slavery, no matter how attractive, anymore.

Mother, you must carry the torch toward our freedom, toward freedom of the human species, which is made up of two genders. And now women must lead the way, must set the captives free, whether or not they know they are captives....

AFTERWORD
by
Dr. Angela Browne-Miller

Violence has many faces and masks itself in countless ways. Revealing to ourselves the multitude of physical and non-physical violences in which we humans engage -- against ourselves, others and our world -- may be immensely disturbing, chillingly honest, perhaps even repulsive. Yet, removing this mask to unveil and examine personal and interpersonal violence for its actual nature may be the purest path to internal and interpersonal peace.

This novel, *Still Chattel After All These Years*, takes us deep into the life and mind of an abused woman caught in a complex situation she does not fully see, at least at first. Her story is played out, (via her husband's illegal business, and their daughter's unusual occupation), against the backdrop of a larger global picture of extreme levels of violence and abuse against women. The picture of the global reality comes into focus as we come to see the anatomy of a modern day marriage rife with confusion, fear, poor communication, and domestic violence. We know this is only one story among millions, and not necessarily a representative story, as everyone's story is different, however this story calls for our attention.

Amidst complicated love and hate, coupled with intrigue, suspicion, danger, fear, attraction, sex, love, as well as concerns of family, friends, business associates, and various federal investigators, *Still Chattel After All These Years* delves into the mind and life of a woman suffering from long term domestic violence. We walk with this main character, Carla, as she travels her own journey of anguish and pain, a journey shared by so many.

Carla falls into a suicidal mindset, a mindset from which it takes virtual shock to recover. Carla eventually emerges from her narrow view of herself, her life, and the world. In this case, her shock is discovering that women all over the world are being abused, that she is not alone in her suffering. And in fact, many of the abuses women around the world are experiencing are so very extreme that Carla cannot even begin to fathom these.

That is, until her own young adult daughter, arriving armed and working for some mysterious organization, wakes Carla up to what is going on around the world, and to what the real trends might be. In fact, Carla's daughter, Sheila, has discovered a serious trend in massively moneyed global slave, organ, baby, and flesh trades. According to Sheila, there is a hidden underground movement to turn the clock back and to re-enslave women. Sheila works for a secret global women's organization dedicated to eliminating this scourge.

Carla can hardly believe her ears. Has her daughter joined some sort of cult? Is there any validity to what her daughter is telling her? Or is all this just to shake Carla out of her own suicidal depression, a state of mind common among severely abused women, even today?

Will Carla, Sheila's mother, begin to see the larger picture? Will she wake up and break out of the roller coaster ride of spousal and self abuse she has lived on for decades? We ask ourselves as we read this story, are we, any of us, or any of the ones we love, actually in any way, in some way, Still Chattel After All These Years? And what exactly does this mean, to be Still Chattel on some level, even after all the advancements that have been made for and by women in our times.

Indeed, so many advancements have taken place in our times. Among these are the increase in opportunities for women worldwide, and the growing efforts to protect women from many forms of abuse and violence: ranging from partner abuse to forced flesh trade work to other extremes in abuse and cruelty in the US and around the world. Yet nations of the world, even individuals within every nation, are at different stages in this process. In fact, many are likely of different understandings of, and minds regarding, this process. Still, we cannot and should not look away from the suffering and pain, even injury and death, that frequently accompany many abuses and violences, including violence in the home between life partners and spouses.

This book, Still Chattel After All These Years, unpacks these issues in a suspenseful, dramatic and deeply touching way. We can see abuse from the inside. We can tell that stopping the clock to look closely at what is taking place when we interact in abusive ways, freeze-framing the process we are partaking in, can allow us to understand close up and personal the intricate working of the energies of two people engaged in harm to themselves and others. These complex dances couples do are highly elaborate, quite interactive, and more readily understood in very slow motion.

Some people spend entire lifetimes mired in very difficult relationships and or the aftermaths of these. For many of them, these problem relationship behaviors become habitual, increasingly difficult, and sometimes even dangerous to break away from without guidance and assistance. What does it take to leave the patterns of confusion, wounds, pain, sadness, and agony behind? Seeing and changing one's role in it all is health-promoting, even essential. Owning one's role does not mean wearing for life a label such as abusee or abuser, survivor or batterer, victim or perpetrator. Labels are only labels and not who we are.

Let's say for a moment that violence is cumulative, and that all violence affects all humanity. Say that on some level, even if we prefer not to, (even if we do not realize we are), we sense, feel and hear pain of violence coming from the other side of the world. Then, any amount of violence hurts us all. Then, any amount of violence – even the slightest and most invisible violence -- which we ourselves can put a stop to, we must stop.

We can create a wave of change by starting at home, in our own interpersonal relations, ***modeling intelligent alternatives to (both physical and non-physical) abuse and violence***. And it is never too late to begin the process of non-violent relating. Any attention to this process which any one can give and share is much needed in this world.

Dr. Angela Browne-Miller
Author, *To Have and To Hurt*
Editor, *Violence and Abuse in Society: Understanding a Global Crisis*

About the Author of
Still Chattel After All These Years
Dr. Angela Browne-Miller

Dr. Angela Browne-Miller, also known as Dr. Angela®, is author of over forty fiction and nonfiction books under this and her pen names. She has served as a consultant to local, state and national governments, and to world wide organizations, regarding social, psychological, political and other issues including but not limited to violence and abuse, domestic violence, women's and men's issues, addiction, human development throughout the lifecycle, the human mind and its workings, learning techniques, behavior change, and consciousness. Dr. Browne-Miller is Editor of the international compendium, Violence and Abuse in Society: Understanding a Global Crisis, and Editor of the International Collection on Addictions. She has also served as author, editor, ghostwriter, coach and advisor to authors around the world. Among her publications are these:

http://www.AngelaBrowne-Miller.com
Also uses pen name:
DR. ANGELA DEANGELIS
(See these and other books by this author listed on
Amazon and at www.DrAngela.com.)

Endings are Beginnings:
Navigating Your Hard Times Into Higher States
Written by Angela DeAngelis.

Embracing Eternity:
The Life Force Does Not Die
Written by Angela DeAngelis.

Transition and Survival Technologies:
Inter-dimensional Consciousness as Healing, Survival and Beyond
Written by Angela DeAngelis.

VOLUME ONE: STILL CHATTEL COLLECTION

Healing Earth in All Her Dimensions:
Personal, Species and Planetary Healing
Written by Angela DeAngelis.

Rewiring Your Self to Break Addictions and Habits:
Overcoming Problem Patterns
Written by Angela Browne-Miller.

To Have and To Hurt:
Seeing, Changing or Escaping Patterns of Abuse in Relationships
Written by Angela Browne-Miller.
Foreword by Arun Ghandi.

Will You Still Need Me:
Finding Friends, Love and Meaning as We Age
Written by Angela Browne-Miller.
Foreword by Evacheska DeAngelis.

Raising Thinking Children and Teens:
Guiding Mental and Moral Development
Written by Angela Browne-Miller.
Foreword by Evacheska DeAngelis.

International Collection on Addictions
Dr. Angela Browne-Miller, Editor.

Violence and Abuse in Society:
Understanding a Global Crisis
Dr. Angela Browne-Miller, Editor.

WHAT FOLLOWS THIS VOLUME, STILL CHATTEL?

Volume Two of the

STILL CHATTEL COLLECTION

Look for the next volumes of
STILL CHATTEL AFTER ALL THESE YEARS.

TO BE NOTIFIED REGARDING
RELEASE DATES OF THESE
AND OTHER VOLUMES,

CONTACT US AT:

INFO@METATERRA.COM

THANK YOU

Readers will also want to read the Maka Shan Saga:

MAKA SHAN

Written by Anatarra Whitewing

Afterword by Dr. Angela Browne-Miller

(cover on following page)

This is the tale of a young woman, Lilith Akashakana, who turns eighteen back in 1970. At eighteen, right after her mother dies, she joins a Native American commune, a pan-tribal tribe, seeking her true roots as she carries Native American blood herself -- a fact which her parents had seemed to her to be ashamed of. Now she feels called to find herself. She also feels called to learn the Tribe's Earth Change survival knowledge she has heard about.

However, she quickly stumbles into confusion and trouble, including rape, captivity, and near loss of life. She also discovers that the US Government is following her, and studying the efforts of some to regain access to sacred lands, portals. She is overwhelmed. Yet, she also finds some of the greatest spiritual teachers one could want to know on one's life journey. And one of these guides seems to be her dead mother, now reaching to her from other realms.

Once escaping the commune, leaving the dear friends and teachers she met there, she is directed by guides she finds along the way to embark on a journey to visit other tribal areas in the Americas, to understand the teachings she was given during the very trying time in the commune. She is called to ancient Mayan ritual grounds. She there finds, much to her surprise, that she actually belongs to an ancient tribe of medicine women who are speaking to her through time.

Published by Metaterra® Publications

STILL CHATTEL AFTER ALL THESE YEARS

MAKA SHAN

VOLUME ONE: MAKA SHAN SAGA

ANATARRA WHITEWING

Afterword by

Dr. Angela Browne-Miller

MAKA SHAN SAGA
Volume Two:
THE GREAT RETURN
BY
ANATARRA WHITE WING

(See cover on next page)

This is the story of a young woman, Lilith Akashakana, whose life has somehow been pulled into a mysterious journey. This is the journey of everyone on the quest for truth about what is really going on now, here on Earth, in our times. Are there ancient secrets that explain our times and the possibility of power shifts and even Earth changes to come? Who knows the truth about all this? And who has a right to access this truth? Lilith Akashakana is determined to access this information she believes is her, our, birthright. She travels to homes of ancient tribes such as the Mayans who know what she has been told is the true medicine and the true truth.

She has broken out of the normal path of life she had been expected to follow, and now is in search of meaning and truth, as well as of ancient survival knowledge teachings. Many events have taken place in her young life, including the recent death of her mother, and her being raped by someone who had access to the survival teachings she was so intent upon learning. Some sort of transfer of power has taken place, and Lilith is being called to know this.

This novel can be read free standing or as the sequel to Maka Shan, which is Volume One of this Maka Shan Saga. Volume One closes with our heroine barely surviving a strange form of captivity, and finally free. Now, in Volume Two, The Great Return, she embarks on a journey to understand the teachings she had absorbed during this very trying time. She finds out, much to her surprise, that there is an ancient tribe of medicine women seeking to come back into the now to influence the course of history and the fate of this Earth. They are calling her, and others like her now, in our times....

THE GREAT RETURN

VOLUME TWO: MAKA SHAN SAGA

ANATARRA WHITEWING

Afterword by

Dr. Angela Browne-Miller

Readers, you will also want to look for the
BLOODWIN SAGA Collection
written by Alias Skye
VOLUME ONE of the
BLOODWIN SAGA COLLECTION:

PROJECT HEARTFIRE

Available as Kindle Ebook and Amazon Paperback.
(see cover on next page)

Fiction: Edgy sci fi, sex, obsession, and romance novel. Psychological thriller. Beautiful, brilliant, professional woman is invited to become partner in a futuristic business worth hundreds of millions. Then, her entire reality is shattered. She behaves unexplainably promiscuously, engaging in intense extramarital sex with two scientists, falling into an intense obsession with one of them, while the other is desperately in love with her, and while both men are working toward global domination via their cutting edge cloning business. Our heroine eventually discovers she has become hooked on a high tech drug which was developed to encourage clones to engage in sexual activity with humans and vice versa. Can she break her addiction? Can she fix her life? Does she know too many secrets about clones now? Are there clones walking among us now, all over the world, today? Read the novel and see.

Project Heartfire
Volume One: Bloodwin Saga
Alias Skye
Afterword by Dr. Angela Browne-Miller
Metaterra Publications

And also look for the
BLOODWIN SAGA Collection
Volume Two:

BLOODWIN MANIFEST

Available as Kindle Ebook and Amazon Paperback.

(See cover on following page.)

Intriguing, exciting, and disturbing, Bloodwin Manifest is Volume Two of the Bloodwin Saga collection. This is an incredible psychological, sci fi, sex, and romance novel. Here, we find walking among us, almost perfect beings, seemingly perfect beings anyway, who are copies of others, clones. Already there are plans to use these clones to achieve control of the planet – of us. What is happening and what are we doing about it?

Read this novel on its own, or as a follow on to Volume One, Project Heartfire. Either way, you will be walked into a world you have never seen, or have not realized you are already seeing. Many readers will want to follow the characters we meet in Volume One, Project Heartfire: Risa, Gavon and Dan – or better stated perhaps—the several Risas, Gavons and even Dans, some of which may not know the others exist.

Bloodwin Manifest
Volume Two: Bloodwin Saga
Alias Skye
Afterword by Dr. Angela Browne-Miller
Metaterra Publications

metaterra®
publications

Still Chattel After All These Years©, written by Angela Browne-Miller, is published by Metaterra® Publications for general distribution to readers all over the world. Metaterra® Publications is an independent publisher dedicated to the furthering of insight, wisdom, truth, learning, creativity, and perception. For other Metaterra® publications, see the Metaterra® website:

http://www.Metaterra.com

See Novels by Title Section

of the Metaterra.com website
and see also Amazon.com/
Look for:

Proxy War© (Volume One: Phantom War© Trilogy)
by E.L. Speed.

Matumba's Legacy©
by E.L. Speed.

Email us to join our mailing list:

INFO@METATERRA.COM

www.ingramcontent.com/pod-product-compliance
Lightning Source LLC
Chambersburg PA
CBHW060806030726
47503CB00002B/353